Charlee Rodgers

About the Author

CHRISTOPHER MOORE is the author of seven novels, including this one. He began writing at age six and became the oldest known child prodigy when, in his early thirties, he published his first novel. His turn-ons are the ocean, playing the toad lotto, and talking animals on TV. His turn-offs are salmonella, traffic, and rude people. Chris enjoys cheese crackers, acid jazz, and otter scrubbing. He lives in an inaccessible island fortress in the Pacific. You can e-mail him at BSFiends@aol.com. Visit the official Christopher Moore website at www.chrismoore.com.

PRACTICAL DEMONKEEPING

PRACTICAL DEMONKEEPING

A Comedy of Horrors

CHRISTOPHER MOORE

Perennial

An Imprint of HarperCollinsPublishers

A hardcover edition of this book was originally published in 1992 by St. Martin's Press. It is reprinted here by arrangement with St. Martin's Press.

HarperCollins books may be purchased for educational, business, or sales promotional use. For information please write: Special Markets Department, HarperCollins Publishers Inc., 10 East 53rd Street, New York, NY 10022.

First Avon Trade Paperback edition published 2000.
Reprinted in Perennial 2003.
Reissued in Perennial 2004.

Designed by Judy Dannecker

Library of Congress Cataloging-in-Publication Data

Moore, Christopher.
   Practical demonkeeping/Christopher Moore.
      p. cm.
    I. Title. II Practical demonkeeping.
PS3563.O594P73   1992   91-3226
813'.54—dc20   CIP

ISBN 0-380-81655-5 (pbk.)
ISBN 0-06-073542-2 (reissue)

04 05 06 07 08 RRD 10 9 8 7 6 5 4 3 2 1

FOR THE DEMONKEEPERS:
KARLENE, KATHY, AND HEATHER

ACKNOWLEDGMENTS

Many thanks to the folks who helped: Darren Westlund and Dee Dee Leichtfuss, for help with the manuscript; the people at the Harmony Pasta Factory and the Pine Tree Inn, for their tolerance and support; Pam Jacobson and Kathe Frahm, for their faith; Mike Molnar, for keeping the machine running; Nick Ellison and Paul Haas, for running the gauntlet for me; and Faye Moore, for mom stuff.

Part 1

SATURDAY NIGHT

Like one that on that lonesome road
Doth walk in fear and dread,
And having once turned round walks on,
And no more turns his head;
Because he knows a frightful fiend
Doth close behind him tread.
—Samuel Taylor Coleridge, *The Rime
of the Ancient Mariner*

1

THE BREEZE

The Breeze blew into San Junipero in the shotgun seat of Billy Winston's Pinto wagon. The Pinto lurched dangerously from shoulder to centerline, the result of Billy trying to roll a joint one-handed while balancing a Coors tallboy and bopping to the Bob Marley song that crackled through the stereo.

"We be jammin' now, mon!" Billy said, toasting The Breeze with a slosh of the Coors.

The Breeze shook his head balefully. "Keep the can down, watch the road, let me roll the doobie," he said.

"Sorry, Breeze," Billy said. "I'm just stoked that we're on the road."

Billy's admiration for The Breeze was boundless. The Breeze was truly cool, a party renaissance man. He spent his days at the beach and his nights in a cloud of sinsemilla. The Breeze could smoke all night, polish off a bottle of tequila, maintain well enough to drive the forty miles back to Pine Cove without arousing the suspicion of a single cop, and be on the beach by nine the next

4 / Christopher Moore

morning acting as if the term *hangover* were too abstract to be considered. On Billy Winston's private list of personal heroes The Breeze ranked second only to David Bowie.

The Breeze twisted the joint, lit it, and handed it to Billy for the first hit.

"What are we celebrating?" Billy croaked, trying to hold in the smoke.

The Breeze held up a finger to mark the question, while he dug the *Dionysian Book of Days: An Occasion for Every Party* from the pocket of his Hawaiian shirt. He flipped through the pages until he found the correct date. "Nambian Independence Day," he announced.

"Bitchin'," Billy said. "Party down for Nambian Independence."

"It says," The Breeze continued, "that the Nambians celebrate their independence by roasting and eating a whole giraffe and drinking a mixture of fermented guava juice and the extract of certain tree frogs that are thought to have magical powers. At the height of the celebration, all the boys who have come of age are circumcised with a sharp stone."

"Maybe we can circumcise a few Techies tonight if it gets boring," Billy said.

Techies was the term The Breeze used to refer to the male students of San Junipero Technical College. For the most part, they were ultraconservative, crew-cut youths who were perfectly satisfied with their role as bulk stock to be turned into tools for industrial America by the rigid curricular lathe of San Junipero Tech.

To The Breeze, the Techies' way of thinking was so foreign that he couldn't even muster a healthy loathing for them. They were simply nonentities. On the other hand, the coeds of S.J. Tech occupied a special place in The Breeze's heart. In fact, finding a few moments of blissful escape between the legs of a nubile coed was the only reason he was subjecting himself to a forty-mile sojourn in the company of Billy Winston.

Billy Winston was tall, painfully thin, ugly, smelled bad, and had a particular talent for saying the wrong thing in almost any situation. On top of it all, The Breeze suspected that Billy was gay.

The idea had been reinforced one night when he dropped in on Billy at his job as night desk clerk at the Rooms-R-Us motel and found him leafing through a *Playgirl* magazine. In Breeze's business one got used to running across the skeletons in people's closets. If Billy's skeleton wore women's underwear, it didn't really matter. Homosexuality on Billy Winston was like acne on a leper.

The up side of Billy Winston was that he had a car that ran and would take The Breeze anywhere he wanted to go. The Breeze's van was currently being held by some Big Sur growers as collateral against the forty pounds of sinsemilla buds he had stashed in a suitcase at his trailer.

"The way I see it," said Billy, "we hit the Mad Bull first. Do a pitcher of margaritas at Jose's, dance a little at the Nuked Whale, and if we don't find any nookie, we head back home for a nightcap at the Slug."

"Let's hit the Whale first and see what's shakin'," The Breeze said.

The Nuked Whale was San Junipero's premier college dance club. If The Breeze was going to find a coed to cuddle, it would be at the Whale. He had no intention of making the drive with Billy back to Pine Cove for a nightcap at the Head of the Slug. Closing up the Slug was tantamount to having a losing night, and The Breeze was through with being a loser. Tomorrow when he sold the forty pounds of grass he would pocket twenty grand. After twenty years blowing up and down the coast, living on nickle-dime deals to make rent, The Breeze was, at last, stepping into the winners' circle, and there was no room for a loser like Billy Winston.

Billy parked the Pinto in a yellow zone a block away from the Nuked Whale. From the sidewalk they could hear the throbbing rhythms of the latest techno-pop dance music.

The unlikely pair covered the block in a few seconds, Billy striding ahead while The Breeze brought up the rear with a laid-back shuffle. As Billy slipped under the neon whale tail and into the club, the doorman—a fresh-faced slab of muscle and crew cut—caught him by the arm.

"Let's see some I.D."

Billy flashed an expired driver's license as Breeze caught up to him and began digging into the pocket of his Day-Glo green surf shorts for his wallet.

The doorman raised a hand in dismissal. "That's okay, buddy, with that hairline you don't need any."

The Breeze ran his hand over his forehead self-consciously. Last month he had turned forty, a dubious achievement for a man who had once vowed never to trust anyone over thirty.

Billy reached around him and slapped two dollar bills into the doorman's hand. "Here," he said, "buy yourself a night with an Inflate-A-Date."

"What!" The doorman vaulted off his stool and puffed himself up for combat, but Billy had already scampered away into the crowded club. The Breeze stepped in front of the doorman and raised his hands in surrender.

"Cut him some slack, man. He's got problems."

"He's going to have some problems," the doorman bristled.

"No, really," The Breeze continued, wishing that Billy had spared him the loyal gesture and therefore the responsibility of pacifying this collegiate cave man. "He's on medication. Psychological problems."

The doorman was unsure. "If this guy is dangerous, get him out of here."

"Not dangerous, just a little squirrelly—he's bipolar Oedipal," The Breeze said with uncharacteristic pomposity.

"Oh," the doorman said, as if it had all become clear. "Well, keep him in line or you're both out."

"No problem." The Breeze turned and joined Billy at the bar amid a crunch of beer-drinking students. Billy handed him a Heineken.

Billy said, "What did you say to that asshole to calm him down?"

"I told him you wanted to fuck your mom and kill your dad."

"Cool. Thanks, Breeze."

"No charge." The Breeze tipped his beer in salute.

Things were not going well for him. Somehow he had been snared into this male-bonding bullshit with Billy Winston, when all he wanted to do was ditch him and get laid.

The Breeze turned and leaned back, scanning the club for a likely candidate. He had set his sights on a homely but tight-assed little blond in leather pants when Billy broke his concentration.

"You got any blow, man?" Billy had shouted to be heard over the music, but his timing was off; the song had ended. Everyone at the bar turned toward The Breeze and waited, as if the next few words he spoke would reveal the true meaning of life, the winning numbers in the state lottery, and the unlisted phone number of God.

The Breeze grabbed Billy by the front of the shirt and hustled him to the back of the club, where a group of Techies were pounding a pinball machine, oblivious to anything but buzzers and bells. Billy looked like a frightened child who had been dragged from a movie theater for shouting out the ending.

"First," The Breeze hissed, waving a trembling finger under Billy's nose to enumerate his point, "first, I do not use or sell cocaine." This was half true. He did not sell since he had done six months in Soledad for dealing—and would go up for five years if he was busted again. He used it only when it was offered or when he needed bait when trolling for women. Tonight he was holding a gram.

"Second, if I did use, I wouldn't want it announced to everybody in San Junipero."

"I'm sorry, Breeze." Billy tried to look small and weak.

"Third," The Breeze shook three stubby fingers in Billy's face, "we have an agreement. If one of us scores, the other one gets cut loose. Well, I think I found someone, so cut loose."

Billy started to shuffle toward the door, head down, his lower lip hanging, like the bloated victim of a lynch mob. After a few steps he turned. "If you need a ride—if things don't work out—I'll be at the Mad Bull."

The Breeze, as he watched the injured Billy skulk away, felt a twinge of remorse.

Forget it, he thought, Billy had it coming. After the deal tomorrow he wouldn't need Billy or any of the quarter-ounce-a-week buyers of his ilk. The Breeze was eager for the time when he could afford to be without friends. He strutted across the dance floor toward the blond in the leather pants.

Having wafted through most of his forty years as a single man, The Breeze had come to recognize the importance of the pickup line. At best, it should be original, charming, concise but lyrical—a catalyst to invoke curiosity and lust. Knowing this, he approached his quarry with the calm of a well-armed man.

"Yo, babe," he said, "I've got a gram of prime Peruvian marching powder. You want to go for a walk?"

"Pardon me?" the girl said, somewhere between astonishment and disgust. The Breeze noticed that she had a wide-eyed, fawnlike look—Bambi with too much mascara.

He gave her his best surfer-boy smile. "I was wondering if you'd like to powder your nose."

"You're old enough to be my father," she said.

The Breeze was staggered by the rejection. As the girl escaped onto the crowded dance floor, he fell back to the bar to consider strategy.

Go on to the next one? Everybody gets tubed now and then; you just have to climb back on the board and wait for the next wave. He scanned the dance floor looking for a chance at the wild ride. Nothing but sorority girls with absolutely perfect hair. No chance. His fantasy of jumping one and using her until her perfect hair was tangled into a hopeless knot at the back of her head had been relegated long ago to the realm of fairy tales and free money.

The energy in San Junipero was all wrong. It didn't matter—he'd be a rich man tomorrow. Best to catch a ride back to Pine Cove. With luck he could get to the Head of the Slug Saloon before last call and pick up one of the standby bitches who still valued good company and didn't require a hundred bucks worth of blow to get upside down with you.

As he stepped into the street a chill wind bit at his bare legs and swept through his thin shirt. Thumbing the forty miles back to Pine Cove was going to suck, big time. Maybe Billy was still at the Mad Bull? No, The Breeze told himself, there are worse things than freezing your ass off.

He shrugged off the cold and fell into a steady stride toward the highway, his new fluorescent yellow deck shoes squeaking with every step. They rubbed his little toe when he walked. After five blocks he felt the blister break and go raw. He cursed himself for becoming another slave to fashion.

Half a mile outside of San Junipero the streetlights ended. Darkness added to The Breeze's list of mounting aggravations. Without trees and buildings to break its momentum, the cold Pacific wind increased and whipped his clothes around him like torn battle flags. Blood from his damaged toe was beginning to spot the canvas of his deck shoe.

A mile out of town The Breeze abandoned the dancing, smiling, and tipping of a ghost-hat that was supposed to charm drivers into stopping to give a ride to a poor, lost surfer. Now he trudged, head down in the dark, his back to traffic, a single frozen thumb thrust into the air beaconing, then changing into a middle finger of defiance as each car passed without slowing.

"Fuck you! You heartless assholes!" His throat was sore from screaming.

He tried to think of the money—sweet, liberating cash, crispy and green—but again and again he was brought back to the cold, the pain in his feet, and the increasingly dismal chance of getting a ride home. It was late, and the traffic was thinning to a car every five minutes or so.

Hopelessness circled in his mind like a vulture.

He considered doing the cocaine, but the idea of entering a too-fast jangle on a lonely, dark road and crashing into a paranoid, teeth-chattering shiver seemed somewhat insane.

Think about the money. The money.

It was all Billy Winston's fault. And the guys in Big Sur; they didn't have to take his van. It wasn't like he had ever ripped anyone off on a big deal before. It wasn't like he was a bad guy. Hadn't he let Robert move into his trailer, rent free, when his old lady threw him out? Didn't he help Robert put a new head gasket in his truck? Hadn't he always played square—let people try the product before buying? Didn't he advance his regulars a quarter-ounce until payday?

In a business that was supposed to be fast and loose, wasn't he a pillar of virtue? Right as rain? Straight as an arrow. . . .

A car pulled up twenty yards behind him and hit the brights. He didn't turn. Years of experience told him that anyone using that approach was only offering a ride to one place, the Iron-bar Hotel. The Breeze walked on, as if he didn't notice the car. He shoved his hands deep into the pockets of his surf shorts, as if fighting the cold, found the cocaine and slipped it into his mouth, paper and all. Instantly his tongue went numb. He raised his hands in surrender and turned, expecting to see the flashing reds and blues of a county sheriff cruiser.

But it wasn't a cop. It was just two guys in an old Chevy, playing games. He could make out their figures past the headlights. The Breeze swallowed the paper the cocaine had been wrapped in. Taken by a burning anger, fueled by blow and blood-lust, he stormed toward the Chevy.

"C'mon out, you fucking clowns."

Someone crawled out of the passenger side. It looked like a child—no, thicker—a dwarf.

The Breeze blew on. "Bring a tire iron, you little shit. You'll need it."

"Wrong," said the dwarf, the voice was low and gravely.

The Breeze pulled up and squinted into the headlights. It wasn't a dwarf, it was a big dude, a giant. Huge, getting bigger as it moved toward him. Too fast. The Breeze turned and started to run. He got three steps before the jaws clamped over his head and shoulders, crunching through his bones as if they were peppermint sticks.

When the Chevy pulled back onto the highway, the only thing left of The Breeze was a single fluorescent-yellow deck shoe. It would be a fleeting mystery to passers-by for two days until a hungry crow carried it away. No one would notice that there was still a foot inside.

Part 2

SUNDAY

All mystical experience is coincidence;
and vice versa, of course.
  —Tom Stoppard, *Jumpers*

2

PINE COVE

The village of Pine Cove lay in a coastal pine forest just south of the great Big Sur wilderness area, on a small natural harbor. The village was established in the 1880s by a dairy farmer from Ohio who found verdant hills around the cove provided perfect fodder for his cows. The settlement, such as it was—two families and a hundred cows—went nameless until the 1890s, when the whalers came to town and christened it Harpooner's Cove.

With a cove to shelter their small whaling boats and the hills from which they could sight the migrating gray whales far out to sea, the whalers prospered and the village grew. For thirty years a greasy haze of death blew overhead from the five-hundred-gallon rendering pots where thousands of whales were boiled down to oil.

When the whale population dwindled and electricity and kerosene became an alternative to whale oil, the whalers abandoned Harpooner's Cove, leaving behind mountains of whale bone and the rusting hulks of their rendering kettles. To this day many of the town's driveways are lined with the bleached arches of whale ribs, and even now, when the great gray whales pass, they rise out of the water a bit and cast a suspicious eye toward the little cove, as if expecting the slaughter to begin again.

After the whalers left, the village survived on cattle ranching and the mining of mercury, which had been discovered in the nearby hills. The mercury ran out about the same time the coastal highway was completed through Big Sur, and Harpooner's Cove became a tourist town.

Passers-through who wanted a little piece of California's burgeoning tourist industry but didn't want to deal with the stress of life in San Francisco or Los Angeles, stopped and built motels, souvenir shops, restaurants, and real estate offices. The hills around Pine Cove were subdivided. Pine forests and pastures became ocean-view lots, sold for a song to tourists from California's central valley who wanted to retire on the coast.

Again the village grew, populated by retirees and young couples who eschewed the hustle of the city to raise their children in a quiet coastal town. Harpooner's Cove became a village of the newly wed and the nearly dead.

In the 1960s the young, environmentally conscious residents decided that the name Harpooner's Cove hearkened back to a time of shame for the village and that the name Pine Cove was more appropriate to the quaint, bucolic image the town had come to depend on. And so, with the stroke of a pen and the posting of a sign—WELCOME TO PINE COVE, GATEWAY TO BIG SUR—history was whitewashed.

The business district was confined to an eight-block section of Cypress Street, which ran parallel to the coast highway. Most of the buildings on Cypress sported facades of English Tudor half-timbering, which made Pine Cove an anomaly among the coastal communities of California with their predominantly Spanish-Moorish architecture. A few of the original structures still stood, and these, with their raw timbers and feel of the Old West, were a thorn in the side of the Chamber of Commerce, who played on the village's English look to promote tourism.

In a half-assed attempt at thematic consistency, several pseudo-authentic, Ole English restaurants opened along Cypress Street to lure tourists with the promise of tasteless English cuisine. (There had even been an attempt by one entrepreneur to establish an authentic English pizza place, but the enterprise was abandoned with the realization that boiled pizza lost most of its character.)

Pine Cove's locals avoided patronage of these restaurants with the duplicity of a Hindu cattle rancher: willing to reap the profits without sampling the product. Locals dined at the few, out-of-the-way cafes that were content with carving a niche out of the hometown market with good food and service rather than gouging an eye out of the swollen skull of the tourist market with over-priced, pretentious charm.

The shops along Cypress Street were functional only in that they moved money from the pockets of the tourists into the local economy. From the standpoint of the villagers, there was nothing of practical use for sale in any of the stores. For the tourist, immersed in the oblivion of vacation spending, Cypress Street provided a bonanza of curious gifts to prove to the folks back home that they had been somewhere. Somewhere where they had obviously forgotten that soon they would return home to a mortgage, dental bills, and an American Express bill that would descend at the end of the month like a financial Angel of Death.

And they bought. They bought effigies of whales and sea otters carved in wood, cast in plastic, brass, or pewter, stamped on key chains, printed on postcards, posters, book covers, and condoms. They bought all sorts of useless junk imprinted with: *Pine Cove, Gateway to Big Sur,* from bookmarks to bath soap.

Over the years it became a challenge to the Pine Cove shopowners to come up with an item so tacky that it would not sell. Gus Brine, owner of the local general store, suggested once at a Chamber of Commerce meeting that the merchants, without compromising their high standards, might put cow manure into jars, imprint the label with *Pine Cove, Gateway to Big Sur,* and market it as authentic gray whale feces. As often happens with matters of money, the irony of Brine's suggestion was lost, a motion was carried, a plan was laid, and if it had not been for a lack of volunteers to do the actual packaging, the shelves of Cypress

Street would have displayed numbered, limited-edition jars of *Genuine Whale Waste*.

The residents of Pine Cove went about their work of fleecing the tourists with a slow, methodical resolve that involved more waiting than activity. Life, in general, was slow in Pine Cove. Even the wind that came in off the Pacific each evening crept slowly through the trees, allowing the villagers ample time to bring in wood and stoke their fires against the damp cold. In the morning, down on Cypress Street, the *Open* signs flipped with a languid disregard for the times posted on the doors. Some shops opened early, some late, and some not at all, especially if it was a nice day for a walk on the beach. It was as if the villagers, having found their little bit of peace, were waiting for something to happen.

And it did.

Around midnight on the night that The Breeze disappeared, every dog in Pine Cove began barking. During the following fifteen minutes, shoes were thrown, threats were made, and the sheriff was called and called again. Wives were beaten, pistols were loaded, pillows were pounded, and Mrs. Feldstein's thirty-two cats simultaneously coughed up hairballs on her porch. Blood pressure went up, aspirin was opened, and Milo Tobin, the town's evil developer, looked out the front window to see his young neighbor, Rosa Cruz, in the nude, chasing twin Pomeranians around her front yard. The strain was too much for his chain-smoker's heart, and he flopped on the floor like a fish and died.

On another hill, Van Williams, the tree surgeon, had reached the limit of his patience with his neighbors, a family of born-again dog breeders whose six Labrador retrievers barked all night long with or without supernatural provocation. With his professional-model chain saw he dropped a hundred-foot Monterey pine tree on their new Dodge Evangeline van.

A few minutes later, a family of raccoons who normally roamed the streets of Pine Cove breaking into garbage cans, were taken, temporarily, with a strange sapience and ignored their normal activities to steal the stereo out of the ruined van and install it in their den that lay in the trunk of a hollow tree.

An hour after the cacophony began, it stopped. The dogs had delivered their message, and as it goes in cases where dogs warn of coming earthquakes, tornadoes, or volcanic eruptions, the message was completely misconstrued. What was left the next morning was a very sleepy, grumpy village brimming with lawsuits and insurance claims, but without a single clue that something was coming.

At six that morning a cadre of old men gathered outside the general store to discuss the events of the night before, never once letting their ignorance of what had happened interfere with a good bull session.

A new, four-wheel-drive pickup pulled into the small parking lot, and Augustus Brine crawled out, jangling his huge key ring as if it were a talisman of power sent down by the janitor god. He was a big man, sixty years old, white haired and bearded, with shoulders like a mountain gorilla. People alternately compared him to Santa Claus and the Norse god Odin.

"Morning, boys," Brine grumbled to the old men, who gathered behind him as he unlocked the door and let them into the dark interior of Brine's Bait, Tackle, and Fine Wines. As he switched on the lights and started brewing the first two pots of his special, secret, dark-roast coffee, Brine was assaulted by a salvo of questions.

"Gus, did you hear the dogs last night?"

"We heard a tree went down on your hill. You hear anything about it?"

"Can you brew some decaf? Doctor says I've got to cut the caffeine."

"Bill thinks it was a bitch in heat started the barking, but it was all over town."

"Did you get any sleep? I couldn't get back to sleep."

Brine raised a big paw to signal that he was going to speak, and the old men fell silent. It was like that every morning: Brine arrived in the middle of a discussion and was immediately elected to the role of expert and mediator.

"Gentlemen, the coffee's on. In regard to the events of last night, I must claim ignorance."

"You mean it didn't wake you up?" Jim Whatley asked from under the brim of a Brooklyn Dodgers baseball cap.

"I retired early last night with two lovely teenage bottles of cabernet, Jim. Anything that happened after that did so without my knowledge or consent."

Jim was miffed with Brine's detachment. "Well, every goddamn dog in town started barking last night like the end of the world was coming."

"Dogs bark," Brine stated. He left off the "big deal"—it was understood from his tone.

"Not every dog in town. Not all at once. George thinks it's supernatural or something."

Brine raised a white eyebrow toward George Peters, who stood by the coffee machine sporting a dazzling denture grin. "And what, George, leads you to the conclusion that the cause of this disturbance was supernatural?"

"Woke up with a hard-on for the first time in twenty years. It got me right up. I thought I'd rolled over on the flashlight I keep by the bed for midnight emergencies."

"How were the batteries, Georgie?" someone interjected.

"I tried to wake up the wife. Whacked her on the leg with it just to get her attention. I told her the bear was charging and I have one bullet left."

"And?" Brine filled the pause.

"She told me to put some ice on it to make the swelling go down."

"Well," Brine said, stroking his beard, "that certainly sounds like a supernatural experience to me." He turned to the rest of the group and announced his judgment. "Gents, I agree with George. As with Lazarus rising from the dead, this unexplained erection is hard evidence of the supernatural at work. Now, if you'll excuse me, I have cash customers to attend to."

The last remark was not meant as a dig toward the old men, whom Brine allowed to drink coffee all day free of charge. Augustus Brine had long ago won their loyalty, and it would have been absurd for any one of them to think of going anywhere else to purchase wine, or cheese, or bait, or gasoline, even though Brine's prices were a good thirty percent higher than the Thrifty-Mart down the street.

Could the pimple-faced clerks at the Thrifty-Mart give advice on which bait was best for rock cod, a recipe for an elegant dill sauce for that same fish, recommend a fine wine to complement the meal, and at the same time ask after the well-being of every family member for three generations by name? They could not! And therein lay the secret of Augustus Brine's ability to run a successful business based entirely on the patronage of locals in an economy catering to tourists.

Brine made his way to the counter, where an attractive woman in a waitress apron awaited, impatiently worrying a five-dollar bill.

"Five dollars worth of unleaded, Gus." She thrust the bill at Brine.

"Rough night, Jenny?"

"Does it show?" Jenny made a show of fixing her shoulder-length auburn hair and smoothing her apron.

"A safe assumption, only," Brine said with a smile that revealed teeth permanently stained by years of coffee and pipe smoke. "The boys tell me there was a citywide disturbance last night."

"Oh, the dogs. I thought it was just my neighborhood. I didn't get to sleep until four in the morning, then the phone rang and woke me up."

"I heard about you and Robert splitting up," Brine said.

"Did someone send out a newsletter or something? We've only been separated a few days." Irritation put an unattractive rasp in her voice.

"It's a small town," Brine said softly. "I wasn't trying to be nosy."

"I'm sorry, Gus. It's just the lack of sleep. I'm so tired I was hallucinating on the way down here. I thought I heard Wayne Newton singing 'What a Friend We Have in Jesus.'"

"Maybe you did."

"The music was coming from a pine tree. I'm telling you, I've been a basket case all week."

Brine reached across the counter and patted her hand. "The only constant in this life is change, but that doesn't mean it's easy. Give yourself a break."

Just then Vance McNally, the local ambulance driver, burst through the door. The radio on his belt made a sizzling sound as if he'd just stepped out of a deep fryer. "Guess who vapor locked last night?" he said, obviously hoping that no one would know.

Everyone turned and waited for his announcement. Vance basked in their attention for a moment to confirm his self-importance. "Milo Tobin," he said, finally.

"The evil developer?" George asked.

"That's him. Sometime around midnight. We just bagged him," Vance said to the group. Then to Brine, "Can I get a pack of Marlboros?"

The old men searched each other's faces for the right reaction to Vance's news. Each was waiting for another to say what they were all thinking, which was, "It couldn't have happened to a nicer guy," or even, "Good riddance," but as they were all aware that Vance's next rude announcement could be about them, they tried to think of something nice to say. You don't park in the handicapped space lest the forces of irony give you a reason to, and you don't speak ill of the dead unless you want to get bagged next.

Jenny saved them. "He sure kept that Chrysler of his clean, didn't he?"

"Sure did."

"The thing sparkled."

"He kept it like new, he did."

Vance smiled at the discomfort he had caused. "See you boys later." He turned to leave and bumped straight into the little man standing behind him.

"Excuse me, fella," Vance said.

No one had seen him come in or had heard the bell over the door. He was an Arab, dark, with a long, hooked nose and old; his skin hung around his piercing gray-blue eyes in folds. He wore a wrinkled, gray flannel suit that was at least two sizes too big. A red stocking cap rode high on the back of his bald head. His rumpled appearance combined with this diminutive size made him look like a ventriloquist's dummy that had spent a long time in a small suitcase.

The little man brandished a craggy hand under Vance's nose and let loose with a string of angry Arabic that swirled through the air like blue on a Damascus blade. Vance backed out the door, jumped into his ambulance, and motored away.

Everyone stood stunned by the ferocity of the little man's anger. Had they really seen blue swirls? Were the Arab's teeth really filed to points? Were, for that moment, his eyes glowing white-hot? It would never be discussed.

Augustus Brine was the first to recover. "Can I help you with something, sir?"

The unnatural light in the Arab's eyes dimmed, and in a humble, obsequious manner he said, "Excuse me, please, but could I trouble you for a small quantity of salt?"

3

TRAVIS

Travis O'Hearn was driving a fifteen-year-old Chevy Impala he had bought in L.A. with money the demon had taken from a pimp. The demon was standing on the passenger seat with his head out the window, panting into the rushing coastal wind with the slobbering exuberance of an Irish setter. From time to time he pulled his head inside the car, looked at Travis, and sang, "Your mother sucks cocks in he-ell, Your mother sucks cocks in he-ell," in a teasing, childlike way. Then he would spin his head around several times for effect.

They had spent the night in a cheap motel north of San Junipero, and the demon had tuned the television to a cable channel that played an uncut version of *The Exorcist*. It was the demon's favorite movie. At least, Travis thought, it was better than the last time, when the demon had seen *The Wizard of Oz* and had spent an entire day pretending to be a flying monkey, or screaming, "And that goes for your little dog, too."

"Sit still, Catch," Travis said. "I'm trying to drive."

The demon had been wired since he had eaten the hitchhiker the night before. The guy must have been on cocaine or speed. Why did drugs affect the demon when poisons did not phase him? It was a mystery.

The demon tapped Travis on the shoulder with a long reptilian claw. "I want to ride on the hood," he said. His voice was like rusty nails rattling in a can.

"Enjoy," Travis said, waving across the dashboard.

The demon climbed out the window and across the front, where he perched like a hood ornament from hell, his forked tongue flying in the wind like a storm-swept pennon, spattering the windshield with saliva. Travis turned on the wipers and was grateful to find that the Chevy was equipped with an interval delay feature.

It had taken him a full day in Los Angeles to find a pimp who looked as if he were carrying enough cash to get them a car, and another day for the demon to catch the guy in a place isolated enough to eat him. Travis insisted that the demon eat in private. When he was eating he became visible to other people. He also tripled in size.

Travis had a recurring nightmare about being asked to explain the eating habits of his traveling companion.

In the dream Travis is walking down the street when a policeman taps him on the shoulder.

"Excuse me, sir," the policeman says.

Travis does a slow-mo Sam Peckenpah turn. "Yes," he says.

The policeman says, "I don't mean to bother you—but that large, scaly fellow over there munching on the mayor—do you know him?" The policeman points toward the demon, who is biting off the head of a man in a pinstriped polyester suit.

"Why, yes, I do," Travis says. "That's Catch, he's a demon. He has to eat someone every couple of days or he gets cranky. I've known him for seventy years. I'll vouch for his lack of character."

The policeman, who has heard it all before, says, "There's a city ordinance against eating an elected official without a permit. May I see your permit, please?"

"I'm sorry," Travis says, "I don't have a permit, but I'll be glad to get one if you'll tell me where to go."

The cop sighs and begins writing on a ticket pad. "You can only get a permit from the mayor, and your friend seems to be finishing him off now. We don't like strangers eating our mayor around here. I'm afraid I'll have to cite you."

Travis protests, "But if I get another ticket, they'll cancel my insurance." He always wondered about this part of the dream; he'd never carried insurance. The cop ignores him and continues to write out the ticket. Even in a dream, he is only doing his job.

Travis thought it terribly unfair that Catch even invaded his dreams. Sleep, at least, should provide some escape from the demon, who had been with him for seventy years, and would be with him forever unless he could find a way to send him back to hell.

For a man of ninety, Travis was remarkably well preserved. In fact, he did not appear to be much over twenty, his age when he had called up the demon. Dark with dark eyes and lean, Travis had sharp features that would have seemed evil if not for the constant look of confusion he wore, as if there were one answer that would make everything in life clear to him if he could only remember the question.

He had never bargained for the endless days on the road with the demon, trying to figure out how to stop the killing. Sometimes the demon ate daily, sometimes he would go for weeks without killing. Travis had never found a reason, a connection, or a pattern to it. Sometimes he could dissuade the demon from killing, sometimes he could only steer him toward certain victims. When he could, he had the demon eat pimps or pushers, those that humanity could do without. But other times he had to choose vagrants and vagabonds, those that would not be missed.

There was a time when he had cried while sending Catch after a hobo or a bag-lady. He'd made friends among the homeless when he was riding the rails with the demon, back before there were so many automobiles. Often a bum who didn't know where his next roof or drink was coming from had shared a boxcar and a bottle with Travis. And Travis had learned that there was no evil in being poor; poverty merely opened one up to evil. But over the years he had learned to push aside the remorse, and time and again Catch dined on bums.

He wondered what went through the minds of Catch's victims just before they died. He had seen them wave their hands before their eyes as if the monster looming before them was an illusion, a trick of the light. He wondered what would happen now, if oncoming drivers could see Catch perched on the front of the Chevy waving like a parade queen from the Black Lagoon.

They would panic, swerve off the narrow road and over the ocean-side bank. Windshields would shatter, and gasoline would explode, and people would die. Death and the demon were never separated for long. *Coming soon to a town near you,* Travis thought. *But perhaps this is the last one.*

As a seagull cry dopplered off to Travis's left, he turned to look out the window over the ocean. The morning sun was reflecting off the face of the waves, illuminating a sparkling halo of spray. For a moment he forgot about Catch and drank in the beauty of the scene, but when he turned to look at the road again, there was the demon, standing on the bumper, reminding him of his responsibility.

Travis pushed the accelerator to the floor and the Impala's engine hesitated, then roared as the automatic transmission dropped into passing gear. When the speedometer hit sixty he locked up the brakes.

Catch hit the roadway face first and skidded headlong, throwing up sparks where his scales scraped the asphalt. He bounced off a signpost and into a ditch, where he lay for a moment trying to gather his thoughts. The Impala fishtailed and came to a stop sideways in the road.

Travis slammed the Chevy into reverse, righted the car, then threw it into drive and screeched toward the demon, keeping the wheels out of the ditch until the moment of impact. The Impala's headlights shattered against Catch's chest. The corner of the bumper caught him in the waist and drove him deep into the mud of the ditch. The engine sputtered to a stop and the damaged radiator hissed a rusty cloud of steam into Catch's face.

The driver's side door was jammed against the ditch, so Travis crawled out the window and ran around the car to see what damage he had done. Catch was lying in the ditch with the bumper against his chest.

"Nice driving, A.J.," Catch said. "You going to try for Indy next year?"

Travis was disappointed. He hadn't really expected to hurt Catch, he knew from experience that the demon was virtually indestructible, but he had hoped at least to piss him off. "Just trying to keep you on your toes," he said. "A little test to see how you hold up under stress."

Catch lifted the car, crawled out, and stood next to Travis in the ditch. "What's the verdict? Did I pass?"

"Are you dead?"

"Nope, I feel great."

"Then you have failed miserably. I'm sorry but I'll have to run you over again."

"Not with this car," the demon said, shaking his head.

Travis surveyed the steam rising from the radiator and wondered whether he might not have been a little hasty in giving way to his anger. "Can you get it out of the ditch?"

"Piece of cake." The demon hoisted the front of the car and began to walk it up onto the berm. "But you're not going to get far without a new radiator."

"Oh, you're all of a sudden an expert mechanic. Mr. help-me-I-can't-change-the-channel-while-the-magic-fingers-is-on all of a sudden has a degree in automotive diagnostics?"

"Well, what do you think?"

"I think there's a town just ahead where we can get it fixed. Didn't you read that sign you bounced off of?" It was a dig. Travis knew the demon couldn't read; in fact, he often watched subtitled movies with the sound off just to irritate Catch.

"What's it say?"

"It says, 'Pine Cove, five miles.' That's where we're going. I think we can limp the car five miles with a bad radiator. If not, you can push."

"You run over me and wreck the car and I get to push?"

"Correct," Travis said, crawling back through the car window.

"At your command, master," Catch said sarcastically.

Travis tried the ignition. The car whined and died. "It won't start. Get behind and push."

"Okay," Catch said. He went around to the back of the car, put his shoulder to the bumper, and began pushing it the rest of the way out of the ditch. "But pushing cars is very hungry work."

4

ROBERT

Robert Masterson had drunk a gallon of red wine, most of a five-liter Coors minikeg, and a half-pint of tequila, and still the dream came.

A desert. A big, bright, sandy bastard. The Sahara. He is naked, tied to a chair with barbed wire. Before him is a great canopied bed covered in black satin. Under the cool shade of the canopy his wife, Jennifer, is making love to a stranger—a young, muscular, dark-haired man. Tears run down Robert's cheeks and crystallize into salt. He cannot close his eyes or turn away. He tries to scream, but every time he opens his mouth a squat, lizardlike monster, the size of a chimpanzee, shoves a saltine cracker into his mouth. The heat and the pain in his chest are agonizing. The lovers are oblivious to his pain. The little reptile man tightens the barbed wire around his chest by twisting a stick. Every time he sobs, the wire cuts deeper. The lovers turn to him in slow motion, maintaining their embrace. They wave to him, a big home-movie wave, postcard smiles. Greetings from the heart of anguish.

Awake, the dream-pain in his chest replaced by a real pain in his head. Light is the enemy. It's out there waiting for you to open your eyes. No. No way.

Thirst—brave the light to slake the thirst—it must be done.

He opened his eyes to a dim, forgiving light. Must be cloudy out. He looked around. Pillows, full ashtrays, empty wine bottles, a chair, a calendar from the wrong year with a picture of a surfer riding a huge swell, pizza boxes. This wasn't home. He didn't live like this. Humans don't live like this.

He was on someone's couch. Where?

He sat up and waited in vertigo until his brain snapped back into his head, which it did with a vengeful impact. Ah, yes, he knew where he was. This was Hangover—Hangover, California. Pine Cove, where he was thrown out of the house by his wife. Heartbreak, California.

Jenny, call Jenny. Tell her that humans don't live this way. No one lives this way. Except The Breeze. He was in The Breeze's trailer.

He looked around for water. There was the kitchen, fourteen miles away, over there at the end of the couch. Water was in the kitchen.

He crawled naked off the couch, across the floor of the kitchen to the sink, and pulled himself up. The faucet was gone, or at least buried under a stack of dirty dishes. He reached into an opening, cautiously searching for the faucet like a diver reaching into an underwater crevice for a moray eel. Plates skidded down the pile and crashed on the floor. He looked at the china shards scattered around his knees and spotted the mirage of a Coors minikeg. He managed a controlled fall toward the mirage and his hand struck the nozzle. It was real. Salvation: hair of the dog in a handy, five-liter disposable package.

He started to drink from the nozzle and instantly filled his mouth, throat, sinuses, aural cavity, and chest hair with foam.

"Use a glass," Jenny would say. "What are you, an animal?" He must call Jenny and apologize as soon as the thirst was gone.

First, a glass. Dirty dishes were strewn across every horizontal surface in the kitchen: the counter, stove, table, breakfast bar, and the top of the refrigerator. The oven was filled with dirty dishes.

Nobody lives like this. He spotted a glass among the miasma. The Holy Grail. He grabbed it and filled it with beer. Mold floated on the settling foam. He threw the glass into the oven and slammed the door before an avalanche could gain momentum.

A clean glass, perhaps. He checked the cupboard where the dishes had once been kept. A single cereal bowl stared out at him. From the bottom of the bowl Fred Flintstone congratulated him, "Good kid! You're a clean-plater!" Robert filled the bowl and sat cross-legged on the floor amid the broken dishes while he drank.

Fred Flintstone congratulated him three times before his thirst abated. Good old Fred. The man's a saint. Saint Fred of Bedrock.

"Fred, how could she do this to me? Nobody can live like this."

"Good kid! You're a clean-plater!" Fred said.

"Call Jenny," Robert said, reminding himself. He stood and staggered through the offal toward the phone. Nausea swept over him and he bounced back through the trailer's narrow hallway and fell into the bathroom, where he retched into the toilet until he passed out. The Breeze called it "talking to Ralph on the Big White Phone." This one was a toll call.

Five minutes later he came to and found the phone. It seemed a superhuman effort to hit the right buttons. Why did they have to keep moving? At last he connected and someone answered on the first ring. "Jenny, honey, I'm sorry. Can I—"

"Thank you for calling Pizza on Wheels. We will open at eleven A.M. and deliveries begin at four P.M. Why cook when—"

Robert hung up. He'd dialed the number written on the phone's emergency numbers sticker instead of his home. Again he chased down the buttons and pegged them one by one. It was like shooting skeet, you had to lead them a little.

"Hello." Jenny sounded sleepy.

"Honey, I'm sorry. I'll never do it again. Can I come home?"

"Robert? What time is it?"

He thought for a moment then guessed, "Noon?"

"It's five in the morning, Robert. I've been asleep about an hour,

Robert. There were dogs barking in the neighborhood all night long, Robert. I'm not ready for this. Good-bye, Robert."

"But Jenny, how could you do it? You don't even like the desert. And you know how I hate saltines."

"You're drunk, Robert."

"Who is this guy, Jenny? What does he have that I don't have?"

"There is no other guy. I told you yesterday, I just can't live with you anymore. I don't think I love you anymore."

"Who do you love? Who is he?"

"Myself, Robert. I'm doing it for myself. Now I'm hanging up for myself. Say good-bye so I don't feel like I'm hanging up on you."

"But, Jenny—"

"It's over. Get on with your life, Robert. I'm hanging up now. Good-bye."

"But—" She hung up. "Nobody lives like this," Robert said to the dial tone.

Get on with your life. Okay, that's a plan. He would clean up this place and clean up his life. Never drink again. Things were going to change. Soon she would remember what a great guy he was. But first he had to go to the bathroom to answer an emergency call from Ralph.

The smoke alarm was screaming like a tortured lamb. Robert, now back on the couch, pulled a cushion over his head and wondered why the Breeze didn't have a sleeper button on his smoke alarm. Then the pounding started. It was a door buzzer, not the smoke alarm.

"Breeze, answer the door!" Robert shouted into the cushion. The pounding continued. He crawled off the couch and waded through the litter to the door.

"Hold on a minute, man. I'm coming." He threw the door open and caught the man outside with his fist poised for another pounding. He was a sharp-faced Hispanic in a raw silk suit. His hair was slicked back and tied in a ponytail with a black silk ribbon. Robert could see a flagship model BMW parked in the driveway.

"Shit. Jehovah's Witnesses must make a lot of money," Robert said.

The Hispanic was not amused. "I need to talk to The Breeze."

At that point Robert realized that he was naked and picked an empty, gallon wine bottle from the floor to cover his privates.

"Come in," Robert said, backing away from the door. "I'll see if he's awake."

The Hispanic stepped in. Robert stumbled down the narrow hall to The Breeze's room. He knocked on the door. "Breeze, there's some big money here to see you." No answer. He opened the door and went in and searched through the piles of blankets, sheets, pillows, beer cans, and wine bottles, but found no Breeze.

On the way back to the living room Robert grabbed a mildewed towel from the bathroom and wrapped it around his hips. The Hispanic was standing in the middle of a small clearing, peering around the trailer with concentrated disgust. It looked to Robert as if he were trying to levitate to avoid having his Italian shoes contact the filth on the floor.

"He's not here," Robert said.

"How do you live like this?" the Hispanic said. He had no discernible accent. "This is subhuman, man."

"Did my mother send you?"

The Hispanic ignored the question. "Where is The Breeze? We had a meeting this morning." He put an extra emphasis on the word *meeting*. Robert got the message. The Breeze had been hinting that he had some big deal going down. The guy must be the buyer. Silk suits and BMWs were not the usual accouterments of The Breeze's clientele.

"He left last night. I don't know where he went. You could check down at the Slug."

"The Slug?"

"Head of the Slug Saloon, on Cypress. He hangs out there sometimes."

The Hispanic tiptoed through the garbage to the door, then paused on the step. "Tell him I'm looking for him. He should call me. Tell him I do not do business this way."

Robert didn't like the commanding tone in the Hispanic's voice. He affected the obsequious tone of an English butler, "And whom shall I say has called, sir?"

"Don't fuck with me, *cabron*. This is business."

Robert took a deep breath, then sighed. "Look, Pancho. I'm hung over, my wife just threw me out, and my life is not worth shit. So if you want me to take messages, you can damn well tell me who the fuck you are. Or should I tell The Breeze to look for a Mexican with a Gucci loafer shoved up his ass? *Comprende, Pachuco?*"

The Hispanic turned on the step and started to reach into his suit coat. Robert felt adrenaline shoot through his body, and he tightened his grip on the towel. Oh, yeah, he thought, pull a gun and I'll snap your eyes out with this towel. He suddenly felt extremely helpless.

The Hispanic kept his hand in his coat. "Who are you?"

"I'm The Breeze's decorator. We're redoing the whole place in an abstract expressionist motif." Robert wondered if he wasn't really trying to get shot.

"Well, smart ass, when The Breeze shows up, you tell him to call Rivera. And you tell him that when the business is done, his decorator is mine. You understand?"

Robert nodded weakly.

"*Adios*, dogmeat." Rivera turned and walked toward the BMW.

Robert closed the door and leaned against it, trying to catch his breath. The Breeze was going to be pissed when he heard about this. Robert's fear was replaced by self-loathing. Maybe Jenny was right. Maybe he had no idea how to maintain a relationship with anybody. He was worthless and weak—and dehydrated.

He looked around for something to drink and vaguely remembered having done this before. *Déjà vu?*

"Nobody lives like this." It was going to change, goddammit. As soon as he found his clothes, he was going to change it.

RIVERA

Detective Sergeant Alphonso Rivera of the San Junipero County Sheriff's Department sat in the rented BMW and cursed. "Fuck, fuck, and double fuck." Then he remembered the transmitter taped to his chest. "Okay, cowboys, he's not here. I should have known. The van's been gone for a week. Call it off."

In the distance he could hear cars starting. Two beige Plymouths drove by a few seconds later, the drivers conspicuously not looking at the BMW as they passed.

What could have gone wrong? Three months setting it all up. He'd gone out on a limb with the captain to convince him that Charles L. Belew, a.k.a. The Breeze, was their ticket into the Big Sur growers' business.

"He's gone down twice for cocaine. If we pop him for dealing, he'll give us everything but his favorite recipe to stay out of Soledad."

"He's small time," the captain had said.

"Yeah, but he knows everybody, and he's hungry. Best of all, he knows he's small time, so he thinks we wouldn't bother with him."

Finally the captain had relented and it had been set up. Rivera could hear him now. "Rivera, if you got made by a drugged-out loser like Belew, maybe we should put you back in uniform, where your high visibility will be an asset. Maybe we can put you in P.R. or recruitment."

Rivera's ass was hanging out worse than that drunken jerk in the trailer. Who was he, anyway? As far as anyone knew, The Breeze lived alone. But this guy seemed to know something. Why else would he give Rivera such a hard time? Maybe he could pull this off with the drunk. Desperate thinking. A long shot.

Rivera memorized the license number of the old Ford truck parked outside The Breeze's trailer. He would run it through the computer when he got back to the station. Maybe he could convince the captain that he still had something. Maybe he did. And then again, maybe he could just climb a stream of angel piss to heaven.

Rivera sat in the file room of the sheriff's office drinking coffee and watching a videotape. After running the license number through the computer, Rivera found that the pickup belonged to a Robert Masterson, age twenty-nine. Born in Ohio, married to

Jennifer Masterson, also twenty-nine. His only prior was a drunk-driving conviction two years ago.

The video was a record of Masterson's breathalyzer test. Several years ago the department had begun taping all breathalyzer tests to avoid legal-defense strategies based on procedural mistakes made by arresting officers during testing.

On the television screen a very drunk Robert W. Masterson (6 ft., 180 lbs., eyes green, hair brown) was spouting nonsense to two uniformed deputies.

"We work for a common purpose. You serve the state with your minds and bodies. I serve the state by opposing it. Drinking is an act of civil disobedience. I drink to end world hunger. I drink to protest the United States' involvement in Central America. I drink to protest nuclear power. I drink . . ."

A sense of doom descended on Rivera as he watched. Unless The Breeze reappeared, his career was in the hands of this tightly wound, loosely wrapped, drunken idiot. He wondered what life might be like as a bank security guard.

On the screen the two officers looked away from their prisoner to the door of the testing room. The camera was mounted in the corner and fitted with a wide-angle lens to cover anything that happened without having to be adjusted. A little Arab man in a red stocking cap had come through the door, and the deputies were telling him that he had the wrong room and to please leave.

"Could I trouble you for a small quantity of salt?" the little man asked. Then he blinked off the screen as if the tape had been stopped and he had been edited out.

Rivera rewound the tape and ran it again. The second time, Masterson performed the test without interruption. The door did not open and there was no little man. Rivera ran it back again: no little man.

He must have dozed off while the tape was running. His subconscious had continued the tape while he slept, inserting the little man's entrance. That was the only viable explanation.

"I don't need this shit," he said. Then he ejected the tape and drained his coffee, his tenth cup of the day.

5

AUGUSTUS BRINE

He was an old man who fished off the beaches of Pine Cove and he had gone eighty-four days without catching a fish. This, however, was of little consequence because he owned the general store and made a comfortable enough living to indulge his passions, which were fishing and drinking California wines.

Augustus Brine was old, but he was still strong and vital and a dangerous man in a fight—although he had had little cause to prove it in over thirty years (except for the few occasions when he picked up a teenage boy by the scruff of the neck and dragged him, terrified, to the stockroom, where he lectured him alternately on the merits of hard work and the folly of shoplifting from Brine's Bait, Tackle, and Fine Wines). And while a weariness had come upon him with age, his mind was still sharp and agile. On any evening one might find him stretched out before his fireplace in a leather chair, toasting his bare feet on the hearth, reading Aristotle, or Lao-tzu, or Joyce.

He lived on a hillside overlooking the Pacific, in a small wooden house he had designed and built himself, so that he might live there alone without having his surroundings seem lonely. During the day, windows and skylights filled the house with light, and even on the most dismal, foggy day, every corner was illuminated. In the evening three stone fireplaces, which took up whole walls in the living room, bedroom, and study, warmed the house. They offered a soft, orange comfort to the old man, who burned cord after cord of red oak and eucalyptus, which he cut and split himself.

When he considered his own mortality, which was seldom, Augustus Brine knew he would die in this house. He had built it on one floor with wide halls and doorways so that if he were ever confined to a wheelchair he might remain self-sufficient until the day when he would take the black pill sent to him by the Hemlock Society.

He kept the house neat and orderly. Not so much because he desired order, for Brine believed chaos to be the way of the world, but because he did not wish to make life difficult for his cleaning lady, who came in once a week to dust and shovel ashes from the fireplaces. He also wished to avoid acquiring the reputation of being a slob, for he knew people's propensity for judging a man on one aspect of his character, and even Augustus Brine was not above some degree of vanity.

Despite his belief that the pursuit of order in a chaotic universe was futile, Brine lived a very ordered life, and this paradox, upon reflection, amused him. He rose each day at five, indulged himself in a half-hour-long shower, dressed, and ate the same breakfast of six eggs and half a loaf of sourdough toast, heavily buttered. (Cholesterol seemed too silent and sneaky to be dangerous, and Brine had decided long ago that until cholesterol gathered its forces and charged him headlong across the plate with Light Brigade abandon, he would ignore it.)

After breakfast, Brine lit his meerschaum pipe for the first time of the day, crawled onto his truck, and drove downtown to open his store.

For the first two hours he puffed around the store like a great white-bearded locomotive, making coffee, selling pastries, trading idle banter with the old men who greeted him each morning, and preparing the store to run under full steam until midnight, under the supervision of a handful of clerks. At eight o'clock the first of Brine's employees arrived to man the register while Brine busied himself ordering what he called Epicurean necessities: pastries, imported cheeses and beers, pipe tobacco and cigarettes, home-made pasta and sauces, freshly baked bread, gourmet coffees, and California wines. Brine believed, like Epicurus, that a good life was one dedicated to the pursuit of simple pleasures, tempered with justice and prudence. Years ago, while working as a bouncer in a whorehouse, Brine had repeatedly seen depressed, angry men turned to gentleness and gaiety by a few moments of pleasure. He had vowed then to someday open a brothel, but when the ramshackle general store with its two gas pumps had been put up for sale, Brine had compromised his dream by buying it and bringing pleasure of a different sort to the public. From time to time, however, a needling suspicion arose in his mind that he had missed his true calling as a madam.

Each day when the orders were finished, Brine selected a bottle of red wine from his shelves, packed it in a basket with some bread, cheese, and bait, and took off for the beach. He passed the rest of the day sitting on the beach in a canvas director's chair sipping wine and smoking his pipe, waiting for the long surf-casting rod to bend with a strike.

On most days Brine let his mind go as clear as water. Without worry or thought he became one with everything around him, neither conscious nor unconscious: the state of Zen *mushin,* or no-mind. He had come to Zen after the fact, recognizing in the writings of Suzuki and Watts an attitude he had come to without discipline, by simply sitting on the beach staring into an empty sky and becoming just as empty. Zen was his religion, and it brought him peace and humor.

On this particular morning Brine was having a difficult time clearing his mind. The visit of the little Arab man to the store vexed him. Brine did not speak Arabic, yet he had understood every word the little man had said. He *had* seen the air cut with swirling blue curses, and he *had* seen the Arab's eyes glow white with anger.

He smoked his pipe, the meerschaum mermaid carved so that Brine's index finger fell across her breasts, and tried to apply some meaning to a situation that was outside the context of his reality. He knew that if he were to accept the fluid of this experience, the cup of his mind had to be empty. But right now he had a better chance of buying bread with moonlight than reaching a Zen calm. It vexed him.

"It is a mystery, is it not?" someone said.

Startled, Brine looked around. The little Arab man stood about three feet from Brine's side, drinking from a large styrofoam cup. His red stocking cap was glistening, damp with the morning spray.

"I'm sorry," Brine said. "I didn't see you come up."

"It is a mystery, is it not? How this dashing figure seems to appear out of nowhere? You must be awestruck. Paralyzed with fear perhaps?"

Brine looked at the withered little man in the rumpled flannel suit and silly red hat. "Very close to paralyzed," he said. "I am Augustus Brine." He extended his hand to the little man.

"Are you not afraid that by touching me you will burst into flames?"

"Is that a danger?"

"No, but you know how superstitious fishermen are. Perhaps you believe that you will be transformed into a toad. You hide your fear well, Augustus Brine."

Brine smiled. He was baffled and amused; it didn't occur to him to be afraid.

The Arab drained his cup and dipped it into the surf to refill it.

"Please call me Gus," Brine said, his hand still extended. "And you are?"

The Arab drained his cup again, then took Brine's hand. His skin had the feel of parchment.

"I am Gian Hen Gian, King of the Djinn, Ruler of the Netherworld. Do not tremble, I wish you no harm."

"I am not trembling," Brine said. "You might go easy on that seawater—it works hell on your blood pressure."

"Do not fall to your knees; there is no need to prostrate yourself before my greatness. I am here in your service."

"Thank you. I am honored," Brine said. Despite the strange happenings in the store, he was having a hard time taking this pompous little man seriously. The Arab was obviously a nuthouse Napoleon. He'd seen hundreds of them, living in cardboard castles and feasting from dumpsters all over America. But this one had some credentials: he could curse in blue swirls.

"It is good that you are not afraid, Augustus Brine. Terrible evil is at hand. You will have to call upon your courage. It is a good sign that you have kept your wits in the presence of the great Gian Hen Gian. The grandeur is sometimes too much for weaker men."

"May I offer you some wine?" Brine extended the bottle of cabernet he had brought from the store.

"No, I have a great thirst for this." He sloshed the cup of seawater. "From a time when it was all I could drink."

"As you wish." Brine sipped from the bottle.

"There is little time, Augustus Brine, and what I am to tell you may overwhelm your tiny mind. Please prepare yourself."

"My tiny mind is steeled for anything, O King. But first, tell me, did I see you curse blue swirls this morning?"

"A minor loss of temper. Nothing really. Would you have had me turn the clumsy dolt into a snake who forever gnaws his own tail?"

"No, the cursing was fine. Although in Vance's case the snake might be an improvement. Your curses were in Arabic, though, right?"

"A language I prefer for its music."

"But I don't speak Arabic. Yet I understood you. You did say, 'May the IRS find that you deduct your pet sheep as an entertainment expense,' didn't you?"

"I can be most colorful and inventive when I am angry." The Arab flashed a bright grin of pride. His teeth were pointed and saw-edged like a shark's. "You have been chosen, Augustus Brine."

"Why me?" Somehow Brine had suspended his disbelief and denied the absurdity of the situation. If there was no order in the universe, then why should it be out of order to be sitting on the beach talking to an Arab dwarf who claimed to be king of the Djinn, whatever the hell that was? Strangely enough, Brine took comfort in the fact that this experience was invalidating every assumption he had ever made about the nature of the world. He had tapped into the Zen of ignorance, the enlightenment of absurdity.

Gian Hen Gian laughed. "I have chosen you because you are a fisherman who catches no fish. I have had an affinity for such men since I was fished from the sea a thousand years ago and released from Solomon's jar. One gets ever so cramped passing the centuries inside a jar."

"And ever so wrinkled, it would seem," Brine said.

Gian Hen Gian ignored Brine's comment. "I found you here, Augustus Brine, listening to the noise of the universe, holding in your heart a spark of hope, like all fishermen, but resolved to be disappointed. You have no love, no faith, and no purpose. You shall be my instrument, and in return, you shall gain the things you lack."

Brine wanted to protest the Arab's judgment, but he realized that it was true. He'd been enlightened for exactly thirty seconds and already he was back on the path of desire and karma. Postenlightenment depression, he thought.

6

THE DJINN'S STORY

Brine said, "Excuse me, O King, but what exactly is a Djinn?"

Gian Hen Gian spit into the surf and cursed, but this time Brine did not understand the language and no blue swirls cut the air.

"I am Djinn. The Djinn were the first people. This was our world long before the first human. Have you not read the tales of Scheherazade?"

"I thought those were just stories."

"By Aladdin's lamplit scrotum, man! Everything is a story. What is there but stories? Stories are the only truth. The Djinn knew this. We had power over our own stories. We shaped our world as we wished it to be. It was our glory. We were created by Jehovah as a race of creators, and he became jealous of us.

"He sent Satan and an army of angels against us. We were banished to the netherworld, where we could not make our stories. Then he created a race who could not create and so would stand in awe of the Creator."

"Man?" Brine asked.

The Djinn nodded. "When Satan drove us into the netherworld, he saw our power. He saw that he was no more than a servant, while Jehovah had given the Djinn the power of gods. He returned to Jehovah demanding the same power. He proclaimed that he and his army would not serve until they were given the power to create.

"Jehovah was sorely angered. He banished Satan to hell, where the angel might have the power he wished, but only over his own army of rebels. To further humiliate Satan, Jehovah created a new race of beings and gave them control over their own destinies, made them masters of their own world. And he made Satan watch it all from hell.

"These beings were parodies of the angels, resembling them physically, but with none of the angels' grace or intelligence. And because he had made two mistakes before, Jehovah made these creatures mortal to keep them humble."

"Are you saying," Brine interrupted, "that the human race was created to irritate Satan?"

"That is correct. Jehovah is infinite in his snottiness."

Brine reflected on this for a moment and regretted that he had not become a criminal at an early age. "And what happened to the Djinn?"

"We were left without form, purpose, or power. The netherworld is timeless and unchanging, and boring—much like a doctor's waiting room."

"But you're here, you're not in the netherworld."

"Be patient, Augustus Brine. I will tell you how I came here. You see, many years passed on Earth and we remained undisturbed. Then was born Solomon the thief."

"You mean King Solomon? Son of David?"

"The thief!" The Djinn spat. "He asked for wisdom from Jehovah that he might build a great temple. To assist him, Jehovah gave him a great silver seal, which he carried in a scepter, and the power to call the Djinn from the netherworld to act as slaves. Solomon was given power over the Djinn on Earth that by all rights belonged to me. And as if that was not enough, the seal also gave him the power to call up the deposed angels from hell. Satan was furious that such power be given to a mortal, which, of course, was Jehovah's plan.

"Solomon called first upon me to help him build his temple. He spread the temple plans before me and I laughed in his face. It was little more than a shack of stone. His imagination was as limited as his intelligence. Nevertheless, I began work on his temple, building it stone by stone as he instructed. I could have built it in an instant had he commanded it, but the thief could only imagine a temple being built as it might be built by men.

"I worked slowly, for even under the reign of the thief, my time on Earth was better than the emptiness of the netherworld. After some time I convinced Solomon that I needed help, and I was given slaves to assist me in the construction. Work slowed even more, for while some of them worked, most stood by and chatted about their dreams of freedom. I have seen that such methods are used today in building your highways."

"It's standard," Brine said.

"Solomon grew impatient with my progress and called from hell one of the deposed angels, a warrior Seraph named Catch. Thus did his troubles begin.

"Catch had once been a tall and beautiful angel, but his time in hell, steeping in his own bitterness, had changed him. When he appeared before Solomon, he was a squat monster, no bigger than a dwarf. His skin was like that of a snake, his eyes like those of a cat. He was so hideous that Solomon would not allow him to be seen by the people of Jerusalem, so he made the demon invisible to all but himself.

"Catch carried in his heart a loathing for humans as deep as Satan himself. I had no quarrel with the race of man. Catch, however, wanted revenge. Fortunately, he did not have the powers of a Djinn.

"Solomon told the slaves who worked on the temple that they were being given divine assistance and that they should behave as if nothing was out of the ordinary, so the people of Jerusalem might not notice the demon's presence. The demon threw himself into the construction, honing huge blocks of stone and hauling them into place.

"Solomon was pleased with the demon's work and told him so. Catch said that the work would go faster if he didn't have to work with a Djinn, so I stood by and watched as the temple rose. From time to time great stones dropped from the walls, crushing the slaves below. While the blood ran, I could hear Catch laughing and shouting 'Whoops' from the top of the wall.

"Solomon believed these killings to be accidents, but I knew them to be murder. It was then that I realized that Solomon's control over the demon was not absolute, and therefore, his control over me must have its limits as well. My first impulse was to try to escape, but if I were wrong, I knew that I would be sent back to the netherworld and all would be lost. Perhaps I could persuade Solomon to set me free by offering him something he could attain only through my power to create.

"Solomon's appetite for women was infamous. I offered to bring him the most beautiful woman he had ever seen if he would allow me to remain on Earth. He agreed.

"I retreated to my quarters and contemplated what sort of woman might most please the idiot king. I had seen his thousand wives and found no common thread among their charms that revealed Solomon's preferences. In the end I was left to my own creativity.

"I gave her fair hair and blue eyes and skin as white and smooth as marble. She was all things that men wish of women in body and mind. She was a virgin with a courtesan's knowledge in the ways of pleasure. She was kind, intelligent, forgiving, and warm with humor.

"Solomon fell in love with the woman as soon as I presented her to him. 'She shines like a jewel', he said. 'Jewel shall be her name.' He spent an hour or more just staring at her, captivated with her beauty. When finally his senses returned, he said, 'We will talk later of your reward, Gian Hen Gian.' Then he took Jewel by the hand and led her to his bedchamber.

"I felt a strength return to me the moment I presented Jewel to the king. I was not free to escape, but for the first time I was able to leave the city without being compelled by some invisible bond to return to Solomon. I went into the desert and spent the night enjoying the freedom I had gained. It was not until I returned the next morning that I realized that Solomon's control over me and the demon depended upon the concentration of his will, as well as the invocations and the seal given to him by Jehovah. The woman, Jewel, had broken his will.

"I found Solomon in his palace weeping one moment, then screaming with rage the next. While I had been away Catch had come to Solomon's bedchamber, not in the form that Solomon recognized, but in the form of a huge monster, taller than two men and as wide as a team of horses, and the slaves could see him as well. While Solomon watched in horror, the demon snatched Jewel from the bed with a single, talonlike hand and bit her head off. Then the monster swallowed the girl's body and reached for Solomon. But some force protected the king, and Solomon commanded the demon to return to his smaller form. Catch laughed in his face and skulked off to the wives' quarters.

"Through the night the palace was filled with the screams of terrified women. Solomon ordered his guards to attack the demon. Catch swatted them away as if they were flies. By dawn the palace was littered with the crushed bodies of the guards. Of Solomon's thousand wives only two hundred remained alive. Catch was gone.

"During the attack Solomon had called upon the power of the seal and prayed to Jehovah to stop the demon. But the king's will was broken, and so it did no good.

"I sensed then that I might escape Solomon's control altogether, and live free, but even the idiot king would eventually make the connection and my fate would lie in the netherworld.

"I bade Solomon allow me to bring Catch to justice. I knew my power to be much greater than the demon's. But Solomon had only the building of the temple by which to judge my powers, and in that example the demon appeared superior. 'Do what you can,' he said. 'If you capture the demon, you may remain on Earth.'

"I found Catch in the great desert, wantonly slaughtering tribes of nomads. When I bound him with my magic, he protested that he had planned to return, for he was enslaved to Solomon by the invocation and could never really escape. He was only having a little sport with the humans, he said. To quiet him, I filled his mouth with sand for the journey back to Jerusalem.

"When I brought Catch to Solomon, the king commanded me to devise a punishment to torment the demon, so that the people of Jerusalem might watch him suffer. I chained Catch to a giant stone outside the palace, then I created a huge bird of prey that swooped on the demon and tore at his liver, which grew back at once, for like the Djinn, the demon was immortal.

"Solomon was pleased with my work. During my absence he had regained his senses somewhat, and thereby his will. I stood before the king awaiting my reward, feeling my powers wane as Solomon's will returned.

"'I have promised that you shall never be returned to the netherworld, and you shall not,' he said. 'But this demon has put me off of immortals more than somewhat, and I do not wish that you be allowed to roam free. You shall be imprisoned in a jar and cast into the sea. Should the time come when you are set free to walk the Earth again, you shall have no power over the realm of man except as is commanded by my will, which shall be from now to the end of time the goodwill of all men. By this you shall be bound.'

"He had a jar fashioned from lead and marked it on all sides with a silver seal. Before he imprisoned me, Solomon promised that Catch would remain chained to the rock until his screams burned into the king's soul—so that Solomon might never lose his will or his wisdom again. He said he would then send the demon back to hell and destroy the tablets with the invocations, as well as the great seal. He swore these things to me, as if he believed the fate of the demon meant something to me. I didn't give a camel's fart about Catch. Then he gave me a last command and sealed the jar. His soldiers cast the jar into the Red Sea.

"For two thousand years I languished inside the jar, my only comfort a trickle of seawater that seeped in, which I drank with relish, for it tasted of freedom.

"When the jar was finally pulled from the sea by a fisherman, and I was released, I cared nothing about Solomon or Catch, only about my freedom. I have lived as a man would live these last thousand years, bound by Solomon's will. Of this Solomon spoke truly, but about the demon, he lied."

The little man paused and refilled his cup in the ocean. Augustus Brine was at a loss. It couldn't possibly be true. There was nothing to corroborate the story.

"Begging your pardon, Gian Hen Gian, but why is none of this told in the Bible?"

"Editing," the Djinn said.

"But aren't you confusing Greek myth with Christian myth? The birds eating the demon's liver sounds an awful lot like the story of Prometheus."

"It was my idea. The Greeks were thieves, no better than Solomon."

Brine considered this for a moment. He was seeing evidence of the supernatural, wasn't he? Wasn't this little Arab drinking seawater as he watched, with no apparent ill effects? And even if some of it could be explained by hallucination, he was pretty sure that he hadn't been the only one to see the strange blue swirls in the store this morning. What if for a moment—just a moment—he took the Arab's outrageous story for the truth? . . .

"If this is true, then how do you know, after all this time, that Solomon lied to you? And why tell me about it?"

"Because, Augustus Brine, I knew you would believe. And I know Solomon lied because I can feel the presence of the demon, Catch. And I'm sure that he has come to Pine Cove."

"Swell," Brine said.

7

ARRIVAL

Virgil Long backed out from under the hood of the Impala, wiped his hands on his coveralls, and scratched at his four-day growth of beard. He reminded Travis of a fat weasel with the mange.

"So you're thinking it's the radiator?" Virgil asked.

"It's the radiator," Travis said.

"It might be the whole engine is gone. You were running pretty quiet when you drove in. Not a good sign. Do you have a charge card?"

Virgil was unprecedented in his inability to diagnose specific engine problems. When he was dealing with tourists, his strategy was usually to start replacing things and keep replacing them until he solved the problem or reached the limit on the customer's credit card, whichever came first.

"It wasn't running at all when I came in," Travis protested. "And I don't have a credit card. It's the radiator, I promise."

"Now, son," Virgil drawled, "I know you think you know what you're talking about, but I got a certificate from the Ford factory there on the wall that says I'm a master mechanic." Virgil pointed a fat finger toward the service station's office. One wall was covered with framed certificates along with a poster of a nude woman sitting on the hood of a Corvette buffing her private parts with a scarf in order to sell motor oil. Virgil had purchased the Master Mechanic certificates from an outfit in New Hampshire: two for five dollars, six for ten dollars, fifteen for twenty. He had gone for the twenty-dollar package. Those who took the time to read the certificates were somewhat surprised to find out that Pine Cove's only service station and car wash had its own factory-certified snowmobile mechanic. It had never snowed in Pine Cove.

"This is a Chevy," Travis said.

"Got a certificate for those, too. You probably need new rings. The radiator's just a symptom, like these broken headlights. You treat the symptom, the disease just gets worse." Virgil had heard that on a doctor show once and liked the sound of it.

"What will it cost to just fix the radiator?"

Virgil stared deep into the grease spots on the garage floor, as if by reading their patterns and by some mystic mode of divination, petrolmancy perhaps, he would arrive at a price that would not alienate the dark young man but would still assure him an exorbitant hourly rate for his labor.

"Hundred bucks." It had a nice round ring to it.

"Fine," Travis said, "Fix it. When can I have it back?"

Virgil consulted the grease spots again, then emerged with a good-ol'-boy smile. "How's noon sound?"

"Fine," Travis said. "Is there a pool hall around here—and someplace I can get some breakfast?"

"No pool hall. The Head of the Slug is open down the street. They got a couple of tables."

"And breakfast?"

"Only thing open this end of town is H.P.'s, a block off Cypress, down from the Slug. But it's a local's joint."

"Is there a problem getting served?"

"No. The menu might throw you for a bit. It—well, you'll see."

Travis thanked the mechanic and started off in the direction of H.P.'s, the demon skulking along behind him. As they passed the self-serve car-wash stalls, Travis noticed a tall man of about thirty unloading plastic laundry baskets full of dirty dishes from the bed of an old Ford pickup. He seemed to be having trouble getting quarters to go into the coin box.

Looking at him, Travis said: "You know, Catch, I'll bet there's a lot of incest in this town."

"Probably the only entertainment," the demon agreed.

The man in the car wash had activated the high-pressure nozzle and was sweeping it back and forth across the baskets of dishes. With each sweep he repeated, "Nobody lives like this. Nobody."

Some of the overspray caught on the wind and settled over Travis and Catch. For a moment the demon became visible in the spray. "I'm melt-ing," Catch whined in perfect Wicked Witch of the West pitch.

"Let's go," Travis said, moving quickly to avoid more spray. "We need a hundred bucks before noon."

JENNY

In the two hours since Jenny Masterson had arrived at the cafe she had managed to drop a tray full of glasses, mix up the orders on three tables, fill the saltshakers with sugar and the sugar dispensers with salt, and pour hot coffee on the hands of two customers who had covered their cups to indicate that they'd had enough—a patently stupid gesture on their part, she thought. The worst of it was not that she normally performed her duties flawlessly, which she did. The worst of it was that everyone was so damned understanding about it.

"You're going through a rough time, honey, it's okay."

"Divorce is always hard."

Their consolations ranged from "too bad you couldn't work it out" to "he was a worthless drunk anyway, you're better off without him."

She'd been separated from Robert exactly four days and everybody in Pine Cove knew about it. And they couldn't just let it lie. Why didn't they let her go through the process without running this cloying gauntlet of sympathy? It was as if she had a big red *D* sewed to her clothing, a signal to the townsfolk to close around her like a hungry amoeba.

When the second tray of glasses hit the floor, she stood amid the shards trying to catch her breath and could not. She had to do something—scream, cry, pass out—but she just stood there, paralyzed, while the busboy cleaned up the glass.

Two bony hands closed on her shoulders. She heard a voice in her ear that seemed to come from very far away. "You are having an anxiety attack, dear. It shall pass. Relax and breathe deeply." She felt the hands gently leading her through the kitchen door to the office in the back.

"Sit down and put your head between your knees." She let herself be guided into a chair. Her mind went white, and her breath caught in her throat. A bony hand rubbed her back.

"Breathe, Jennifer. I'll not have you shuffling off this mortal coil in the middle of the breakfast shift."

In a moment her head cleared and she looked up to see Howard Phillips, the owner of H.P.'s, standing over her.

He was a tall, skeletal man, who always wore a black suit and button shoes that had been fashionable a hundred years ago. Except for the dark depressions on his cheeks, Howard's skin was as white as a carrion worm. Robert had once said that H.P. looked like the master of ceremonies at a chemotherapy funfest.

Howard had been born and raised in Maine, yet when he spoke, he affected the accent of an erudite Londoner. "The prospect of change is a many-fanged beast, my dear. It is not, however, appropriate to pay fearful obeisance to that beast by cowering in the ruins of my stemware while you have orders up."

"I'm sorry, Howard. Robert called this morning. He sounded so helpless, pathetic."

"A tragedy, to be sure. Yet as we sit, ensconced in our grief, two perfectly healthy daily specials languish under the heat lamps metamorphosing into gelatinous invitations to botulism."

Jenny was relieved that in his own, cryptically charming way, Howard was not giving her sympathy but telling her to get off her ass and live her life. "I think I'm okay now. Thanks, Howard."

Jenny stood and wiped her eyes with a paper napkin she took from her apron. Then she went off to deliver her orders. Howard, having exhausted his compassion for the day, closed the door of his office and began working on the books.

When Jenny returned to the floor, she found that the restaurant had cleared except for a few regular customers and a dark young man she didn't recognize, who was standing by the PLEASE WAIT TO BE SEATED sign. At least he wouldn't ask about Robert, thank God. It was a welcome relief.

Not many tourists found H.P.'s. It was tucked in a tree-lined cul-de-sac off Cypress Street in a remodeled Victorian bungalow. The sign outside, small and tasteful, simply read, CAFE. Howard did not believe in advertising, and though he was an Anglophile at heart—loving all things British and feeling that they were somehow superior to their American counterparts—his restaurant displayed none of the ersatz British decor that might draw in the tourists. The cafe served simple food at fair prices. If the menu exhibited Howard Phillips's eccentricity in style, it did not discourage the locals from eating at his place. Next to Brine's Bait, Tackle, and Fine Wines, H.P.'s Cafe had the most loyal clientele in Pine Cove.

"Smoking or nonsmoking?" Jenny asked the young man. He was very good-looking, but Jenny noticed this only in passing. She was conditioned by years of monogamy not to dwell on such things.

"Nonsmoking," he said.

Jenny led him to a table in the back. Before he sat down, he pulled out the chair across from him, as if he were going to put his feet up.

"Will someone be joining you?" Jenny asked, handing him a menu. He looked up at her as if he were seeing her for the first time. He stared into her eyes without saying a word.

Embarrassed, Jenny looked down. "Today's special is Eggs-Sothoth—a fiendishly toothsome amalgamation of scrumptious ingredients so delicious that the mere description of the palatable gestalt could drive one mad," she said.

"You're joking?"

"No. The owner insists that we memorize the daily specials verbatim."

The dark man kept staring at her. "What does all that mean?" he asked.

"Scrambled eggs with ham and cheese and a side of toast."

"Why didn't you just say that?"

"The owner is a little eccentric. He believes that his daily specials may be the only thing keeping the Old Ones at bay."

"The Old Ones?"

Jenny sighed. The nice thing about regular customers is she didn't have to keep explaining Howard's weird menu to them. This guy was obviously from out of town. But why did he have to keep staring at her like that?

"It's his religion or something. He believes that the world was once populated by another race. He calls them the Old Ones. For some reason they were banished from Earth, but he believes that they are trying to return and take over."

"You're joking?"

"Stop saying that. I'm not joking."

"I'm sorry." He looked at the menu. "Okay, give me an Eggs-Sothoth with a side order of The Spuds of Madness."

"Would you like coffee?"

"That would be great."

Jenny wrote out the ticket and turned to put the order in at the kitchen window.

"Excuse me," the man said.

Jenny turned in midstep. "Yes?"

"You have incredible eyes."

"Thanks." She felt herself blush as she headed off to get his coffee. She wasn't ready for this. She needed some sort of break between being married and being divorced. Divorce leave? They had pregnancy leave, didn't they?

When she returned with his coffee, she looked at him for the first time as a single woman might. He was handsome, in a sharp, dark sort of way. He looked younger than she was, twenty-three, maybe twenty-four. She was studying his clothes and trying to get a feel for what he did for a living when she ran into the chair he had pushed out from the table and spilled most of the coffee into the saucer.

"God, I'm sorry."

"It's okay," he said. "Are you having a bad day?"

"Getting worse by the minute. I'll get you another cup."

"No," he raised a hand in protest. "Its fine." He took the cup and saucer from her, separated them, and poured the coffee back into the cup. "See, good as new. I don't want to add to your bad day."

He was staring again.

"No, you're fine. I mean, I'm fine. Thanks." She felt like a geek. She cursed Robert for causing all this. If he hadn't . . . No, it wasn't Robert's fault. She'd made the decision to end the marriage.

"I'm Travis." The man extended his hand. She took it, tentatively.

"Jennifer—" She was about to tell him that she was married and that he was nice and all. "I'm not married," she said. She immediately wanted to disappear into the kitchen and never come back.

"Me either," Travis said. "I'm new in town." He didn't seem to notice how awkward she was. "Look, Jennifer, I'm looking for an address and I wonder if you could tell me how to find it? Do you know how to get to Cheshire Street?"

Jenny was relieved to be talking about anything but herself. She rattled off a series of streets and turns, landmarks and signs, that would lead Travis to Cheshire Street. When she finished, he just looked at her quizzically.

"I'll draw you a map," she said. She took a pen from her apron, bent over the table, and began drawing on a napkin.

Their faces were inches apart. "You're very beautiful," he said.

She looked at him. She didn't know whether to smile or scream. *Not yet,* she thought. *I'm not ready.*

He didn't wait for her to respond. "You remind me of someone I used to know."

"Thank you . . ." She tried to remember his name. ". . . Travis."

"Have dinner with me tonight?"

She searched for an excuse. None came. She couldn't use the one she had used for a decade—it wasn't true anymore. And she hadn't been alone long enough to brush up on some new lies. In fact, she felt that she was somehow being unfaithful to Robert just by talking to this guy. But she *was* a single woman. Finally she wrote her phone number under the map on the napkin and handed it to him.

"My number's on the bottom. Why don't you call me tonight, around five, and we'll take it from there, okay?"

Travis folded the napkin and put it in his shirt pocket. "Until tonight," he said.

"Oh, spare me!" a gravely voice said. Jenny turned toward the voice, but there was only the empty chair.

To Travis she said, "Did you hear that?"

"Hear what?" Travis glared at the empty chair.

"Nothing," Jenny said, "I'm starting to go over the edge, I think."

"Relax," Travis said. "I won't bite you." He shot a glance at the chair.

"Your order is up. I'll be right back."

She retrieved the food from the window and delivered it to Travis. While he ate, she stood behind the counter separating coffee filters for the lunch shift, occasionally looking up and smiling at the dark, young man, who paused between bites and smiled back.

She was fine, just fine. She was a single woman and could do any damned thing she wanted to. She could go out with anyone she wanted to. She was young and attractive and she had just made her first date in ten years—sort of.

Over all of her affirmations her fears flew up and perched like a murder of crows. It occurred to her that she didn't have the slightest idea what she was going to wear. The freedom of single life had suddenly become a burden, a mixed blessing, herpes on the pope's ring. Maybe she wouldn't answer the phone when he called.

Travis finished eating and paid his bill, leaving her far too large a tip.

"See you tonight," he said.

"You bet." She smiled.

She watched him walk across the parking lot. He seemed to be talking to someone as he walked. Probably just singing. Guys did that right after they made a date, didn't they? Maybe he was just a whacko?

For the hundredth time that morning she resisted the urge to call Robert and tell him to come home.

8

ROBERT

Robert loaded the last of the laundry baskets full of dishes into the bed of the pickup. The sight of a truckload of clean dishes did not raise his spirits nearly as much as he thought it would. He was still depressed. He was still heartbroken. And he was still hung over.

For a moment he thought that washing the dishes might have been a mistake. Having created a single bright spot, no matter how small, seemed to make the rest of his life look even more dismal by contrast. Maybe he should have just gone with the downward flow, like the pilot who pushes down the stick to pull out of an uncontrolled spin.

Secretly, Robert believed that if things got so bad that he couldn't see his way out, something would come along and not only save him from disaster but improve his life overall. It was a skewed brand of faith that he had developed through years of watching television—where no problem was so great that it could not be surmounted by the last commercial break—and through two events in his own life.

As a boy in Ohio he had taken his first summer job at the local county fair, picking up trash on the midways. The job had been great fun for the first two weeks. He and the other boys on the cleanup crew spent their days wandering the midways using long sticks, with nails extending from one end, to spear paper cups and hot dog wrappers as if they were hunting lions on the Serengeti. They were paid in cash at the end of each day. The next day they spent their pay on games of chance and repeated rides on the Zipper, which was the beginning of Robert's lifelong habit of exchanging money for dizziness and nausea.

The day after the fair ended, Robert and the boys were told to report to the livestock area of the fairgrounds. They arrived before dawn, wondering what they would do now that the colorful carny trailers and rides were gone and the midways were as barren as airport runways.

The man from the county met them outside the big exhibition barns with a dump truck, a pile of pitchforks, and some wheelbarrows. "Clean out those pens, boys. Load the manure on the truck," he had said. Then he went away, leaving the boys unsupervised.

Robert had loaded only three forkfuls when he and the boys ran out of the barn gasping for breath, the odor of ammonia burning in their noses and lungs.

Again and again they tried to clean the stables only to be overcome by the stench. As they stood outside the barn, swearing and complaining, Robert noticed something sticking up out of the morning fog on the adjacent show ground. It looked like the head of a dragon.

It was beginning to get light, and the boys could hear banging and clanging and strange animal noises coming from the show ground. They stared into the fog, trying to make out the shapes moving there, glad for the distraction from their miserable task.

When the sun broke over the trees to the east of the fairgrounds, a scraggly man in blue work clothes walked out of the mist toward the barn. "Hey, you kids," he shouted, and they all prepared to be admonished for standing around instead of working. "You want to work for the circus?"

The boys dropped their pitchforks as if they were red-hot rods of steel and ran to the man. The dragon had been a camel. The strange noises were the trumpeting of elephants. Under the mist a crew of men were unrolling the big top of the Clyde Beatty Circus.

Robert and the boys worked all morning beside the circus people, lacing together the bright-yellow canvas panels of the tent and fitting together giant sections of aluminum poles that would support the big top.

It was hot, sweaty, heavy work, and it was wonderful and exciting. When the poles lay out across the canvas, cables were hitched to a team of elephants and the poles were hoisted skyward. Robert thought his heart would burst with excitement. The canvas was connected by cables to a winch. The boys watched in awe as the big top rose up the poles like a great yellow dream.

It was only one day. But it was glorious, and Robert thought of it often—of the roustabouts who sipped from their hip flasks and called each other by the names of their home states or towns. "Kansas, bring that strut over here. New York, we need a sledge over here." Robert thought of the thick-thighed women who walked the wire and flew on the trapeze. Their heavy makeup was grotesque up close but beautiful at a distance when they were flying through the air above the crowd.

That day was an adventure and a dream. It was one of the finest in Robert's life. But what had impressed him was that it had come right when things seemed the most bleak, when everything had gone, literally, to shit.

The next time Robert's life took a nosedive he was in Santa Barbara, and his salvation arrived in the form of a woman.

He had come to California with everything he owned packed into a Volkswagen Beetle, determined to pursue a dream that he thought would begin at the California border with music by the Beach Boys and a long, white beach full of shapely blondes dying for the company of a young photographer from Ohio. What he found was alienation and poverty.

Robert had chosen the prestigious photography school in Santa

Barbara because it was reputed to be the best. As photographer for the high school yearbook he had gained a reputation as one of the best photographers in town, but in Santa Barbara he was just another teenager among hundreds of students who were, if anything, more skilled than he.

He took a job in a grocery store, stocking shelves from midnight to eight in the morning. He had to work full-time to pay his exorbitant tuition and rent, and soon he fell behind in his assignments. After two months he had to leave school to avoid flunking out.

He found himself in a strange town with no friends and barely enough money to survive. He started drinking beer every morning with the night crew in the parking lot. He drove home in a stupor and slept through the day until his next shift. With the added expense of alcohol, Robert had to hock his cameras to pay rent, and with them went his last hope for a future beyond stocking shelves.

One morning after his shift the manager called him into the office.

"Do you know anything about this?" The manager pointed to four jars of peanut butter that lay open on his desk. "These were returned by customers yesterday." On the smooth surface of the peanut butter in each jar was etched, "Help, I'm trapped in Supermarket Hell!"

Robert stocked the glass aisle. There was no denying it. He had written the messages one night during his shift after drinking several bottles of cough medicine he had stolen from the shelves.

"Pick up your check on Friday," the manager said.

He shuffled away, broke, unemployed, two thousand miles from home, a failure at nineteen. As he left the store, one of the cashiers, a pretty redhead about his age, who was coming in to open the store, stopped him.

"Your name is Robert, isn't it?"

"Yes," he said.

"You're the photographer, aren't you?"

"I was." Robert was in no mood to chat.

"Well, I hope you don't mind," she said, "but I saw your portfolio sitting in the break room one morning and I looked at it. You're very good."

"I don't do it anymore."

"Oh, that's too bad. I have a friend who's getting married on Saturday, and she needs a photographer."

"Look," Robert said, "I appreciate the thought, but I just got fired and I'm going home to get hammered. Besides, I hocked my cameras."

The girl smiled, she had incredible blue eyes. "You were wasting your talent here. How much would it cost to get your cameras out of hock?"

Her name was Jennifer. She paid to get his cameras out of hock and showered him with praise and encouragement. Robert began to make money picking up weddings and Bar Mitzvahs, but it wasn't enough to make rent. There were too many good photographers competing in Santa Barbara.

He moved into her tiny studio apartment.

After a few months of living together they were married and they moved north to Pine Cove, where Robert would find less competition for photography jobs.

Once again, Robert had sunk to a lifetime low, and once again Dame Fate had provided him with a miraculous rescue. The sharp edges of Robert's world were rounded by Jennifer's love and dedication. Life had been good, until now.

Robert's world was dropping out from under him like a trapdoor and he found himself in a disoriented free-fall. Trying to control things by design would only delay his inevitable rescue. The sooner he hit bottom, he reasoned, the sooner his life would improve.

Each time this had happened before, things had gotten a little worse only to get a little better. One day the good times had to keep on rolling, and all of life's horseshit would turn to circuses. Robert had faith that it would happen. But to rise from the ashes you had to crash and burn first. With that in mind, he took his last ten dollars and headed down the street to the Head of the Slug Saloon.

9

THE HEAD OF THE SLUG

Mavis Sand, the owner of the Head of the Slug Saloon, had lived
so long with the Specter of Death hanging over her shoulders that
she had started to think of him as one might regard a comfortable
old sweater. She had made her peace with Death a long time ago,
and Death, in return, had agreed to whittle away at Mavis rather
than take her all at once.

In her seventy years, Death had taken her right lung, her gall
bladder, her appendix, and the lenses of both eyes, complete with
cataracts. Death had her aortic heart valve, and Mavis had in its
place a steel and plastic gizmo that opened and closed like the
automatic doors at the Thrifty Mart. Death had most of Mavis's
hair, and Mavis had a polyester wig that irritated her scalp.

She had also lost most of her hearing, all of her teeth, and her
complete collection of Liberty dimes. (Although she suspected a
ne'er-do-well nephew rather than Death in the disappearance of
the dimes.)

Thirty years ago she had lost her uterus, but that was at a time when doctors were yanking them so frequently that it seemed as if they were competing for a prize, so she didn't blame Death for that.

With the loss of her uterus Mavis grew a mustache that she shaved every morning before leaving to open the saloon. At the Slug she ambled around behind the bar on a pair of stainless steel ball and sockets, as Death had taken her hips, but not before she had offered them up to a legion of cowboys and construction workers.

Over the years Death had taken so much of Mavis that when her time finally came to pass into the next world, she felt it would be like slipping slowly into a steaming-hot bath. She was afraid of nothing.

When Robert walked into the Head of the Slug, Mavis was perched on her stool behind the bar smoking a Taryton extra-long, lording over the saloon like the quintessential queen of the lipstick lizards. After each few drags on her cigarette she applied a thick paste of fire-engine-red lipstick, actually getting a large percentage of it where it was supposed to go. Each time she butted a Taryton she sprayed her abysmal cleavage and behind her ears with a shot of Midnight Seduction from an atomizer she kept by her ashtray. On occasion, when she had rendered herself wobbly by too many shots of Bushmill's, she would shoot perfume directly into one of her hearing aids, causing a short circuit and making the act of ordering drinks a screaming ordeal. To avoid the problem, someone had once given her a pair of earrings fashioned from cardboard air fresheners shaped like Christmas trees, guaranteed to give Mavis that new car smell. But Mavis insisted that it was Midnight Seduction or nothing, so the earrings hung on the wall in a place of honor next to the plaque listing the winners of the annual Head of the Slug eight-ball tournament and chili cook-off, known locally as "The Slugfest."

Robert stood by the bar trying to get his eyes to adjust to the smoky darkness of the Slug.

"What can I get for you, sweet cheeks?" Mavis asked, batting her false eyelashes behind pop-bottle-thick, rhinestone-rimmed glasses. They put Robert in mind of spiders trying to escape a jar.

He fingered the ten-dollar bill in his pocket and climbed onto the bar stool. "A draft, please."

"Hair of the dog?"

"Does it show?" Robert asked in earnest.

"Not much. I was just going to ask you to close your eyes before you bled to death." Mavis giggled like a coquettish gargoyle, then burst into a coughing fit. She drew a mug of beer and set it in front of Robert, taking his ten and replacing it with nine ones.

Robert took a long pull from the beer as he turned on the stool and looked around the bar.

Mavis kept the bar dimly lit except for the lights over the pool tables, and Robert's eyes were still adjusting to the darkness. It occurred to him that he had never seen the floor of the saloon, which stuck to his shoes when he walked. Except for the occasional crunch underfoot identifying a piece of popcorn or a peanut shell, the floor of The Slug was a murky mystery. Whatever was down there should be left alone to evolve, white and eyeless, in peace. He promised himself to make it to the door before he passed out.

He squinted into the lights over the pool tables. There was a heated eight-ball match going on at the back table. A half dozen locals had gathered at the end of the bar to watch. Society called them the hard-core unemployed; Mavis called them the daytime regulars. On the table Slick McCall was playing a dark young man Robert did not recognize. The man seemed familiar, though, and for some reason, Robert found that he did not like him.

"Who's the stranger?" Robert asked Mavis over his shoulder. Something about the young man's aquiline good looks repelled Robert, like biting down on tin foil with a filling.

"New meat for Slick," Mavis said. "Came in about fifteen minutes ago and wanted to play for money. Shoots a pretty lame stick, if you ask me. Slick is keeping his cue behind the bar until the money gets big enough."

Robert watched the wiry Slick McCall move around the table, stopping to drill a solid ball into the side pocket with a bar cue. Slick left himself without a following shot. He stood and ran his fingers over his greased-back brown hair.

He said, "Shit. Snookered myself." Slick was on the hustle.

The phone rang and Mavis picked it up. "Den of iniquity. Den mother speaking. No, he ain't here. Just a minute." She covered the mouthpiece and turned to Robert. "You seen The Breeze?"

"Who's calling?"

Into the phone, "Who's calling?" Mavis listened for a moment, then covered the mouthpiece again. "It's his landlord."

"He's out of town," Robert said. "He'll be back soon."

Mavis conveyed the message and hung up. The phone rang again immediately.

Mavis answered, "Garden of Eden. Snake speaking." There was a pause. "What am I, his answering service?" Pause. "He's out of town; he'll be back soon. Why don't you guys take a social risk and call him at home?" Pause. "Yeah, he's here." Mavis shot a glance at Robert. "You want to talk to him? Okay." She hung up.

"That for The Breeze?" Robert asked.

Mavis lit a Taryton. "He got popular all of a sudden?"

"Who was it?"

"Didn't ask. Sounded Mexican. Asked about you."

"Shit," Robert said.

Mavis set him up with another draft. He turned to watch the game. The stranger had won. He was collecting five dollars from Slick.

"Guess you showed me, pard," Slick said. "You gonna give a chance to win my money back?"

"Double or nothing," the stranger said.

"Fine. I'll rack 'em." Slick pushed the quarters into the coin slot on the side of the pool table. The balls dropped into the gutter and Slick began racking them.

Slick was wearing a red-and-blue polka-dotted polyester shirt with long, pointed collars that had been fashionable around the time that disco died—about the same time that Slick had stopped brushing his teeth, Robert guessed. Slick wore a perpetual brown and broken grin, a grin that was burned into the memories of countless tourists who had strayed into the Slug to be fleeced at the end of Slick's intrepid cue.

The stranger reared back and broke. His stick made the sickly vibrato sound of a miscue. The cue ball rocketed down the table, barely grazing the rack, then bounced off two corner rails and made a beeline toward the corner pocket where the stranger stood.

"Sorry, brother," Slick said, chalking his cue and preparing to shoot the scratch.

When it reached the corner pocket, the cue ball stopped dead on the lip. Almost as an afterthought, one of the solid balls moved out of the pack and fell into the opposite corner with a plop.

"Damn," Slick said. "That was some pretty fancy English. I thought you'd scratched for sure."

"Was that a solid?" the stranger asked.

Mavis leaned over the bar and whispered to Robert. "Did you see that ball stop? It should have been a scratch."

"Maybe there's a piece of chalk on the table that stopped it," Robert speculated.

The stranger made two more balls in an unremarkable fashion, then called a straight-in shot on the three ball. When he shot, the cue ball curved off his stick, describing a C-shaped curve, and sunk the six ball in the opposite corner.

"I said the three ball!" the stranger shouted.

"I know you did," Slick said. "Looks like you were a little heavy on the English. My shot."

The stranger seemed to be angry at someone, but it wasn't Slick. "How can you confuse the six with the three, you idiot?"

"You got me," said Slick. "Don't be so hard on yourself, pard. You're up one game already."

Slick ran four balls, then missed a shot that was so obvious it made Robert wince. Slick's hustles were usually more subtle.

"Five in the side!" the stranger shouted. "Got that? Five!"

"I got it," Slick said. "And all these folks got it along with half the people out in the street. You don't need to yell, pard. This is just a friendly game."

The stranger bent over the table and shot. The five ball careened off the cue ball, headed for the rail, then changed its path and curved into the side pocket. Robert was amazed, as were all the observers. It was an impossible shot, yet they all had seen it.

"Damn," Slick said to no one in particular, then to Mavis, "Mavis, when was the last time you leveled this table?"

"Yesterday, Slick."

"Well, it sure as shit went catywumpus fast. Give me my cue, Mavis."

Mavis waddled to the end of the bar and pulled out a three-foot-long black leather case. She handled it carefully and presented it to Slick with reverence, a decrepit Lady of the Lake presenting a hardwood Excaliber to the rightful king. Slick flipped the case open and screwed the cue together, never taking his eyes off the stranger.

At the sight of the cue the stranger smiled. Slick smiled back. The game was defined. Two hustlers recognized each other. A tacit agreement passed between them: *Let's cut the bullshit and play.*

Robert had become so engrossed in watching the tension between the two men and trying to figure out why the stranger angered him so, that he failed to notice that someone had slipped onto the stool next to him. Then she spoke.

"How are you, Robert?" Her voice was deep and throaty. She placed her hand on his arm and gave it a sympathetic squeeze. Robert turned and was taken aback by her appearance. She always affected him that way. She affected most men that way.

She was wearing a black body stocking, belted at the waist with wide leather in which she had tucked a multitude of chiffon scarves that danced around her hips when she walked like diaphanous ghosts of Salome. Her wrists were adorned with layers of silver bangles; her nails were sculptured long and lacquered black. Her eyes were wide and green, set far apart over a small, straight nose and full lips, glossed blood red. Her hair hung to her waist, blue-black. An inverted silver pentagram dangled between her breasts on a silver chain.

"I'm miserable," Robert said. "Thanks for asking, Ms. Henderson."

"My friends call me Rachel."

"Okay. I'm miserable, Ms. Henderson."

Rachel was thirty-five but she could have passed for twenty if it weren't for the arrogant sensuality with which she moved and the mocking smile in her eyes that evinced experience, confidence, and guile beyond any twenty-year-old. Her body did not betray her age; it was her manner. She went through men like water.

Robert had known her for years, but her presence never failed to awaken in him a feeling that his marital fidelity was nothing more than an absurd notion. In retrospect, perhaps it was. Still, she made him feel uneasy.

"I'm not your enemy, Robert. No matter what you think. Jenny has been thinking about leaving you for a long time. We didn't have anything to do with it."

"How are things with the coven?" Robert asked sarcastically.

"It's not a coven. The Pagan Vegetarians for Peace are dedicated to Earth consciousness, both spiritual and physical."

Robert drained his fifth beer and slammed the mug down on the bar. "The Pagan Vegetarians for Peace are a group of bitter, ball-biting, man haters, dedicated to breaking up marriages and turning men into toads."

"That's not true and you know it."

"What I know," Robert said, "is that within a year of joining, every woman in your coven has divorced her husband. I was against Jenny getting into this mumbo jumbo from the beginning. I told her you would brainwash her and you have."

Rachel reared back on the bar stool like a hissing cat. "You believe what you want to believe, Robert. I show women the Goddess within. I put them in touch with their own personal power; what they do with it is their own business. We aren't against men. Men just can't stand to see a woman discover herself. Maybe if you'd exalted Jenny's growth instead of criticizing, she'd still be around."

Robert turned away from her and caught a glimpse of himself in the mirror behind the bar. He was overcome by a wave of self-loathing. She was right. He covered his face with his hands and leaned forward on the bar.

"Look, I didn't come here to fight with you," Rachel said. "I saw your truck outside and I thought you might be able to use a little money. I have some work for you. It might take your mind off the hurt."

"What?" Robert said through his hands.

"We're sponsoring the annual tofu sculpture contest at the park this year. We need someone to take pictures for the poster and the press package. I know you're broke, Robert."

"No," he said, without looking up.

"Fine. Suit yourself." Rachel slid off the stood and started to leave.

Mavis sat another beer in front of Robert and counted his money on the bar. "Very smooth," she said. "You've got four bucks left to your name."

Robert looked up. Rachel was almost to the door. "Rachel!"

She turned and waited, an elegant hand on an exquisite hip.

"I'm staying at The Breeze's trailer." He told her the phone number. "Call me, okay?"

Rachel smiled. "Okay, Robert, I'll call." She turned to walk out.

Robert called out to her again. "You haven't seen The Breeze, have you?"

Rachel grimaced. "Robert, just being in the same room with The Breeze makes me want to take a bath in bleach."

"Come on, he's a fun guy."

"He's a fun-gus," Rachel said.

"But have you seen him?"

"No."

"Thanks," he said. "Call me."

"I will." She turned and walked out. When she opened the door, light spilling in blinded Robert. When his vision returned, a little man in a red stocking cap was sitting next to him. He hadn't seen him come in.

To Mavis the little man said, "Could I trouble you for a small quantity of salt?"

"How about a margarita with extra salt, handsome?" Mavis batted her spider-lashes.

"Yes, that will be good. Thank you."

Robert looked the little man over for a moment, then turned away to watch the pool game while he contemplated his destiny.

Maybe this job for Rachel was his way out. Strange, though, things didn't seem to be bad enough yet. And the idea that Rachel could be his fairy godmother in disguise made him smile. No, the downward spiral to salvation was going quite nicely. The Breeze was missing. The rent was due. He had made enemies with a crazed Mexican drug dealer, and it was driving him nuts trying to figure out where he had seen the stranger at the pool table.

The game was still going strong. Slick was running the balls with machinelike precision. When he did miss, the stranger cleared the table with a series of impossible, erratic, curving shots, while the crowd watched with their jaws hanging, and Slick broke into a nervous sweat.

Slick McCall had been the undisputed king of eight ball at the Head of the Slug Saloon since before it had been called the Head of the Slug. The bar had been the Head of the Wolf for fifty years, until Mavis grew tired of the protests of drunken environmentalists, who insisted that timber wolves were an endangered species and that the saloon was somehow sanctioning their killing. One day she had taken the stuffed wolf head that hung over the bar to the Salvation Army and had a local artist render a giant slug head in fiberglass to replace it. Then she changed the sign and waited for some half-wit from the Save the Slugs Society to show up and protest. It never happened. In business, as in politics, the public is ever so tolerant of those who slime.

Years ago, Slick and Mavis had come to a mutually beneficial business agreement. Mavis allowed Slick to make his living on her pool table, and in return, Slick agreed to pay her twenty percent of his winnings and to excuse himself from the Slug's annual eight-ball tournament. Robert had been coming into the Slug for seven years and in that time he had never seen Slick rattled over a pool game. Slick was rattled now.

Occasionally some tourist who had won the Sheep's Penis Kansas Nine-Ball tournament would come into the Slug puffed up like the omnipotent god of the green felt, and Slick would return him to Earth, deflating his ego with gentle pokes from his custom-made, ivory-inlaid cue. But those fellows played within the known laws of physics. The dark stranger played as if Newton had been dropped on his head at birth.

To his credit, Slick played his usual methodical game, but Robert could tell that he was afraid. When the stranger sank the eight ball in a hundred-dollar game, Slick's fear turned to anger and he threw his custom cue across the room like a crazed Zulu.

"Goddammit, boy, I don't know how you're doing it, but no one can shoot like that." Slick was screaming into the stranger's face, his fists were balled at his sides.

"Back off," the stranger said. All the boyishness drained from his face. He could have been a thousand years old, carved in stone. His eyes were locked on Slick's. "The game is over." He might have been stating that "water is wet." It was truth. It was deadly serious.

Slick reached into the pocket of his jeans, fished out a handful of crumpled twenties, and threw them on the table.

The stranger picked up the bills and walked out.

Slick retrieved his stick and began taking it apart. The daytime regulars remained silent, allowing Slick to gather his dignity.

"That was like a fucking bad dream," he said to the onlookers.

The comment hit Robert like a sock full of birdshot. He suddenly remembered where he had seen the stranger. The dream of the desert came back to him with crippling clarity. He turned back to his beer, stunned.

"You want a margarita?" Mavis asked him. She was holding a baseball bat she had pulled from under the bar when things had heated up at the pool table.

Robert looked to the stool next to him. The little man was gone.

"He saw that guy make one shot and ran out of here like his ass was on fire," Mavis said.

Robert picked up the margarita and downed its frozen contents in one gulp, giving himself an instant headache.

Outside on the street Travis and Catch headed toward the service station.

"Well, maybe you should learn to shoot pool if you're going to get money this way."

"Maybe you could pay attention when I call a shot."

"I didn't hear you. I don't understand why we just don't steal our money."

"I don't like to steal."

"You stole from the pimp in L.A."

"That was okay."

"What's the difference?"

"Stealing is immoral."

"And cheating at pool isn't?"

"I didn't cheat. I just had an unfair advantage. He had a custom-made pool cue. I had you to push the balls in."

"I don't understand morality."

"That's not surprising."

"I don't think you understand it either."

"We have to pick up the car."

"Where are we going?"

"To see an old friend."

"You say that everywhere we go."

"This is the last one."

"Sure."

"Be quiet. People are looking."

"You're trying to be tricky. What's morality?"

"It's the difference between what is right and what you can rationalize."

"Must be a human thing."

"Exactly."

10

AUGUSTUS BRINE

Augustus Brine sat in one of his high-backed leather chairs massaging his temples, trying to formulate a plan of action. Rather than answers, the question, *Why me?* repeated in his mind like a perplexing mantra. Despite his size, strength, and a lifetime of learning, Augustus Brine felt small, weak, and stupid. *Why me?*

A few minutes before, Gian Hen Gian had rushed into the house babbling in Arabic like a madman. When Brine finally calmed him down, the genie had told him he had found the demon.

"You must find the dark one. He must have the Seal of Solomon. You must find him!"

Now the genie was sitting in the chair across from Brine, munching potato chips and watching a videotape of a Marx Brothers movie.

The genie insisted that Brine take some sort of action, but he had no suggestions on how to proceed. Brine examined the options and found them wanting. He could call the police, tell them that a genie had told him that an invisible man-eating demon had invaded Pine Cove, and spend the rest of his life under sedation: not good. Or, he could find the dark one, insist that he send the demon back to hell, and be eaten by the demon: not good. Or he could find the dark one, sneak around hoping that he wasn't noticed by an invisible demon that could be anywhere, steal the seal, and send the demon back to hell himself, but probably get eaten in the process: also, not good. Of course he could deny that he believed the story, deny that he had seen Gian Hen Gian drink enough saltwater to kill a battalion, deny the existence of the supernatural altogether, open an impudent little bottle of merlot, and sit by his fireplace drinking wine while a demon from hell ate his neighbors. But he did believe it, and that option, too, was not good. For now he decided to rub his temples and think, *Why me?*

The genie would be no help at all. Without a master he was as powerless as Brine himself. Without the seal and invocation, he could have no master. Brine had run through the more obvious courses of action with Gian Hen Gian to have each doomed in succession. No, he could not kill the demon: he was immortal. No, he could not kill the dark one: he was under the protection of the demon, and killing him, if it were possible, might release the demon to his own will. To attempt an exorcism would be silly, the genie reasoned; would some mingy prelate be able to override the power of Solomon?

Perhaps they could separate the demon from his keeper— somehow force the dark one to send the demon back. Brine started to ask Gian Hen Gian if it was feasible but stopped himself. Tears were coursing down the genie's face.

"What's the matter?" Brine asked.

Gian Hen Gian kept his eyes trained on the television screen, where Harpo Marx was pulling a collection of objects from his coat, objects obviously too large to be stored there.

"It has been so long since I have seen one of my own kind. This one who does not speak, I do not recognize him, but he is Djinn. What magic!"

Brine considered for a moment the possibility that Harpo Marx might have been one of the Djinn, then berated himself for even thinking about it. Too much had happened today that was outside the frame of his experience and it had opened him up to thinking that anything was possible. If he weren't careful, he would lose his sense of judgment completely.

"You've been here a thousand years and you've never seen a movie before?" Brine asked.

"What is a movie?"

Slowly and gently, Augustus Brine explained to the king of the Djinn about the illusion created by motion pictures. When he finished, he felt like he had just raped the tooth fairy in front of a class of kindergartners.

"Then I am alone still?" the genie said.

"Not completely."

"Yes," the genie said, eager to leave the moment behind, "but what are you going to do about Catch, Augustus Brine?"

11

EFFROM

Effrom Elliot awoke that morning eagerly anticipating his nap. He'd been dreaming about women, about a time when he had hair and choices. He hadn't slept well. Some barking dogs had awakened him during the night, and he wished he could sleep in, but as soon as the sun broke through his bedroom window, he was wide awake, without a hope of getting back to sleep and recapturing his dream until nap time. It had been that way since he had retired, twenty-five years ago. As soon as his life had eased so that he might sleep in, his body would not let him.

He crept from bed and dressed in the half-light of the bedroom, putting on corduroys and a wool flannel shirt the wife had laid out for him. He put on his slippers and tiptoed out of the bedroom, palming the door shut so as not to wake the wife. Then he remembered that the wife was gone to Monterey, or was it Santa Barbara? Anyway, she wasn't home. Still, he continued his morning routine with the usual stealth.

In the kitchen he put on the water for his morning cup of decaf.

Outside the kitchen window the hummingbirds were already hovering up to the feeder, stopping for drinks of red sugar water on their route through the wife's fuchias and honeysuckle. He thought of the hummingbirds as the wife's pets. They moved too fast for his tastes. He had seen a nature show on television that said that their metabolism was so fast that they might not even be able to see humans. The whole world had gone the way of the hummingbirds as far as Effrom was concerned. Everything and everybody was too fast, and sometimes he felt invisible.

He couldn't drive anymore. The last time he had tried, the police had stopped him for obstructing traffic. He had told the cop to stop and smell the flowers. He told the cop that he had been driving since before the cop was a glimmer in his daddy's eye. It had been the wrong approach. The policeman took his license. The wife did all the driving now. Imagine it—when he had taught her to drive, he had to keep grabbing the wheel to keep her from putting the Model T into the ditch. What would the snot-nosed cop say about that?

The water was beginning to boil on the stove. Effrom rummaged through the old tin bread box and found the package of chocolate-covered graham crackers the wife had left for him. In the cupboard the jar of Sanka sat next to the real coffee. Why not? The wife was gone, why not live a little? He took the regular coffee from the shelf and set about finding the filters and filter holder. He hadn't the slightest idea where they were kept. The wife took care of that sort of thing.

He finally found the filters, the holder, and the serving carafe on the shelf below. He poured some coffee into the filter, eyeballed it, and poured in some more. Then he poured the water over the grounds.

The coffee came through strong and black as the kaiser's heart. He poured himself a cup and there was still a little left in the carafe. No sense wasting it. He opened the kitchen window, and after fumbling with the lid for a moment, poured the remaining coffee into the hummingbird feeder.

"Live a little, boys."

He wondered if the coffee might not speed them up to the point where they just burnt up in the atmosphere. He toyed with the idea of watching for a while, then he remembered that his exercise show was about to start. He picked up his graham crackers and coffee and headed for the living room and his big easy chair in front of the RCA.

He made sure the sound was turned down, then turned on the old console set. When the picture came on, a young blond woman in iridescent tights was leading three other young women through a series of stretches. Effrom guessed that there was music playing from the way they moved, but he always watched with the sound turned off so as not to wake the wife. Since he had discovered his exercise program, the women in his dreams all wore iridescent tights.

The girls were all on their backs now, waving their legs in the air. Effrom munched his graham crackers and watched in fascination. Time was when a man had to spend the better part of a week's pay to see a show like that. Now you could get it on cable for only. . . . Well, the wife took care of the cable bill, but he guessed that it was pretty cheap. Life was grand.

Effrom considered going out to his workshop and getting his cigarettes. A smoke would go good right now. After all, the wife was gone. Why should he sneak around in his own house? No, the wife would know. And when she confronted him, she wouldn't yell, she would just look at him. She would get that sad look in her blue eyes and she would say, "Oh, Effrom." That's all, "Oh, Effrom." And he would feel as if he had betrayed her. Nope, he could wait until his show was over and go smoke in his workshop, where the wife would never dare to set foot.

Suddenly the house felt very empty. It was like a great vacant warehouse where the slightest noise rattles in the rafters. A presence was missing.

He never saw the wife until she knocked on his workshop door at noon to call him to lunch, but somehow he felt her absence, as if the insulation had been ripped from around him, leaving him raw to the elements. For the first time in a long time Effrom felt afraid. The wife was coming back, but maybe someday she would be gone forever. Someday he would really be alone. He wished for a moment that he would die first, then thinking of the wife alone, knocking on the workshop door from which he would never emerge, made him feel selfish and ashamed.

He tried to concentrate on the exercise show but found no solace in spandex tights. He rose and turned off the TV. He went to the kitchen and put his coffee in the sink. Outside the window the hummingbirds went about their business, shimmering in the morning sun. A sense of urgency came over him. It became suddenly very important to get to his workshop and finish his latest carving. Time seemed as fleeting and fragile as the little birds. In his younger days he might have met the feeling with a naive denial of his own mortality. Age had given him a different defense, and his thoughts returned to the image of he and the wife going to bed together and never waking, their lives and memories going out all at once. This too, he knew, was a naive fantasy. When the wife got home he was going to give her hell for going away, he knew that for sure.

Before unlocking his workshop he set the alarm on his watch to go off at lunchtime. If he worked through lunch he might miss his nap. There was no sense in wasting the day just because the wife was out of town.

When the knock came on his workshop door, Effrom thought at first that the wife had come home early to surprise him with lunch. He ground out his cigarette in an empty toolbox that he kept for that purpose. He blew the last lungful of smoke into the exhaust fan he had installed "to take out the sawdust."

"Coming. Just a minute," he said. He revved up one of his high-speed polishing tools for effect. The knocking continued and Effrom realized that it was not coming from the inside door that the wife usually knocked on, but from the one leading out into the front yard. *Probably Jehovah's Witnesses.* He climbed down from his stool, checked the pockets of his corduroys for quarters, and found one. If you bought a *Watchtower* from them, they would go away, but if they caught you without spare change, they would be on you like soul-saving terriers.

Effrom threw the door open and the young man outside jumped

back. He was dressed in a black sweatshirt and jeans—rather casual, Effrom thought, for someone carrying the formal invitation to the end of the world.

"Are you Effrom Elliot?" he asked.

"I am." Effrom said. He held out his quarter. "Thanks for stopping by, but I'm busy, so you can just give me my *Watchtower* and I'll read it later."

"Mr. Elliot, I'm not a Jehovah's Witness."

"Well, I have all the insurance I can afford, but if you leave me your card, I'll give it to the wife."

"Is your wife still alive, Mr. Elliot?"

"Of course she's alive. What did you think? I was going to tape your business card to her tombstone? Son, you're not cut out to be a salesman. You should get an honest job."

"I'm not a salesman, Mr. Elliot. I'm an old friend of your wife's. I need to talk to her. It's very important."

"She ain't home."

"Your wife's name is Amanda, right?"

"That's right. But don't you try any of your sneaky tricks. You ain't no friend of the wife or I'd know you. And we got a vacuum cleaner that'd suck the hide off a bear, so go away." Effrom started to close the door.

"No, please, Mr. Elliot. I really need to speak to your wife."

"She ain't home."

"When will she be home?"

"She's coming home tomorrow. But I'm warning you, son, she's even tougher than I am on flimflam men. Mean as a snake. You'd be best to just pack up your carpetbag and go look for honest work."

"You were a World War One veteran, weren't you?"

"I was. What of it?"

"Thank you, Mr. Elliot. I'll be back tomorrow."

"Don't bother."

"Thank you, Mr. Elliot."

Effrom slammed the door. His angina wrenched his chest like a scaly talon. He tried to breathe deeply while he fingered a nitroglycerin pill from his shirt pocket. He popped it into his mouth, and it dissolved on his tongue immediately. In a few seconds the pain in his chest subsided. Maybe he would skip lunch today, go right to his nap.

Why the wife kept sending in those cards about insurance was beyond him. Didn't she know that "no salesman will call" was one of the three great lies? He resolved again to give her hell when she got home.

When Travis got back into the car, he tried to hide his excitement from the demon. He fought the urge to shout "Eureka!" to pound on the steering wheel, to sing hallelujah at the top of his lungs. It might finally be coming to an end. He wouldn't let himself think about it. It was only a long shot, but he felt closer than he ever had to being free of the demon.

"So, how's your old friend?" Catch said sarcastically. They had played this scene literally thousands of times. Travis tried to assume the same attitude he always had when faced with those failures.

"He's fine," Travis said. "He asked about you." He started the car and pulled away from the curb slowly. The old Chevy's engine sputtered and tried to die, then caught.

"He did?"

"Yeah, he couldn't understand why your mother didn't eat her young."

"I didn't have a mother."

"Do you think she'd claim you?"

Catch grinned. "Your mother wet herself before I finished her."

The anger came sliding back over the years. Travis shut off the engine.

"Get out and push," he said. Then he waited. Sometimes the demon would do exactly what he said, and other times Catch laughed at him. Travis had never been able to figure out the inconsistency.

"No," Catch said.

"Do it."

The demon opened the car door. "Lovely girl you're going out with tonight, Travis."

"Don't even think about it."

The demon licked his chops. "Think what?"

"Get out."

Catch got out. Travis left the Chevy in drive. When the car started moving, Travis could hear the demon's clawed feet cutting furrows in the asphalt.

Just one more day. Maybe.

He tried to think of the girl, Jenny, and it occurred to him that he was the only man he had ever heard of who had waited until he was in his nineties before going on his first date. He didn't have the slightest idea why he had asked her out. Something about her eyes. There was something there that reminded him of happiness, his own happiness. Travis smiled.

12

JENNIFER

When Jennifer arrived home from work, the phone was ringing. She ran to the phone, then stopped with her hand on the receiver, checked her watch, and decided to let the answering machine get it. It was too early to be Travis.

The machine clicked and began its message, Jennifer cringed as she heard Robert's voice on the answer tape. "You've reached the studios of Photography in the Pines. Please leave your name and number at the tone."

The machine beeped and Robert's voice continued, "Honey, pick up if you're there. I'm so sorry. I need to come home. I don't have any clean underwear. Are you there? Pick up, Jenny. I'm so lonely. Call me, okay? I'm still at The Breeze's. When you get in—"

The machine cut him off.

Jennifer ran the tape back and listened to the other messages. There were nine others, all from Robert. All whining, drunken, pleading for forgiveness, promising changes that would never happen.

Jenny reset the machine. On the message pad next to the phone she wrote, "Change message on machine." There was a list of notes to herself: clean beer out of refrigerator; pack up darkroom; separate records, tapes, books. All were designed to wash reminders of Robert out of her life. Right now, though, she needed to wash the residue of eight hours of restaurant work off her body. Robert used to grab her and kiss her as she came in the door. "The smell of grease drives me mad," he'd say.

Jenny went to the bathroom to run her bath. She opened various bottles and poured them into the water: *Essential Algae, revitalizes the skin, all natural.* "It's from France," the clerk had said with import, as if the French had mastered the secret of bathwater along with the elements of rudeness; a dash of *Amino Extract, all vegetable protein in an absorbable form.* "Makes stretch marks as smooth as if you'd spackled them," the clerk had said. He'd been a drywall man moonlighting at the cosmetic counter and was not yet versed in the nomenclature of beauty. Two capfuls of *Herbal Honesty, a fragrant mix of organically grown herbs harvested by the loving hands of spiritually enlightened descendants of the Mayans.* And last, a squeeze of *Female E,* vitamin E oil and dong quai root extract, *to bring out the Goddess in every woman.* Rachel had given her the *Female E* at the last meeting of the Pagan Vegetarians for Peace when Jenny had consulted the group about divorcing Robert. "You're just a little *yanged* out," Rachel had said. "Try some of this."

When Jenny finished adding all the ingredients, the water was the soft, translucent green of cheese mold. It would have come as a great surprise to Jennifer that two hundred miles north, in the laboratories of the Stanford Primordial Slime Research Building, some graduate students were combining the very same ingredients (albeit under scientific names) in a climate-controlled vat, in an attempt to replicate the original conditions in which life had first evolved on Earth. It would have further surprised her that if she had turned on a sunlamp in the bathroom (the last element needed), her bath water would have stood up and said "Howdy," immediately qualifying her for the Nobel prize and millions in grant money.

While Jennifer's chance at scientific immortality bubbled away in the tub, she counted her tips, forty-seven dollars and thirty-two cents' worth of change and dollar bills, into a gallon jar, then marked the total into a logbook on her dresser. It wasn't much, but it was enough. Her tips and wages provided enough to make the house payment, pay utilities, buy food, and keep her Toyota and Robert's truck in marginal running order. She made enough to keep alive Robert's illusion that he was making it as a professional photographer. What little he made on the occasional wedding or senior portrait went into film and equipment, or, for the most part, wine. Robert seemed to think that the key to his creativity was a corkscrew.

Keeping Robert's photography business buoyant was Jennifer's rationalization for putting her own life on hold and wasting her time working as a waitress. It seemed that she had always been on hold, waiting for her life to start. In school they told her if she worked hard and got good grades, she would get into a good college. Hold, please. Then there had been Robert. Work hard, be patient, the photography will take off, and we'll have a life. She'd hitched herself to that dream and put her life on hold once again. And she had kept pumping energy into the dream long after it had died in Robert.

It happened one morning after Robert had been up drinking all night. She had found him in front of the television with empty wine bottles lined up in front of him like tombstones.

"Don't you have a wedding to shoot today?"

"I'm not going to do it. I don't feel up to it."

She had gone over the edge, screaming at him, kicking wine bottles around the room, and finally, storming out. Right then she resolved to start her life. She was almost thirty and she'd be damned if she'd spend the rest of her life as the grieving widow of someone else's dream.

She asked him to leave that afternoon, then called a lawyer.

Now that her life had finally started, she had no idea what she was going to do. Slipping into the tub, she realized she was, in fact, nothing more than a waitress and a wife.

Once again she fought the urge to call Robert and ask him to come home. Not because she loved him—the love had worn so thin it was hard to perceive—but because he was her purpose, her direction, and most important, her excuse for being mediocre.

Sitting in the safety of her bathroom, she found she was afraid. This morning, Pine Cove had seemed like a sweatbox, closing in on her and cutting off her breath. Now Pine Cove and the world seemed a very large and hostile place. It would be easy to slip under the warm water and never come up, escape. It wasn't a serious consideration, just a momentary fantasy. She was stronger than that. Things weren't hopeless, just difficult. Concentrate on the positive, she told herself.

There was this guy Travis. He seemed nice. He was very good-looking, too. Everything is fine. This is not an end, it's a beginning.

Her paltry attempt at positive thinking suddenly dissolved into a whole agenda of first-date fears, which somehow seemed more comfortable than the limitless possibilities of positive thinking because she had been through them before.

She took a bar of deodorant soap from the soap dish, lost her grip, and dropped it into the water. The splash covered the faint death gasp the water let out as the soap's toxic chemicals hit it.

Part 3

SUNDAY NIGHT

Millions of spiritual creatures walk the Earth.
Unseen, both when we wake and when we sleep.

—John Milton

13

NIGHTFALL

Overall, the village of Pine Cove was in a cranky mood. No one had slept well Saturday night. Through most of Sunday the weekend tourists were finding ugly chips in Pine Cove's veneer of small-town charm.

Shopkeepers had been abrupt and sarcastic when asked the usual inane questions about whales and sea otters. Waiters and waitresses lost their tolerance for complaints about the unpalatable English food they served and either snapped at their customers outright, or intentionally gave them bad service. Motel desk clerks indulged themselves by arbitrarily changing check-out times, refusing reservations, and turning on the NO VACANCY signs every time someone pulled up to the office, proclaiming that they had just filled their last room.

Rosa Cruz, who was a chambermaid at the Rooms-R-Us Motel, slipped "sanitized for your protection" bands across all the toilets without even lifting the lids. That afternoon, when a guest protested and she was called on the carpet by the manager, who stood over the toilet in room 103, pointing to a floating turd as if it were a smoking murder weapon, Rosa said, "Well, I sanitized that, too."

It might have been declared Tourist Abuse Day in Pine Cove for all the injustices that were inflicted on unsuspecting travelers. As far as the locals were concerned, the world would be a better place if every tourist decided to hang bug-eyed and blue-tongued by his camera strap from a motel shower rod.

As the day wore into evening and the tourists vacated the streets, the residents of Pine Cove turned to each other to vent their irritability. At the Slug, Mavis Sand, who was stocking her bar for the evening, and who was a keen observer of social behavior, had watched the tension grow in her customers and herself all afternoon.

She must have told the story of Slick McCall's eight-ball match with the dark stranger thirty times. Mavis usually enjoyed the telling and retelling of the events that occurred in The Head of the Slug (even to the point of keeping a microcassette recorder under the bar to save some of her better versions). She allowed the tales to grow into myths and legends as she replaced truths forgotten with details fabricated. Often a tale that started out as a one-beer anecdote would become, in the retelling, a three-beer epic (for Mavis let no glass go dry when she was telling a story). Storytelling, for Mavis, was just good business.

But today people had been impatient. They wanted Mavis to draw a beer and get to the point. They questioned her credibility, denied the facts, and all but called her a liar. The story was too fantastic to be taken at face value.

Mavis lost her patience with those who asked about the incident, and they did ask. News travels fast in a small town.

"If you don't want to know what happened, don't ask," Mavis snapped.

What did they expect? Slick McCall was an institution, a hero, in his own greasy way. The story of his defeat should be an epic, not an obituary.

Even that good-looking fellow who owned the general store had rushed her through the story. What was his name, Asbestos Wine?

No, Augustus Brine. That was it. Now, there was a man she could spend some time under. But he, too, had been impatient, and had rushed out of the bar without even buying a drink. It had pissed her off.

Mavis watched her own mood changes like the needle on a barometer. Given her current crankiness, the social climate in the Slug tonight would be stormy; she predicted fights. The liquor she stocked into the well that evening was diluted to half strength with distilled water. If people were going to get drunk and break up her place, it was going to cost them.

In her heart of hearts, she hoped she would get an opportunity to whack someone with her baseball bat.

AUGUSTUS

As darkness fell on Pine Cove that evening, Augustus Brine was filled with an uncharacteristic feeling of dread. In the past he had always seen sunset as a promise, a beginning. As a young man sunset had been a call to romance and excitement, more recently it signaled a time of rest and contemplation. Tonight it was not sunset, the promise, but sundown, the threat. With nightfall the full weight of his responsibility fell across his back like a leaden yoke, and try as he might, Brine could not shrug it off.

Gian Hen Gian had convinced him that he must find the one that commanded the demon. Brine had driven to the Head of the Slug, and after enduring a barrage of lewd advances from Mavis Sand, he was able to pry out of her the direction the dark stranger had gone when he left the bar. Virgil Long, the mechanic, gave him a description of the car and tried to convince him that his truck needed a tune-up.

Brine had then returned home to discuss a course of action with the king of the Djinn, who was engrossed in his fourth Marx Brothers movie.

"But how did you know he was coming here?" Brine asked.

"It was a feeling."

"Then why can't you get a feeling of where he is now?"

"You must find him, Augustus Brine."

"And do what?"

"Get the Seal of Solomon and send Catch back to hell."

"Or get eaten."

"Yes, there is that possibility."

"Why don't you do it? He can't hurt you."

"If the dark one has the Seal of Solomon, then I too could become his slave. This would not be good. You must do it."

The biggest problem for Brine was that Pine Cove was small enough that he could actually search the entire town. In Los Angles or San Francisco he might have been able to give up before starting, open a bottle of wine, and let the mass of humanity bear the responsibility while he sank into a peaceful fog of nonaction.

Brine had come to Pine Cove to avoid conflict, to pursue a life of simple pleasures, to meditate and find peace and oneness with all things. Now, forced to act, he realized how deluded he had become. Life was action, and there was no peace this side of the grave. He had read about the kendo swordsman, who affected the Zen of controlled spontaneity, never anticipating a move so that he might never have to correct his strategy to an unanticipated attack, but always ready to act. Brine had removed himself from the flow of action, built his life into a fortress of comfort and safety without realizing that his fortress was also a prison.

"Think long and hard on your fate, Augustus Brine," the Djinn said around a mouthful of potato chips. "Your neighbors pay for this time with their lives."

Brine pushed himself out of the chair and stormed into his study. He riffled through the drawers of the desk until he found a street map of Pine Cove. He spread the map out on the desk and began to divide the village into blocks with a red marker. Gian Hen Gian came into the study while he worked.

"What will you do?"

"Find the demon," Brine said through gritted teeth.

"And when you find him?"

"I don't know."

"You are a good man, Augustus Brine."

"You are a pain in the ass, Gian Hen Gian." Brine gathered up the map and headed out of the room.

"If it be so, then so be it," the Djinn shouted after him. "But I am a grand pain in the ass."

Augustus Brine did not answer. He was already making his way to his truck. He drove off feeling quite alone and afraid.

ROBERT

Augustus Brine was not alone in his feeling of dread at the onset of evening. Robert returned at sunset to The Breeze's trailer to find three threatening messages on the answering machine: two from the landlord, and one ominous threat from the drug dealer in the BMW. Robert played the tape back three times in hope of finding a message from Jennifer, but it was not there.

He had failed miserably in his attempt to crash and burn at the Slug, running out of money long before passing out. The job offer from Rachel wasn't enough either. Thinking it over, nothing would really be enough. He was a loser, plain and simple. No one was going to rescue him this time, and he wasn't up to pulling himself up by his own bootstraps.

He had to see Jenny. She would understand. But he couldn't go looking like this, a three-day growth of beard, clothes he had slept in, reeking of sweat and beer. He stripped off his clothes and walked into the bathroom. He took some shaving cream and a razor from the medicine cabinet and stepped into the shower.

Maybe if he showed up looking like he had some self-respect, she would take him back. She had to be missing him, right? And he wasn't sure he could spend another night alone, thinking about it, going though the nightmare.

He turned on the shower and the breath jumped from his body. The water was ice cold. The Breeze hadn't paid the gas bill. Robert steeled himself to endure the cold shower. He had to look good if he was going to rebuild his life.

Then the lights went out.

RIVERA

Rivera was sitting in a coffee shop near the police station sipping from a cup of decaf, smoking a cigarette, waiting. In his fifteen years on the force he estimated that ten of them had been spent in waiting. For once, though, he had the warrants, the budget, the manpower, and probable cause, but he had no suspect.

It had to go down tomorrow, one way or another. If The Breeze showed up, then Rivera was in line for a promotion. If, however, he had gotten wind of the sting, then Rivera would take down the drunk in the trailer and hope that he knew something. It was a dismal prospect. Rivera envisioned his task force swooping in with sirens blaring, lights flashing, only to chalk up a bust for unsafe vehicle, perhaps unlawful copying of a videotape, or tearing the tag off a mattress. Rivera shivered at the thought and ground out his cigarette in the ashtray. He wondered if they would let him smoke when he was working behind the counter at Seven-Eleven.

THE BREEZE

When the jaws of the demon had clamped down on him, The Breeze felt a moment of pain, then a light-headedness and a floating feeling he had come to associate with certain kinds of hallucinogenic mushrooms. Then he looked down to see the monster stuffing his body into its gaping mouth. It looked funny, and the ethereal Breeze giggled to himself. No, this was more like the feeling of nitrous oxide than mushrooms, he thought.

He watched the monster shrink and disappear, then the door to the old Chevy opened and closed. The car sped off and The Breeze felt himself bouncing on the air currents in its wake. Death was fine with The Breeze. Sort of the ultimate acid trip, only cheaper and with no side effects.

Suddenly he found himself in a long tunnel. At the end he saw a bright light. He had seen a movie about this once; you were supposed to go toward the light.

Time had lost meaning for The Breeze. He floated down the tunnel, for a whole day, but to him it seemed only minutes. He was just riding the buzz. Everything was copacetic. As he approached the light, he could make out the figures of people waiting for him. That's right: your family and friends welcome you to the next life. The Breeze prepared himself for a truly bitchin' party on the astral plane.

Coming out of the tunnel, The Breeze was enveloped by an intense white light. It was warm and comforting. The people's faces came into view and as The Breeze floated up to them, he realized that he owed every one of them money.

PREDATORS

While night fell on some like a curtain of foreboding, others were meeting the advent of darkness with excited anticipation. Creatures of the night were rising from their resting places and venturing forth to feed on their unsuspecting victims.

They were feeding machines, armed with tooth and claw, instinctively driven to seek out their prey, gifted with stealth and night vision, perfectly adapted to the hunt. When they stalked the streets of Pine Cove, no one's garbage cans were safe.

When they awakened that evening, they found a curious machine in their den. The supernatural sentience they had experienced the night before had passed, and they retained no memory of having stolen the tape player. They might have been frightened by the noise, but the battery had long since run down. They would push the machine out of the den when they returned, but now there was a scent on the wind that drove them to the hunt with urgent hunger. Two blocks away, Mrs. Eddleman had discarded a particularly gamey tuna-fish salad, and their acute olfactory systems had picked up the scent even while they slept.

The raccoons bounded into the night like wolves on the fold.

JENNIFER

For Jenny, evening came as a mix of blessing and curses. The call from Travis had come at five, as promised, and she found herself elated at being wanted but also thrown into a quandary about what to wear, how to behave, and where to go. Travis had left it up to her. She was a local and knew the best places to go, he had said, and he was right. He had even asked her to drive.

As soon as she had hung up, she ran to the garage for the shop vac to clean out her car. While she cleaned, she ran possibilities through her mind. Should she pick the most expensive restaurant? No, that might scare him away. There was a romantic Italian place south of town, but what if he got the wrong idea? Pizza was too informal for a dinner date. Burgers were out of the question. She was a vegetarian. English food? No—why punish the guy?

She found herself resenting Travis for making her decide. Finally she opted for the Italian place.

When the car was clean, she returned to the house to pick out what she would wear. She dressed and undressed seven times in the next half hour and finally decided on a sleeveless black dress and heels.

She posed before the full-length mirror. The black dress definitely was the best. And if she splashed marinara sauce on it, the stain wouldn't show. She looked good. The heels showed off her calves nicely, but you could also see the light-red hair on her legs. She hadn't thought about it until now. She rummaged through her drawers, found some black panty hose and slipped them on.

That problem taken care of, she resumed her posing, affecting the bored, pouty look she had seen on fashion models in magazines. She was thin and fairly tall, and her legs were tight and muscular from waiting tables. Pretty nice for a thirty-year-old broad, she thought. Then she raised her arms and stretched languidly. Two curly tufts of armpit hair stared at her from the mirror.

It was natural, unpretentious, she thought. She had stopped

shaving about the same time she had stopped eating meat. It was all part of getting in touch with herself, of getting connected to the Earth. It was a way to show that she did not conform to the female ideal created by Hollywood and Madison Avenue, that she was a natural woman. Did the Goddess shave her armpits? She did not. But the Goddess was not going out on her first date in over ten years.

Jenny suddenly realized how unaware she had become of her appearance in the last few years. Not that she had let herself go, but the changes she had made away from makeup and complicated hairstyles had been so slow she had hardly noticed. And Robert hadn't seemed to notice, or at least he had not objected. But that was the past. Robert was in the past, or he would be soon.

She went to the bathroom in search of a razor.

BILLY WINSTON

Billy Winston had no such dilemma about shaving. He did his legs and underarms as a matter of course every time he showered. The idea of conforming to a diet soft-drink ideal of the perfect woman didn't bother him in the least. On the contrary, Billy felt compromised by the fact that he had to maintain his appearance as a six-foot-three-inch tall man with a protruding Adam's apple in order to keep his job as night auditor at the Rooms-R-Us Motel. In his heart, Billy was a buxom blond vixen named Roxanne.

But Roxanne had to stay in the closet until Billy finished doing the motel's books, until midnight, when the rest of the staff left the motel and Billy was alone on the desk. Only then could Roxanne dance through the night on her silicon chip slippers, stroking the libidos of lonely men and breaking hearts. When the iron tongue of midnight told twelve, the sex fairy would find her on-line lovers. Until then, she was Billy Winston, and Billy Winston was getting ready to go to work.

He slipped the red silk panties and garter belt over his long, thin legs, then slowly worked the black, seamed stockings up, teasing himself in the full-length mirror at the end of the bed. He smiled coyly at himself as he clipped the garters into place. Then he put on his jeans and flannel shirt and laced up his tennis shoes. Over his shirt pocket he pinned his name badge: Billy Winston, Night Auditor.

It was a sad irony, Billy thought, that the thing he loved most, being Roxanne, depended on the thing he liked least, his job. Each evening he awoke feeling a mix of excitement and dread. Oh, well, a joint would get him through the first three hours of his shift, and Roxanne would get him through the last five.

He dreamed of the day when he could afford his own computer and become Roxanne anytime he wanted. He would quit his job and make his living like The Breeze: fast and loose. Just a few more months behind the desk and he would have the money he needed.

CATCH

Catch was a demon of the twenty-seventh order. In the hierarchy of hell this put him far below the archdemons like Mammon, master of avarice, but far above the blue-collar demons like Arrrgg, who was responsible for leeching the styrofoam taste into take-out coffee.

Catch had been created as a servant and a destroyer and endowed with a simplemindedness that suited those roles. His distinction in hell was that he had spent more time on Earth than any other demon, where, in the company of men, he had learned to be devious and ambitious.

His ambition took the form of looking for a master who would allow him to indulge himself in destruction and terror. Of all the masters that Catch had served since Solomon, Travis had been the worst. Travis had an irritating streak of righteousness that grated on Catch's nerves. In the past, Catch had been called up by devious men who limited the demon's destruction only to keep his presence secret from other men. Most of the time this was accomplished by the death of all witnesses. Catch always made sure that there were witnesses.

With Travis, Catch's need for destruction was controlled and allowed to build inside him until Travis was forced to unleash him. Always it was someone Travis had chosen. Always it was in private. And it was never enough for Catch's appetite.

Serving under Travis, his mind always seemed foggy and the fire inside him confined to a smolder. Only when Travis directed him toward a victim did he feel crispness in his thoughts and a blazing in his nature. The times were too few. The demon longed again for a master with enemies, but his thoughts were never clear enough to devise a plan to find one. Travis's will was overpowering.

But today the demon had felt a release. It had started when Travis met the woman in the cafe. When they went to the old man's house, he felt a power surge through him unlike anything he had felt in years. Again, when Travis called the girl, the power had increased.

He began to remember what he was: a creature who had brought kings and popes to power and in turn had usurped others. Satan himself, sitting on his throne in the great city of Pandemonium, had spoken to a multitude of hellish hosts, "In our exile, we must be beholden unto Jehovah for two things: one, that we exist, and two, that Catch has no ambition." The fallen angels laughed with Catch at the joke, for that was a time before Catch had walked among men. Men had been a bad influence on Catch.

He would have a new master; one who could be corrupted by his power. He had seen her that afternoon in the saloon and sensed her hunger for control over others. Together they would rule the world. The key was near; he felt it. If Travis found it, Catch would be sent back to hell. He had to find it first and get it into the hands of the witch. After all, it was better to rule on Earth than to serve in hell.

14

DINNER

Travis parked the Chevy on the street in front of Jenny's house. He turned off the engine and turned to Catch.

"You stay here, you understand. I'll be back in a little while to check on you."

"Thanks, Dad."

"Don't play the radio and don't beep the horn. Just wait."

"I promise. I'll be good." The demon attempted an innocent grin and failed.

"Keep an eye on that." Travis pointed to an aluminum suitcase on the backseat.

"Enjoy your date. The car will be fine."

"What's wrong with you?"

"Nothing," Catch grinned.

"Why are you being so nice?"

"It's good to see you getting out."

"You're lying."

"Travis, I'm crushed."

"That would be nice," Travis said. "Now, don't eat anybody."

"I just ate last night. I don't even feel hungry. I'll just sit here and meditate."

Travis reached into the inside pocket of his sport coat and pulled out a comic book. "I got this for you." He held it out to the demon. "You can look at it while you wait."

The demon fumbled the comic book away from Travis and spread it out on the seat. "Cookie Monster! My favorite! Thanks, Travis."

"See you later."

Travis got out of the car and slammed the door. Catch watched him walk across the yard. "I already looked at this one, asshole," he hissed to himself. "When I get a new master, I will tear your arms off and eat them while you watch."

Travis looked back over his shoulder. Catch waved him on with his best effort at a smile.

The doorbell rang precisely at seven. Jenny's reactions went like this: *don't answer it, change clothes, answer it and feign sickness, clean the house, redecorate, schedule plastic surgery, change hair color, take a handful of Valium, appeal to the Goddess for divine intervention, stand here and explore the possibilities of paralyzing panic.*

She opened the door and smiled. "Hi."

Travis stood there in jeans and a gray herringbone tweed jacket. He was transfixed.

"Travis?" Jenny said.

"You're beautiful," he said finally.

They stood in the doorway, Jenny blushing, Travis staring. Jenny had decided to stick with the black dress. Evidently it had been the right choice. A full minute passed without a word between them.

"Would you like to come in?"

"No."

"Okay." She shut the door in his face. Well, that hadn't been so bad. Now she could put on some sweatpants, load the refrigerator onto a tray, and settle down for a night in front of the television.

There was a timid knock on the door. Jenny opened it again. "Sorry, I'm a little nervous," she said.

"It's all right," Travis said. "Shall we go?"

"Sure. I'll get my purse." She closed the door in his face.

There was an uncomfortable silence between them while they drove to the restaurant. Typically, this would be the time for trading life stories, but Jenny had resolved not to talk about her marriage, which closed most of her adult life to conversation, and Travis had resolved not to talk about the demon, which eliminated most of the twentieth century.

"So," Jenny said, "do you like Italian food?"

"Yep," Travis said. They drove in silence the rest of the way to the restaurant.

It was a warm night and the Toyota had no air conditioning. Jenny didn't dare roll down the window and risk blowing her hair. She had spent an hour styling and pinning it back so that it fell in long curls to the middle of her back. When she began to perspire, she remembered that she still had two wads of toilet paper tucked under her arms to stop the bleeding from shaving cuts. For the next few minutes all she could think of was getting to a restroom where she could remove the spotted wads. She decided not to mention it.

The restaurant, the Old Italian Pasta Factory, was housed in an old creamery building, a remnant of the time when Pine Cove's economy was based on livestock rather than tourism. The concrete floors remained intact, as did the corrugated steel roof. The owners had taken care to preserve the rusticity of the structure, while adding the warmth of a fireplace, soft lighting, and the traditional red-and-white tablecloths of an Italian restaurant. The tables were small but comfortably spaced, and each was decorated with fresh flowers and a candle. The Pasta Factory, it was agreed, was the most romantic restaurant in the area.

As soon as the hostess seated them, Jenny excused herself to the restroom.

"Order whatever wine you want," she said, "I'm not picky."

"I don't drink, but if you want some . . ."

"No, that's fine. It'll be a nice change."

As soon as Jenny left, the waitress—an efficient-looking woman in her thirties—came to the table.

"Good evening, sir. What can I bring you to drink this evening?" She pulled her order pad out of her pocket in a quick, liquid movement, like a gunslinger drawing a six-shooter. A career waitress, Travis thought.

"I thought I'd wait for the lady to return," he said.

"Oh, Jenny. She'll have an herbal tea. And you want, let's see . . ." She looked him up and down, cross-referenced him, pigeonholed him, and announced, "You'll have some sort of imported beer, right?"

"I don't drink, so . . ."

"I should have known." The waitress slapped her forehead as if she'd just caught herself in the middle of a grave error, like serving the salad with plutonium instead of creamy Italian. "Her husband is a drunk; it's only natural that she'd go out with a nondrinker on the rebound. Can I bring you a mineral water?"

"That would be fine," Travis said.

The waitress's pen scratched, but she did not look at the order pad or lose her "we aim to please" smile. "And would you like some garlic bread while you're waiting?"

"Sure," Travis said. He watched the waitress walk away. She took small, quick, mechanical steps, and was gone to the kitchen in an instant. Travis wondered why some people seemed to be able to walk faster than he could run. They're professionals, he thought.

Jenny took five minutes to get all the toilet paper unstuck from her underarms, and there had been an embarrassing moment when another woman came into the restroom and found her before the mirror with her elbow in the air. When she returned to the table, Travis was staring over a basket of garlic bread.

She saw the herbal tea on the table and said, "How did you know?"

"Psychic, I guess," he said. "I ordered garlic bread."

"Yes," she said, seating herself.

They stared at the garlic bread as if it were a bubbling caldron of hemlock.

"You like garlic bread?" she asked.

"Love it. And you?"

"One of my favorites," she said.

He picked up the basket and offered it to her. "Have some?"

"Not right now. You go ahead."

"No thanks, I'm not in the mood." He put the basket down.

The garlic bread lay there between them, steaming with implications. They, of course, must both eat it or neither could. Garlic bread meant garlic breath. There might be a kiss later, maybe more. There was just too damn much intimacy in garlic bread.

They sat in silence, reading the menu; she looking for the cheapest entree, which she had no intention of eating; and he, looking for the item that would be the least embarrassing to eat in front of someone.

"What are you going to have?" she asked.

"Not spaghetti," he snapped.

"Okay." Jenny had forgotten what dating was like. Although she couldn't remember for sure, she thought that she might have gotten married to avoid ever having to go through this kind of discomfort again. It was like driving with the emergency brake set. She decided to release the brake.

"I'm starved. Pass the garlic bread."

Travis smiled. "Sure." He passed it to her, then took a piece for himself. They paused in midbite and eyed each other across the table like two poker players on the bluff. Jenny laughed, spraying crumbs all over the table. The evening was on.

"So, Travis, what do you do?"

"Date married women, evidently."

"How did you know?"

"The waitress told me."

"We're separated."

"Good," he said, and they both laughed.

They ordered, and as dinner progressed they found common ground in the awkwardness of the situation. Jenny told Travis about her marriage and her job. Travis made up a history of working as a traveling insurance salesman with no real ties to home or family.

In a frank exchange of truth for lies, they found they liked each other—were, in fact, quite taken with one another.

They left the restaurant arm in arm, laughing.

15

RACHEL

Rachel Henderson lived alone in a small house that lay amid a grove of eucalyptus trees at the edge of the Beer Bar cattle ranch. The house was owned by Jim Beer, a lanky, forty-five-year-old cowboy who lived with his wife and two children in a fourteen-room house his grandfather had built on the far side of the ranch. Rachel had lived on the ranch for five years. She had never paid any rent.

Rachel had met Jim Beer in the Head of the Slug Saloon when she first arrived in Pine Cove. Jim had been drinking all day and was feeling the weight of his rugged cowboy charisma when Rachel sat down on the bar stool next to him and put a newspaper on the bar.

"Well, darlin', I'm damned if you're not a fresh wind on a stale pasture. Can I buy you a drink?" The banjo twang in Jim's accent was pure Oklahoma, picked up from the hands that had worked the Beer Bar when Jim was a boy. Jim was the third generation of Beers to work the ranch and would probably be the last. His teenage son, Zane Grey Beer, had decided early on that he would rather ride a surfboard than a horse. That was part of the reason that Jim was drinking away the afternoon at the Slug. That, and the fact that his wife had just purchased a new Mercedes turbo-diesel wagon that cost the annual net income of the Beer Bar Ranch.

Rachel unfolded the classified section of the *Pine Cove Gazette* on the bar. "Just an orange juice, thanks. I'm house hunting today." She curled one leg under herself on the bar stool. "You don't know anybody that has a house for rent, do you?"

Jim Beer would look back on that day many times in the years to come, but he could never quite remember what had happened next. What he did remember was driving his pickup down the back road into the ranch with Rachel following behind in an old Volkswagen van. From there his memory was a montage of images: Rachel naked on the small bunk, his turquoise belt buckle hitting the wooden floor with a thud, silk scarves tied around his wrists, Rachel bouncing above him—riding him like a bronco—climbing back into his pickup after sundown, sore and sweaty, leaning his forehead on the wheel of the truck and thinking about his wife and kids.

In the five years since, Jim Beer had never gone near the little house on the far side of the ranch. Every month he penciled the rent collected into a ledger, then deposited cash from his poker fund in the business checking account to cover it.

A few of his friends had seen him leave the Head of the Slug with Rachel that afternoon. When they saw him again, they ribbed him, made crude jokes, and asked pointed questions. Jim answered the jibes by pushing his summer Stetson back on his head and saying: "Boys, all I got to say is that male menopause is a rough trail to ride." Hank Williams couldn't have sung it any sadder.

After Jim left that evening Rachel picked several gray hairs from the bunk's pillow. Around the hairs she carefully tied a single red thread, which she knotted twice. Two knots were enough for the bond she wanted over Jim Beer. She placed the tiny bundle in a babyfood jar, labeled it with a marking pen, and stored it away in a cupboard over the kitchen sink.

Now the cupboard was full of jars, each one containing a similar bundle, each bundle tied with a red thread. The number of knots in the thread varied. Three of the bundles were tied with four knots. These contained the hair of men Rachel had loved. Those men were long gone.

The rest of Rachel's house was decorated with objects of power: eagle feathers, crystals, pentagrams, and tapestries embroidered with magic symbols. There was no evidence of a past in Rachel's house. Any photos she had of herself had been taken after she arrived in Pine Cove.

People who knew Rachel had no clue as to where she had lived or who she had been before she came to town. They knew her as a beautiful, mysterious woman who taught aerobics for a living. Or they knew her as a witch. Her past was an enigma, which was just the way she wanted it.

No one knew that Rachel had grown up in Bakersfield, the daughter of an illiterate oil-field worker. They didn't know that she had been a fat, ugly little girl who spent most of her life doing degrading things for disgusting men so that she might receive some sort of acceptance. Butterflies do not wax nostalgic about the time they spent as caterpillars.

Rachel had married a crop-duster pilot who was twenty years her senior. She was eighteen at the time.

It happened in the front seat of a pickup truck in the parking lot of a roadhouse outside of Visalia, California. The pilot, whose name was Merle Henderson, was still breathing hard and Rachel was washing the foul taste out of her mouth with a lukewarm Budweiser. "If you do that again, I'll marry you," Merle gasped.

An hour later they were flying over the Mojave desert, heading for Las Vegas in Merle's Cessna 152. Merle came at ten thousand feet. They were married under a neon arch in a ramshackle, concrete-block chapel just off the Vegas strip. They had known each other exactly six hours.

Rachel regarded the next eight years of her life as her term on the wheel of abuse. Merle Henderson deposited her in his house trailer by the landing strip and kept her there. He allowed her to visit town once a week to go to the laundromat and the grocery store. The rest of her time was spent waiting on or waiting for Merle and helping him work on his planes.

Each morning Merle took off in the crop duster, taking with him the keys to the pickup. Rachel spent the days cleaning up the trailer, eating, and watching television. She grew fatter and Merle began to refer to her as his fat little mama. What little self-esteem she had drained away and was absorbed by Merle's overpowering male ego.

Merle had flown helicopter gunships in Vietnam and he still talked about it as the happiest time in his life. When he opened the tanks of insecticide over a field of lettuce, he imagined he was releasing air-to-ground missiles into a Vietnamese village. The Army had sensed a destructive edge in Merle, Vietnam had honed it to razor sharpness, and it had not dulled when he came home. Until he married Rachel, he released his pent-up violence by starting fights in bars and flying with dangerous abandon. With Rachel waiting for him at home, he went to bars less often and released his aggression on her in the form of constant criticism, verbal abuse, and finally, beatings.

Rachel bore the abuse as if it were a penance sent down by God for the sin of being a woman. Her mother had endured the same sort of abuse from her father, with the same resignation. It was just the way things worked.

Then, one day, while Rachel was waiting at the laundromat for Merle's shirts to dry, a woman approached her. It was the day after a particularly vicious beating and Rachel's face was bruised and swollen.

"It's none of my business," the woman said. She was tall and stately and in her mid-forties. She had a way about her that frightened Rachel, a presence, but her voice was soft and strong. "But when you get some time, you might read this." She held out a pamphlet to Rachel and Rachel took it. The title was *The Wheel of Abuse*.

"There are some numbers in the back that you can call. Everything will be okay," the woman said.

Rachel thought it a strange thing to say. Everything was okay. But the woman had impressed her, so she read the pamphlet.

It talked about human rights and dignity and personal power. It spoke to Rachel about her life in a way that she had never thought possible. *The Wheel of Abuse* was her life story. How did they know?

Mostly it talked about courage to change. She kept the pamphlet and hid it away in a box of tampons under the bathroom sink. It stayed there for two weeks. Until the morning she ran out of coffee.

She could hear the sound of Merle's plane disappearing in the distance as she stared into the mirror at the bloody hole where her front teeth used to be. She dug out the pamphlet and called one of the numbers on the back.

Within a half hour two women arrived at the trailer. They packed Rachel's belongings and drove her to the shelter. Rachel wanted to leave a note for Merle, but the two women insisted that it was not a good idea.

For the next three weeks Rachel lived at the shelter. The women at the shelter cared for her. They gave her food and understanding and affection, and in return they asked only that she acknowledge her own dignity. When she made the call to Merle to tell him where she was, they all stood by her.

Merle promised that it would all change. He missed her. He needed her.

She returned to the trailer.

For a month Merle did not hit her. He did not touch her at all. He didn't even speak to her.

The women at the shelter had warned her about this type of abuse: the withdrawal of affection. When she brought it up to Merle one evening while he was eating, he threw a plate in her face. Then he proceeded to give her the worst beating of her life. Afterward he locked her outside the trailer for the night.

The trailer was fifteen miles from the nearest neighbor, so Rachel was forced to cower under the front steps to escape the cold. She was not sure she could walk fifteen miles.

In the middle of the night Merle opened the door and shouted, "By the way, I ripped the phone out, so don't waste your time thinking about it." He slammed and locked the door.

When the sun broke in the east, Merle reappeared. Rachel had crawled under the trailer, where he could not reach her. He lifted the plastic skirting and shouted to her, "Listen, bitch, you'd better be here when I get home or you'll get worse."

Rachel waited in the darkness under the trailer until she heard the biplane roar down the strip. She climbed out and watched the plane climb gradually into the distance. Although it hurt her face, and the cuts on her mouth split open, she couldn't help smiling. She had discovered her personal power. It lay hidden under the trailer in a five-gallon asphalt can, now half full of aviation grade motor oil.

A policeman came to the trailer that afternoon. His jaw was set with the stoic resolve of a man who knows he has an unpleasant task to perform and is determined to do it, but when he saw Rachel sitting on the steps of the trailer, the color drained from his face and he ran to her. "Are you all right?"

Rachel could not speak. Garbled sounds bubbled from her broken mouth. The policeman drove her to the hospital in his cruiser. Later, after she had been cleaned up and bandaged, the policeman came to her room and told her about the crash.

It seemed that Merle's biplane lost power after a pass over a field. He was unable to climb fast enough to avoid a high-tension tower and flaming bits of Merle were scattered across a field of budding strawberries. Later, at the funeral, Rachel would comment, "It was how he would have wanted to go."

A few weeks later a man from the Federal Aviation Administration came around the trailer asking questions. Rachel told him that Merle had beat her, then had stormed out to the plane and taken off. The F.A.A. concluded that Merle, in his anger, had forgotten to check out his plane thoroughly before taking off. No one ever suspected Rachel of draining the oil out of the plane.

16

HOWARD

Howard Phillips, the owner of H.P.'s Cafe, had just settled down in the study of his stone cottage when he looked out the window and saw something moving through the trees.

Howard had spent most of his adult life trying to prove three theories he had formulated in college: one, that before man had walked the Earth there had been a powerful race of intelligent beings who had achieved a high level of civilization, then for some unknown reason had disappeared; two, that the remnants of their civilization still existed underground or under the ocean, and through extreme cunning and guile had escaped detection by man; and three, that they were planning to return as masters of the planet in a very unfriendly way.

What lurked in the woods outside Howard Phillips's cottage was the first physical evidence of his theories that he had ever encountered. He was at once elated and terrified. Like the child who is delighted by the idea of Santa Claus, then cries and cowers behind its mother when confronted with the corpulent red-suited reality of a department-store Santa, Howard Phillips was not fully prepared for a physical manifestation of what he had long believed extant. He was a scholar, not an adventurer. He preferred his experiences to come secondhand, through books. Howard's idea of adventure was trying whole wheat toast with his daily ham and eggs instead of the usual white bread.

He stared out the window at the creature moving in the moonlight. It was very much like the creatures he had read about in ancient manuscripts: bipedal like a man, but with long, apelike arms; reptilian. Howard could see scales reflecting in the moonlight. The one inconsistency that bothered him was its size. In the manuscripts, these creatures, who were said to be kept as slaves by the Old Ones, had always been small in stature, no more than a few feet tall. This one was enormous—four, maybe five meters tall.

The creature stopped for moment, then turned slowly and looked directly at Howard's window. Howard resisted the urge to dive to the floor and so stood staring straight into the eyes of the nightmare.

The creature's eyes were the size of car headlamps and they glowed a faint orange around slotted, feline pupils. Long, pointed scales lay back against its head, giving the impression of ears. They stood there, staring at each other, the creature and the man, neither moving, until Howard could bear it no longer. He grabbed the curtains and pulled them shut, almost ripping them from the rod in the process. Outside he could hear the sound of laughter.

When he dared to peak through the gap in the curtains, the creature was gone.

Why hadn't he been more scientific in his observation? Why hadn't he run for his camera? For all his work at putting together clues from arcane grimoirs to prove the existence of the Old Ones, people had labeled him a crackpot. One photograph would have convinced them. But he had missed his chance. Or had he?

Suddenly it occurred to Howard that the creature had seen him. Why should the Old Ones be so careful not to be discovered for so long, then walk in the moonlight as if out for a Sunday stroll?

Perhaps it had not moved on at all but was circling the house to do away with the witness.

First he thought of weapons. He had none in the house. Many of the old books in his library had spells for protection, but he had no idea where to start looking. Besides, the verge of panic was not the ideal mental state in which to do research. He might still be able to bolt to his old Jaguar and escape. Then again, he might bolt into the claws of the creature. All these thoughts passed through his mind in a second.

The phone. He snatched the phone from his desk and dialed. It seemed forever for the dial to spin, but finally there was a ring and a woman's voice at the other end.

"Nine-one-one, emergency," she said.

"Yes, I wish to report a lurker in the woods."

"What is your name, sir?"

"Howard Phillips."

"And what is the address you are calling from?"

"Five-oh-nine Cambridge Street, in Pine Cove."

"Are you in any immediate danger?"

"Well, yes, that *is* why I called."

"You say you have a prowler. Is he attempting to enter the house?"

"Not yet."

"You *have* seen the prowler?"

"Yes, outside my window, in the woods."

"Can you describe him?"

"He is an abomination of such abysmal hideousness that the mere recollection of this monstrosity perambulating in the dark outside my domicile fills me with the preternatural chill of the charnel house."

"That would be about how tall?"

Howard paused to think. Obviously the law enforcement system was not prepared to deal with perversions from the transcosmic gulfs of the nethermost craters of the underworld. Yet he needed assistance.

"The fiend stands two meters," he said.

"Could you see what he was wearing?"

Again Howard considered the truth and rejected it. "Jeans, I believe. And a leather jacket."

"Could you tell if he was armed?"

"Armed? I should say so. The beast is armed with monstrous claws and a toothed maw of the most villainous predator."

"Calm down, sir. I am dispatching a unit to your home. Make sure the doors are locked. Stay calm, I'll stay on the line until the officers arrive."

"How long will that be?"

"About twenty minutes."

"Young woman, in twenty minutes I shall be little more than a shredded memory!" Howard hung up the phone.

It had to be escape, then. He took his greatcoat and car keys from the foyer and stood leaning against the front door. Slowly he slipped the lock and grabbed the door handle.

"On three, then," he said to himself.

"One." He turned the door handle.

"Two." He bent, preparing to run.

"Three!" He didn't move.

"All right, then. Steel yourself, Howard." He started the count again.

"One." Perhaps the beast was not outside.

"Two." If it was a slave creature, it wasn't dangerous at all.

"Three!" He did not move.

Howard repeated the process of counting, over and over, each time measuring the fear in his heart against the danger that lurked outside. Finally, disgusted with his own cowardliness, he threw the door open, and bolted into the dark.

17

BILLY

Billy Winston was on the final stretch of the nightly audit at the Rooms-R-Us Motel. His fingers danced across the calculator like a spastic Fred Astaire. The sooner he finished, the sooner he could log onto the computer and become Roxanne. Only thirty-seven of the motel's one hundred rooms were rented tonight, so he was going to finish early. He couldn't wait. He needed Roxanne's ego boost after being ditched by The Breeze the night before.

He hit the total button with a flourish, as if he had just played the final note of a piano concerto, then wrote the figure into the ledger and slammed the book.

Billy was alone in the motel. The only sound was the hum of the fluorescent lights. From the windows by his desk he had a 180-degree view of the highway and the parking lot, but there was nothing to see. At that time of night a car or two passed every half hour or so. Just as well. He didn't like distractions while he was being Roxanne.

Billy pushed a stool up to the front counter behind the computer. He typed in his access code and logged on.

WITKSAS: HOW'S YOUR DOG, SWEETIE? SEND: PNCV-CAL

The Rooms-R-Us Motel chain maintained a computer network for making reservations at their motels all over the world. From any location a desk clerk could contact any of the two hundred motels in the chain by simply entering a seven-letter code. Billy had just sent a message to the night auditor in Wichita, Kansas. He started at the green phosphorescent screen, waiting for an answer.

PNCVCAL: ROXANNE! MY DOG IS LONELY. HELP ME, BABY. WITKSAS

Wichita was on line. Billy punched up a reply.

WITKSAS: MAYBE HE NEEDS A LITTLE DISCIPLINE. I COULD SMOTHER HIM IF YOU WANT. SEND: PNCVCAL

There was a pause while Billy waited.

PNCVCAL: YOU WANT TO HOLD HIS POOR FUZZY FACE BETWEEN YOUR MELONS UNTIL HE BEGS? IS THAT IT? WITKSAS

Billy thought for a moment. This was why they loved him. He couldn't just throw them an answer they could get from any sleazebeast. Roxanne was a goddess.

WITKSAS: YES. AND BEAT HIM SOFTLY ON THE EARS. BAD DOG. BAD DOG. SEND: PNCVCAL

Again Billy waited for the response. A message appeared on the screen.

WHERE ARE YOU DARLING? I MISS YOU. TULSOKL.

It was his lover from Tulsa. Roxanne could handle two or three at once, but she wasn't in the mood for it right now. She was feeling a little crampy. Billy adjusted his crotch, his panties were riding up a bit. He typed two messages.

WITKSAS: GO PET YOUR DOGGIE FOR A WHILE. AUNTIE ROXANNE WILL CHECK ON YOU IN A WHILE. SEND: PNCVCAL

TULSOKL: TOOK AN EVENING OFF TO SHOP FOR

SOMETHING LACY TO WEAR FOR YOU. I HOPE YOU DON'T FIND IT TOO SHOCKING. SEND: PNCVCAL

While he was waiting for a response from Oklahoma, Billy dug into his gym bag for his red high heels. He liked to hook the stiletto heels into the rungs of the stool while he talked to his lovers. When he glanced up, he thought he saw something moving out in the parking lot. Probably just a guest getting something from the car.

PNCVCAL: YOU SWEET LITTLE THING, YOU COULD NEVER SHOCK ME. TELL ME WHAT YOU BOUGHT. TUL-SOKL

Billy started to type in a modest description of a lace teddy he had seen in a catalog.

To the guy in Tulsa, Roxanne was a shy little flower; to Wichita she was a dominatrix. The desk clerk in Seattle saw her as a leather-clad biker chick. The old man in Arizona thought she was a struggling single mother of two, barely making it on a desk clerk's salary. He always wanted to send her money. There were ten of them in all. Roxanne gave them what they needed. They loved her.

Billy heard the double doors of the lobby open, but he did not look up. He finished typing his message and pressed the SEND button. "Can I help you," he said mechanically, still not looking up.

"You betcha," a voice said. Two huge reptilian hands clacked down on the counter about four feet on each side of Billy. He looked up into the open mouth of the demon coming at his face. Billy pushed back from the keyboard. His heel caught in the rung of the stool and he went over backward as the giant maw snapped shut above him. Billy let loose a long, sirenlike scream and began scrambling on his hands and knees behind the counter toward the back office. Looking back over his shoulder, he saw the demon crawling over the counter after him.

Once in the office, Billy leapt to his feet and slammed the door. As he turned to run out the back door, he heard the door fly open and slam against the wall.

The back door of the office led into a long corridor of rooms.

Billy pounded on the doors as he passed. No one opened a door, but there were angry shouts from inside the rooms.

Billy turned and saw the demon filling the far end of the corridor. It was in a crouch, moving down the corridor on all fours, crawling awkward and batlike in the confined space. Billy dug in his pocket for his pass key, found it, and ran down the hallway and around the corner. Making the corner, he twisted his ankle. White pain shot up his leg, and he cried out. He limped to the closest door. The images of women in horror movies who twisted their ankles and feebly fell into the clutches of the monster raced through his head. Damn high heels.

He fumbled the key into the lock while looking back down the hallway. The door opened and Billy fell into the room just as the monster rounded the corner behind him.

He kicked the stiletto heel off his good foot, vaulted up and hopped across the empty room to the sliding glass door. The safety bar was set. He fell to his knees and began clawing at it. The only light in the room was coming from the hallway, and suddenly that was eclipsed. The monster was working its way through the doorway.

"What the fuck are you!" Billy screamed.

The monster stopped just inside the room. Even crouching over, its shoulders hit the ceiling. Billy cowered by the sliding door, still clawing under the curtains at the safety bar. The monster looked around the room, its huge head turning back and forth like a searchlight. To Billy's amazement, it reached around and turned on the lights. It seemed to be studying the bed.

"Does that have Magic Fingers?" it said.

"What!" Billy said. It came out a scream.

"That bed has Magic Fingers, right?"

Billy pulled the safety bar loose and hurled it at the monster. The heavy steel bar hit the monster in the face and rattled to the floor. The monster showed no reaction. Billy reached for the latch on the door and started to pull it open.

The monster scuttled forward, reached over Billy's head, and pushed the door shut with one clawed finger. Billy yanked on the door but it was held fast. He collapsed under the monster with a long, agonizing wail.

"Give me a quarter," the monster said.

Billy looked up into the huge lizard face. The monster's grin was nearly two feet wide. "Give me a quarter!" it repeated.

Billy dug into his pocket, came out with a handful of change, and timidly held it up to the monster.

Still holding the door shut with one hand, the monster reached down with the other and plucked a quarter from Billy's hand with two claws, using them like chopsticks.

"Thanks," it said. "I love Magic Fingers."

The demon let go of the door. "You can go now," it said.

Before he could think about it, Billy threw the door open and dove through. He was climbing to his feet when something caught him by the leg from behind and dragged him back into the room.

"I was just kidding. You can't go."

The monster held Billy upside down by his leg while it dropped the quarter into the little metal box on the nightstand.

Billy flailed in the air, screaming and clawing at the demon, ripping his fingernails against its scales. The monster took Billy into its arms like a teddy bear and lay back on the bed. Its feet hung off the end and nearly touched the dresser on the opposite wall.

Billy could not scream; there was no breath for a scream. The monster let go with one arm and placed one long claw at Billy's ear.

"Don't you just love Magic Fingers?" it said. Then it drove the claw though Billy's brain.

18

RACHEL

After Merle died and Rachel observed a respectable period of mourning, which was precisely the same amount of time it took the courts to transfer Merle's property to her, she sold the Cessna and the trailer, bought herself a Volkswagen van, and on the advice of the women at the shelter, headed for Berkeley. In Berkeley, they insisted, she would find a community of women who could help her stay off the wheel of abuse. They were right.

The women in Berkeley welcomed Rachel with open arms. They helped her find a place to live, enrolled her in exercise and self-actualization courses, taught her to defend herself, nurture herself, and most important, to respect herself. She lost weight and grew strong. She thrived.

Within a year she took the remainder of her inheritance and bought a lease on a small studio adjacent to the University of California campus and began teaching high-intensity aerobics. She soon gained a reputation as a tough, domineering bitch of an instructor. There was a waiting list to get into her classes. The fat little girl had come into her own as a beautiful and powerful woman.

Rachel taught six classes a day, putting herself through the rigors of each workout along with her students. After a few months of that regimen, she fell ill, waking one morning to find that she had just enough strength to call the women in her classes to cancel, and no more. One of her students, a statuesque, gray-haired woman in her forties named Bella, appeared at Rachel's door a few hours later.

Once through the door Bella began giving orders. "Take off your clothes and get back in bed. I'll bring you some tea in a moment." Her voice was deep and strong, yet somehow soothing. Rachel did as she was told. "I don't know what you think you've done to deserve the punishment you are giving yourself, Rachel," Bella said, "but it has to stop."

Bella sat on the edge of Rachel's bed and watched while Rachel drank the tea. "Now lie on your stomach and relax."

Bella applied fragrant oil to Rachel's back and began rubbing, first with long, slow strokes that spread the oil, then gradually digging her fingers into the muscles until Rachel thought she would cry out in pain. When the message was finished, Rachel felt even more exhausted than before. She fell into a deep sleep.

When Rachel awoke, Bella repeated the process, forcing Rachel to drink the bitter tea, then kneading her muscles until they ached. Again, Rachel slept.

When Rachel awoke the fourth time, Bella again served her the tea, but this time she had Rachel lie on her back to receive her massage. Bella's hands played gently over her body, lingering between her legs and on her breasts. Through the drugged haze of the tea, Rachel noticed that the older woman was almost naked and had rubbed her own body with the same fragrant oils that she used on Rachel.

It didn't occur to Rachel to resist. Since Bella had come through the door, she had been giving orders and Rachel had obeyed. In the dim light of Rachel's little apartment they became lovers. It had been two years since Rachel had been with a man. Trading soft caresses with Bella, she didn't care if she was ever again.

When Rachel was back on her feet, Bella introduced her to a group of women who met at Bella's house once a week to perform ceremonies and rituals. Among these women Rachel learned about a new power she carried within herself, the power of the Goddess. Bella tutored her in the machinations of white magic and soon Rachel was leading the coven in rituals, while Bella looked on like a proud mother.

"Modulate your voice," Bella told her. "No matter what you are saying it should sound like a chant to the Goddess. The coven should be taken with the chant. That is the meaning of enchantment, my dear."

Rachel gave up her apartment and moved into Bella's restored Victorian house near the U.C. campus. For the first time in her life, she felt truly happy. Of course, it didn't last.

One afternoon she came home to find Bella in bed with a bald and bewhiskered professor of music. Rachel was livid. She threatened the professor with a fireplace poker and chased him, half-naked, into the street. He exited clutching his tweed jacket and corduroy slacks in front of him.

"You said you loved me!" Rachel screamed at Bella.

"I do love you, dear." Bella did not seem the least bit upset. Her voice was deep and modulated like a chant. "This was about power, not love."

"If I wasn't filling your needs, you should have said something."

"You are the most wonderful lover I have known, dear Rachel. But Dr. Mendenhall holds the mortgage on our house. That loan is interest free, in case you hadn't noticed."

"You whore!"

"Aren't we all, dear?"

"I'm not."

"You are. I am. The Goddess is. We all have our price. Be it love, or money, or power, Rachel. Why do you think the women in your exercise classes put themselves through so much pain?"

"You're changing the subject."

"Answer me," Bella demanded. "Why?"

"They want a sound body. They want a strong vessel to carry a strong spirit."

"They don't give a rat's ass about a strong spirit. They want a tight ass so men will want them. They will deny it to the death, but it's true. The sooner you realize that, the sooner you will realize your own power."

"You're sick. This goes against everything you've ever taught me."

"This is the most important thing I ever will teach you, so listen! Know your price, Rachel."

"No."

"You think I'm some cheap slut, do you? You think you're above selling yourself? How much rent have you ever paid here?"

"I offered. You said it didn't matter. I loved you."

"That's your price, then."

"It's not. It's love."

"Sold!" Bella climbed out of bed and strode across the room, her long gray hair flying behind her. She took her robe from the closet, threw it around herself, and tied the sash. "Love me for what I am, Rachel. Just as I love you for what you are. Nothing has changed. Dr. Mendenhall will be back, whimpering like a puppy. If it will make you feel better, you can be the one that takes him. Maybe we can do it together."

"You're sick. How could you even suggest such a thing?"

"Rachel, as long as you see men as human beings, we are going to have a problem. They are inferior beings, incapable of love. How could a few moments of animal friction with a subhuman affect us? What we have between us?"

"You sound like a man caught with his pants down."

Bella sighed. "I don't want you around the others until you calm down. There's some money in my jewelry box. Why don't you take it and go down to Esalen for a week or so. Think this over. You'll feel better when you get back."

"What about the others?" Rachel asked. "How do you think they'll feel when they find out that all the magic, all the spiritualism you preach, is just so much bullshit?"

"Everything is true. They follow me because they admire my power. This is part of that power. I haven't betrayed anyone."

"You've betrayed me."

"If you feel that way, then perhaps you'd better leave." Bella went into the bathroom and began drawing a bath. Rachel followed her.

"Why should I leave? I could just tell them. I know as much as you do now. I could lead them."

"Dear Rachel." Bella was adding oils to her bath and not looking up. "Didn't you learn anything from killing your husband? Destruction is a man's way."

Rachel was stunned. She had told Bella about the accident but not that she had caused it. She had told no one.

Bella looked up at her at last. "You can stay if you wish. I still love you."

"I'll go."

"I'm sorry, Rachel. I thought you were more highly evolved." Bella slipped out of her robe and into her bath. Rachel stood in the doorway staring down at her.

"I love you," she said.

"I know you do, dear. Now, go pack your things."

Rachel couldn't bear the idea of staying in Berkeley. Everywhere she went she encountered reminders of Bella. She loaded up her van and spent a month driving around California, looking for a place where she might fit in. Then, one morning while reading the paper over breakfast, she spotted a column called "California Facts." It was a simple list of figures that informed readers of obscure facts such as which California county produces the most pistachios (Sacramento), where one had the best chance of having one's car stolen (North Hollywood), and tucked amid a mélange of seemingly insignificant demographics, which California town had the highest per capita percentage of divorced women (Pine Cove). Rachel had found her destination.

Now, five years later, she was firmly set in the community, respected by the women and feared and lusted after by the men. She had moved slowly, recruiting into her coven only women who sought her out—mostly women who were on the verge of leaving their husbands and who needed something to shore them up during the divorce process. Rachel provided them with the support they required, and in return they gave her their loyalty.

Just six months ago she initiated the thirteenth and final member of the coven.

At last she was able to perform the rituals that she had worked so hard to learn from Bella. For years they seemed ineffective, and Rachel attributed their failure to not having a full coven. Now she was starting to suspect that the Earth magic they were trying to perform just did not work—that there was no real power to be had.

She could lead the coven to attempt anything, and on her command they would do it. That was a power of sorts. She could extract favors from men with no more than a seductive glance and in that, there was a power. But none of it was enough. She wanted the magic to work. She wanted real power.

Catch had sensed Rachel's lust for power in the Head of the Slug that afternoon, recognizing in her what he had seen in his ruthless masters before Travis. That night, while Rachel lay in the dark of her cabin, contemplating her own impotence, the demon came to her.

She had locked the door that night, more out of habit than need, as there was very little crime in Pine Cove. Around nine she heard someone try the doorknob and she sat upright in bed.

"Who is it?"

As if in answer, the door bent slowly inward and the doorjamb cracked, then splintered away. The door opened, but there was no one behind it. Rachel pulled the quilt up around her chin and scooted up into the corner of the bed.

"Who is it?"

A voice growled out of the darkness, "Don't be afraid. I will not hurt you."

The moon was bright. If someone was there, she should have been able to see his silhouette in the doorway, but strain as she might, she saw nothing.

"Who are you? What do you want?"

"No—what do you want?" the voice said.

Rachel was truly frightened; the voice was coming from an empty spot not two feet away from her bed.

"I asked you first," she said. "Who are you?"

"Ooooooooooo, I am the ghost of Christmas past."

Rachel poked herself in the leg with her thumbnail to make sure she was not dreaming. She wasn't. She found herself speaking to the disembodied voice in spite of herself.

"Christmas is months away."

"I know. I lied. I'm not the ghost of Christmas past. I saw that in a movie once."

"Who are you!" Rachel was near hysteria.

"I am all your dreams come true."

Someone must have planted a speaker somewhere in the house. Rachel's fear turned to anger. She leapt from bed to find the offending device. Two steps out of bed she ran into something and fell to the floor. Something that felt like claws wrapped around her waist. She felt herself being lifted and put back on the bed. Panic seized her. She began to scream as her bladder let go.

"Stop it!" The voice drowned her screams and rattled the windows of the cabin. "I don't have time for this."

Rachel cowered on the bed. She was panting and felt herself getting light-headed. She started to sink back into unconsciousness, but something caught her by the hair and yanked her back. Her mind searched for a touchstone in reality. A ghost—it was a ghost. Did she believe in ghosts? Perhaps it was time to start. Maybe it was him, returned for revenge.

"Merle, is that you?"

"Who?"

"I'm sorry, Merle, I had to . . ."

"Who is Merle?"

"You're not Merle?"

"Never heard of him."

"Then, who—what in the hell are you?"

"I am the defeat of your enemies. I am the power you crave. I am, live and direct from hell, the demon Catch! Ta-da!" There was a clicking on the floor like a tap-dancing step.

"You're an Earth spirit?"

"Er, uh, yes, an Earth spirit. That's me, Catch, the Earth spirit."

"But I didn't think the ritual worked."

"Ritual?"

"We tried to call you up at the meeting last week, but I didn't think it worked because I didn't draw the circle of power with a virgin blade that had been quenched in blood."

"What did you use?"

"A nail file."

There was a pause. Had she offended the Earth spirit? Here was the first evidence that her magic could work and she had blown it by compromising the materials called for in the ritual.

"I'm sorry," she said, "but it's not easy to find a blade that's been quenched in blood."

"It's okay."

"If I had known, I . . ."

"No really, it's okay."

"Are you offended, Great Spirit?"

"I am about to bestow the greatest power in the world upon a woman who draws circles in the dirt with nail files. I don't know. Give me a minute."

"Then you will grant harmony to the hearts of the women in the coven?"

"What the fuck are you talking about?" the voice said.

"That is why we summoned you, O Spirit—to bring us harmony."

"Oh, yeah, harmony. But there is a condition."

"Tell me what you require of me, O Spirit."

"I will return to you later, witch. If I find what I am looking for, I will need you to renounce the Creator and perform a ritual. In return you will be given the command of a power that can rule the Earth. Will you do this?"

Rachel could not believe what she was hearing. Accepting that her magic worked was a huge step, yet she was speaking to the evidence. But to be offered the power to rule the world? She wasn't sure her career in exercise instruction had prepared her for this.

"Speak, woman! Or would you rather spend your life collecting gobs of hair from shower drains and fingernail parings from ashtrays?"

"How do you know about that?"

"I was destroying pagans when Charlemagne was alive. Now, answer; there is a hunger rising in me and I must go."

"Destroying pagans? I thought the Earth spirits were benevolent."

"We have our moments. Now, will you renounce the Creator?"

"Renounce the Goddess, I don't know . . ."

"Not the Goddess! The Creator!"

"But the Goddess . . ."

"Wrong. The Creator, the All-Powerful. Help me out here, babe—I'm not allowed to say his name."

"You mean the Christian God?"

"Bingo! Will you renounce him?"

"I did that a long time ago."

"Good. Wait here. I will be back."

Rachel searched for a last word, but nothing came. She heard a rustling in the leaves outside and ran to the door. In the moonlight she could see the shapes of cattle standing in the nearby pasture and something moving among them. Something that was growing larger as it moved away toward town.

19

JENNY'S HOUSE

Jenny parked the Toyota behind Travis's Chevy and killed the lights.

"Well?" Travis said.

Jenny said, "Would you like to come in?"

"Well." Travis acted as if he had to think about it. "Yes, I'd love to."

"Give me a minute to go in and clear a path, okay?"

"No problem, I need to check on something in my car."

"Thanks." Jenny smiled with relief.

They got out of the car. Jenny went into the house. Travis leaned against the door of the Chevy and waited for her to get inside. Then he threw open the car door and peeked inside.

Catch was sitting on the passenger side, his face stuck in a comic book. He looked up at Travis and grinned.

"Oh, you're back."

"Did you play the radio?"

"No way."

"Good. It's wired into the battery directly; it'll drain the current."

"Didn't touch it."

Travis glanced at the suitcase on the backseat. "Keep an eye on that."

"You got it."

Travis didn't move.

"Is there something wrong?"

"Well, you're being awfully agreeable."

"I told you, I'm just glad to see you having a good time."

"You may have to stay the night in the car. You aren't hungry, are you?"

"Get a grip, Travis. I just ate last night."

Travis nodded. "I'll check on you later, so stay here." Travis closed the car door.

Catch jumped to his feet and watched over the dashboard while Travis went into the house. Ironically, they were both thinking the same thing: *in a little while this will all be over.*

Catch coughed and a red spiked heel shot out of his mouth and bounced off the windshield, spattering the glass with hellish spit.

Robert had parked his truck a block away from his old house and walked up, hoping and dreading that he would catch Jenny with another man. As he approached the house, he saw the old Chevy parked in front of her Toyota.

He had run through this scene a hundred times in his mind. Walk out of the dark, catch her with the guy, and shout "Ah ha!" Then things got sketchy.

What was the point? He didn't really want to catch her at anything. He wanted her to come to the door with tears streaming down her cheeks. He wanted her to throw her arms around him and beg him to come home. He wanted to assure her that everything would be fine and forgive her for throwing him out. He had run that scene through his mind a hundred times as well. After they made love for the third time, things got sketchy.

The Chevy was not part of his preconceived scenes. It was like a preview, a teaser. It meant that someone was in the house with

Jenny. Someone who, unlike Robert, had been invited. New scenes ran through his mind: knocking on the door, having Jenny answer, looking around her shoulder to see another man sitting on the couch, and being sent away. He couldn't stand that. It was too real.

Maybe it wasn't a guy at all. Maybe it was one of the women from the coven who had stopped over to comfort Jenny in her time of need. Then the dream came back to him. He was tied to a chair in the desert again, watching Jenny make love with another man. The little monster was shoving saltines in his mouth.

Robert realized he had been standing in the middle of the street staring at the house for several minutes, torturing himself. Just be adult about it. Go up and knock on the door. If she is with someone else, just excuse yourself and come back later. He felt an ache rising in his chest at the thought.

No, just walk away. Go back to The Breeze's trailer and call her tomorrow. The thought of another night alone with his heartbreak increased the ache in his chest.

Robert's indecision had always angered Jenny. Now it was paralyzing him. "Just pick a direction and go, Robert," she would say. "It can't be any worse than sitting here pitying yourself."

But it's the only thing I'm good at, he thought.

A truck rounded the corner and started slowly to roll up the street. Robert was galvanized into action. He ran to the Chevy and ducked behind it. *I'm hiding in front of my own house. This is silly,* he thought. Still, it was as if anyone who passed would know how small and weak he was. He didn't want to be seen.

The truck slowed almost to a stop as it passed the house, then the driver gunned the engine and sped off. Robert stayed in a crouch behind the Chevy for several minutes before he moved.

He had to know.

"Just pick a direction and go." He decided to peek in the windows. There were two windows in the living room, about six feet off the ground. Both were old-style, weighted-sash types. Jenny had planted geraniums in the window boxes outside. If the window boxes were strong enough, he could hoist himself up and peek through the gap in the drawn curtains.

Spying on your own wife was sleazy. It was dirty. It was perverse. He thought about it for a moment, then made his way across the yard to the windows. Sleazy, dirty, and perverse would be improvements over how he felt now.

He grabbed the edge of the window box and tested his weight against it. It held. He pulled himself up, hooked his chin on the window box, and peered through the gap in the curtains.

They were on the couch, facing away from him: Jenny and some man. For a moment he thought Jenny was naked, then he saw the thin straps of her black dress. She never wore that dress anymore. It gave out the wrong kind of message, she used to say, meaning it was too sexy.

He stared at them in fascination, caught by the reality of his fear like a deer caught in car headlights. The man turned to say something to Jenny, and Robert caught his profile. It was the guy from the nightmare, the guy he had seen in the Slug that afternoon.

He couldn't look any longer. He lowered himself to the ground. A knot of sad questions beat at him. Who was this guy? What was so great about this guy? What does he have that I don't? Worst of all, how long has this been going on?

Robert stumbled away from the house toward the street. They were sitting in his house, on his couch—the couch he and Jenny had saved up to buy. How could she do that? Didn't everything in the house remind her of their marriage? How could she sit on his couch with some other man? Would they screw in his bed? The ache rose up in his chest at the thought, almost doubling him over.

He thought about trashing the guy's car. It was pretty trashed already, though. Flatten the tires? Break the windshield? Piss in the gas tank? No, then he would have to admit to spying. But he had to do something.

Maybe he could find something in the car that would tell him who this home wrecker was. He peered through the Chevy's windows. Nothing much to see: a few fast-food wrappers, a comic book on the front seat, and a Haliburton suitcase on the backseat. Robert recognized it immediately. He used to carry his four-by-five camera in the same model suitcase. He had sold the camera and given the suitcase to The Breeze for rent.

Was this guy a photographer? One way to find out. He hesitated, his hand on the car door handle. What if the guy came out while Robert was rummaging through the car? What would he do? Fuck it. The guy was rummaging through his life, wasn't' he? Robert tried the door. It was unlocked. He threw it open and reached in.

20

EFFROM

He was a soldier. Like all soldiers, in his spare moments he was thinking of home and the girl who waited for him there. He sat on a hill looking out over the rolling English countryside. It was dark, but his eyes had adjusted during his long guard duty. He smoked a cigarette and watched the patterns the full moon made on the hills when the low cloud cover parted.

He was a boy, just seventeen. He was in love with a brown-haired, blue-eyed girl named Amanda. She had down-soft hair on her thighs that tickled his palms when he pushed her skirt up around her hips. He could see the autumn sun on her thighs, even though he was staring over the spring-green hills of England.

The clouds opened and let the moon light up the whole countryside.

The girl pulled his pants down around his knees.

The trenches were only four days away. He took a deep drag on the cigarette and stubbed it out in the grass. He let the smoke out with a sigh.

The girl kissed him hard and wet and pulled him down on her.

A shadow appeared on the distant hill, black and sharply defined. He watched the shadow undulate across the hills. It can't be, he thought. They never fly under a full moon. But the cloud cover?

He looked in the sky for the airship but could see nothing. It was silent except for the crickets singing sex songs. The countryside was still but for the shadow. He lost the vision of the girl. Everything was the huge, cigar-shaped shadow moving toward him, silent as death.

He knew he should run, sound the alarm, warn his friends, but he just sat, watching. The shadow eclipsed the moonlight and he shivered, the airship was directly over him. He could just hear the engines as it passed. Then he was bathed in moonlight, the shadow behind him. He had survived. The airship had held its bellyful of death. Then he heard the explosions begin behind him. He turned and watched the flashes and fires in the distance, listened to the screams, as his friends at the base woke to find themselves on fire. He moaned and curled into a ball, flinching each time a bomb exploded.

Then he woke up.

There was no justice; Effrom was sure of it. Not an iota, not one scintilla, not a molecule of justice in the world. If there was justice, would he be plagued by nightmares from the war? If there was any justice would he be losing sleep over something that had happened over seventy years ago? No, justice was a myth, and it had died like all myths, strangled by the overwhelming reality of experience.

Effrom was too uncomfortable to mourn the passing of justice. The wife had put the flannel sheets on the bed to keep him cozy and warm in her absence. (They still slept together after all those years; it never occurred to them to do any different.) Now the sheets were heavy and cold with sweat. Effrom's pajamas clung to him like a rain-blown shroud.

After missing his nap, he had gone to bed early to try to recapture his dreams of spandex-clad young women, but his subconscious had conspired with his stomach to send him a nightmare instead. Sitting on the edge of the bed, he could feel his stomach bubbling away like a cannibal's caldron, trying to digest him from the inside out.

To say that Effrom was not a particularly good cook was an understatement akin to saying that genocide is not a particularly effective public relations strategy. He had decided that Tater Tots would provide as good a meal as anything, without challenging his culinary abilities. He read the cooking instructions carefully, then did some simple mathematics to expedite the preparation: twenty minutes at 375 degrees would mean only eleven minutes at 575 degrees. The results of his calculation resembled charcoal briquettes with frozen centers, but because he was in a hurry to get to bed, he drowned the suffering Tots in catsup and ate them anyway. Little did he know that their spirits would return carrying nightmare images of the zeppelin attack. He had never been so frightened, even in the trenches, with bullets flying overhead and mustard gas on the wind. That shadow moving silently across the hills had been the worst.

But now, sitting on the edge of the bed, he felt the same paralyzing fear. Though the dream was fading, instead of the relief of finding himself safe, at home, in bed, he felt he had awakened into something worse than the nightmare. Someone was moving in the house. Someone was thrashing around like a two-year-old in a pan-rattling contest.

Whoever it was, was coming through the living room. The house had a wooden floor and Effrom knew its every squeak and creak. The creaks were moving up the hall. The intruder opened the bathroom door, two doors from Effrom's bedroom.

Effrom remembered the old pistol in his sock drawer. *Was there time?* Effrom shook off his fear and hobbled to the dresser. His legs were stiff and wobbly and he nearly fell into the front of the dresser.

The floor was creaking outside the guest bedroom. He heard the guest room door open. *Hurry!*

He opened the dresser drawer and dug around under his socks until he found the pistol. It was a British revolver he had brought home from the war—a Webley, chambered for .45 automatic cartridges. He broke the pistol open like a shotgun and looked into the cylinders. Empty. Holding the gun open, he dug under his socks for the bullets. Three cartridges were held in a plate of steel shaped like a half-moon so the pistol's six cylinders could be loaded in two quick motions. The British had developed the system so they could use the same rimless cartridges in their revolvers that the Americans used in their Colt automatics.

Effrom located one of the half-moon clips and dropped it into the pistol. Then he started searching for the sound.

The doorknob of his room started to turn. *No time.* He flipped the gun upward and it slammed shut, only half loaded. The door slowly started to swing open. Effrom aimed the Webley at the center of the door and pulled the trigger.

The gun clicked, the hammer fell on an empty chamber. He pulled the trigger again and the gun fired. Inside the small bedroom the gun's report sounded like the end of the world. A large, ragged hole appeared in the door. From the hall came the high-pitched scream of a woman. Effrom dropped the gun.

For a moment he stood there, gunfire and the scream echoing in his head. Then he thought of his wife. "Oh my God! Amanda!" He ran forward. "Oh my God, Amanda. Oh my . . ." He threw the door open, leapt back, and grabbed his chest.

The monster was down on its hands and knees. His arms and head filled the doorway. He was laughing.

"Fooled you, fooled you," the monster chanted.

Effrom backed into the bed and fell. His mouth moved like wind-up chatter dentures, but he made no sound.

"Nice shot, old fella'," the monster said. Effrom could see the squashed remains of the .45 bullet just above the monster's upper lip, stuck like an obscene beauty mark. The monster flipped the bullet off with a single claw. The heavy slug thudded on the carpet.

Effrom has having trouble breathing. His chest was growing tighter with each breath. He slid off the bed to the floor.

"Don't die, old man. I have questions for you. You can't imagine how pissed I'll be if you die now."

Effrom's mind was a white blur. His chest was on fire. He sensed someone talking to him, but he couldn't understand the words. He tried to speak, but no words would come. Finally he found a breath. "I'm sorry, Amanda. I'm sorry," he gasped.

The monster crawled into the room and laid a hand on Effrom's chest. Effrom could feel the hand, hard and scaly, through his pajamas. He gave up.

"No!" the monster shouted. "You will not die!"

Effrom was no longer in the room. He was sitting on a hill in England, watching the shadow of death floating toward him across the fields. This time the zeppelin was coming for him, not the base. He sat on the hill and waited to die. *I'm sorry, Amanda.*

"No, not tonight."

Who said that? He was alone on the hill. Suddenly he became aware of a searing pain in his chest. The shadow of the airship began to fade, then the whole English countryside dissolved. He could hear himself breathing. He was back in the bedroom.

A warm glow filled his chest. He looked up and saw the monster looming over him. The pain in his chest subsided. He grabbed one of the monster's claws and tried to pry it from his chest, but it remained fast, not biting into the flesh, just laid upon it.

The monster spoke to him: "You were doing so good with the gun and everything. I was thinking, 'This old fuck really has some gumption.' Then you go and start drooling and wheezing and ruining a perfectly good first impression. Where's your self-respect?"

Effrom felt the warmth on his chest spreading to his limbs. His mind wanted to switch off, dive under the covers of unconsciousness and hide until daylight, but something kept bringing him back.

"Now, that's better, isn't it?" The monster removed his hand and backed to the corner of the bedroom, where he sat cross-legged looking like the Buddha of the lizards. His pointy ears scraped against the ceiling when he turned his head.

Effrom looked at the door. The monster was perhaps eight feet away from it. If he could get through it, maybe . . . How fast could a beast that size move in the confines of the house?

"Your jammies are all wet," the monster said. "You should change or you'll catch your death."

Effrom was amazed at the reality shift his mind had made. He was accepting this! A monster was in his house, talking to him, and he was accepting it. No, it couldn't be real.

"You're not real," he said.

"Neither are you," the monster retorted.

"Yes I am," Effrom said, feeling stupid.

"Prove it," the monster said.

Effrom lay on the bed thinking. Much of his fear had been replaced by a macabre sense of wonder.

He said: "I don't have to prove it. I'm right here."

"Sure," the monster said, incredulously.

Effrom climbed to his feet. Upon rising he realized that the creak in his knees and the stiffness he had carried in his back for forty years were gone. Despite the strangeness of this situation, he felt great.

"What did you do to me?"

"Me? I'm not real. How could I do anything?"

Effrom realized he had backed himself into a metaphysical corner, from which the only escape was acceptance.

"All right," he said, "you're real. What did you do to me?"

"I kept you from croaking."

Effrom made a connection at last. He had seen a movie about this: aliens who come to Earth with the power to heal. Granted, this wasn't the cute little leather-faced, lightbulb-headed alien from the movie, but it was no monster. It was a perfectly normal person from another planet.

"So," Effrom said, "do you want to use the phone or something?"

"Why?"

"To phone home. Don't you want to phone home?"

"Don't play with me, old man. I want to know why Travis was here this afternoon."

"I don't know anyone named Travis."

"He was here this afternoon. You spoke with him—I saw it."

"You mean the insurance man? He wanted to talk to my wife."

The monster moved across the room so quickly that Effrom almost fell back on the bed to avoid him. His hopes of making it through the door dissolved in an instant. The monster loomed over him. Effrom could smell his fetid breath.

"He was here for the magic and I want it now, old man, or I'll hang your entrails from the curtain rods."

"He wanted to talk to the wife. I don't know nothin' about any magic. Maybe you should have landed in Washington. They run things from there."

The monster picked Effrom up and shook him like a rag doll.

"Where is your wife, old man?"

Effrom could almost hear his brain rattling in his head. The monster's hand squeezed the breath out of him. He tried to answer, but all he could produce was a pathetic croak.

"Where?" The monster threw him on the bed.

Effrom felt the air burn back into his lungs. "She's in Monterey, visiting our daughter."

"When will she be back? Don't lie. I'll know if you are lying."

"How will you know?"

"Try me. Your guts should go well with this decor."

"She'll be home in the morning."

"That's enough," the monster said. He grabbed Effrom by the shoulder and dragged him through the door. Effrom felt his shoulder pop out of its socket and a grinding pain flashed across his chest and back. His last thought before passing out was, *God help me, I've killed the wife.*

21

AUGUSTUS BRINE

"I found them. The car is parked in front of Jenny Masterson's house." Augustus Brine stormed into the house carrying a grocery bag in each arm.

Gian Hen Gian was in the kitchen pouring salt from a round, blue box into a pitcher of Koolaid.

Brine set the bags down on the hearth. "Help me bring some of this stuff in. There's more bags in the truck."

The genie walked to the fireplace and looked in the bags. One was filled with dry-cell batteries and spools of wire. The other was full of brown cardboard cylinders about four inches long and an inch in diameter. Gian Hen Gian took one of the cylinders out of the bag and held it up. A green, waterproof fuse extended from one end.

"What are these?"

"Seal bombs," Brine said. "The Department of Fish and Game distributes them to fishermen to scare seals away from their lines and nets. I had a bunch at the store."

"Explosives are useless against the demon."

"There are five more bags in the truck. Would you bring them in, please?" Brine began to lay the seal bombs out in a line on the hearth. "I don't know how much time we have."

"What am I, some scrounging servant? Am I a beast of burden? Should I, Gian Hen Gian, king of the Djinn, be reduced to bearing loads for an ignorant mortal who would attack a demon from hell with firecrackers?"

"O King," Brine said, exasperated, "please bring in the goddamn bags so I can finish this before dawn."

"It is useless."

"I'm not going to try to blow him up. I just want to know where he is. Unless you can use your great power to restrain him, O King of the Djinn."

"You know I cannot."

"The bags!"

"You are a stupid, mean-spirited man, Augustus Brine. I've seen more intelligence in the crotch lice of harem whores."

The genie walked out the door and his diatribe faded into the night. Brine was methodically wrapping the fuses of the seal bombs with thin monofilament silver wire designed to heat up when a current was applied. It was an inexact method of detonation, but Brine had no access to blasting caps at this hour of the morning.

The genie returned in a moment carrying two grocery bags.

"Put them on the chairs." Brine gestured with his head.

"These bags are filled with flour," Gian Hen Gian said. "Are you going to bake bread, Augustus Brine?"

22

TRAVIS AND JENNY

There was something about her that made Travis want to dump his life out on the coffee table like a pocket full of coins; let her sort through and keep what she wanted. If he was still here in the morning, he'd tell her about Catch, but not now.

"Do you like traveling?" Jenny asked.

"I'm getting tired of it. I could use a break."

She sipped from a glass of red wine and pulled her skirt down for the tenth time. There was still a neutral zone between them on the couch.

She said, "You don't seem like any insurance salesman I've ever known. I hope you don't mind my saying, but usually insurance men dress in loud blazers and reek of cheap cologne. I've never met one that seemed sincere about anything."

"It's a job." Travis hoped she wouldn't ask about the details of his job. He didn't know a thing about insurance. He had decided on the career because Effrom Elliot had mistaken him for an insurance man that afternoon, so it was the first thing that came to mind.

"When I was a kid, an insurance man came to our house to sell my father some life insurance," Jenny said. "He gathered the family together in front of the fireplace and took our picture with a Polaroid camera. It was a nice picture. My father was standing at one side of us all, looking proud. As we were passing the picture around, the insurance man snatched the picture out of my father's hands and said, 'What a nice family.' Then he ripped my father out of the picture and said, 'Now what will they do?' I burst into tears. My father was frightened."

Travis said: "I'm sorry, Jenny." Perhaps he should have told her he was a brush salesman. Did she have any traumatic brush-salesman stories?

"Do you do that, Travis? Do you frighten people for a living?"

"What do you think?"

"Like I said, you don't seem like an insurance man."

"Jennifer, I need to tell you something . . ."

"It's okay. I'm sorry, I got a little heavy on you. You do what you do. I never thought I'd be waiting tables at this age."

"What did you want to do? I mean, when you were a little girl, what did you want to be when you grew up?"

"Honestly?"

"Of course."

"I wanted to be a mom. I wanted to have a family and a man who loved me and a nice house. Pretty unambitious, huh?"

"No, there's nothing wrong with that. What happened?"

She drained her wineglass and poured herself another from the bottle on the coffee table. "You can't have a family alone."

"But?"

"Travis, I don't want to ruin the evening by talking more about my marriage. I'm trying to make some changes."

Travis let it go. She picked up his silence as understanding and brightened.

"So, what did you want to do when you grew up?"

"Honestly?"

"Don't tell me you wanted to be a housewife, too."

"When I was growing up that's all any girl wanted to be."

"Where did you grow up, Siberia?"

"Pennsylvania. I grew up on a farm."

"And what did the farm boy from Pennsylvania want to be when he grew up?"

"A priest."

Jenny laughed. "I never knew anyone who wanted to be a priest. What did you do while the other boys were playing army, give last rights to the dead?"

"No, it wasn't like that. My mother always wanted me to be a priest. As soon as I was old enough, I went away to seminary. It didn't work out."

"So you became an insurance man. I suppose that works. I read once that all religions and insurance companies are supported by the fear of death."

"That's pretty cynical," the demonkeeper said.

"I'm sorry, Travis. I don't have much faith in the concept of an all-powerful being that would glorify war and violence."

"You should."

"Are you trying to convert me?"

"No, it's just that I know, absolutely, that God exists."

"No one knows anything absolutely. I'm not without faith. I have my own beliefs, but I have my doubts, too."

"So did I."

"Did? What happened, did the Holy Spirit come to you in the night and say, 'Go forth and sell insurance'?"

"Something like that." Travis forced a smile.

"Travis, you are a very strange man."

"I really didn't want to talk about religion."

"Good. I'll tell you my beliefs in the morning. You'll be quite shocked, I'm sure."

"I doubt that, I really do . . . Did you say 'in the morning'?"

Jenny held her hand out to him. Inside she was unsure of what she was doing, but it seemed fine—at least it didn't feel wrong.

"Did I miss something?" Travis asked. "I thought you were angry with me."

"No, why would I be angry at you?"

"Because of my faith."

"I think it's cute."

"Cute? Cute! You think the Roman Catholic Church is cute? A hundred popes are rolling in their graves, Jenny."

"Good. They aren't invited. Move over here."

"Are you sure?" he said. "You've had a lot of wine."

She was not sure at all, nevertheless she nodded to him. She was single, right? She liked him, right? Well, hell, it was started now.

He slid down the couch to her side and took her in his arms. They kissed, awkwardly at first; he was too aware of himself and she was still wondering if she should have invited him in in the first place. He held her tighter and she arched her back and pushed against him and they both forgot their reservations. The world outside ceased to exist. When they finally broke the kiss, he buried his face in her hair and held her tight so she could not pull away and see the tears in his eyes.

"Jenny," he said softly, "it's been a long time . . ."

She shushed him and dug her hands into his hair. "Everything will be fine. Just fine."

Perhaps it was because they were both afraid, or perhaps it was because they really didn't know each other; it might even have been that by playing a role they would not have to face anything but the moment. The roles they played throughout the night changed. First, each gave when the other needed, and later, when need was no longer an issue, they played their roles out to felicity. It progressed thusly: she was the comforter, he the comforted; then he was the understanding counselor, she the confused confessor; she became the nurse, he the patient in traction; he took the role of the naive stable boy, she the seductive duchess; he was the drill sergeant, she the raw recruit; she was the cruel master, he the helpless slave girl.

The small hours of the morning found them naked on the kitchen floor after Travis had played a rampaging Godzilla to Jennifer's unsuspecting Tokyo. They were crouched over a cooking toaster oven, each with a table knife loaded with butter, poised like executioners waiting for the signal to drop their blades. They polished off a loaf of toast, a half-pound of butter, a quart of tofu ice cream, a box of whole wheat cream-sandwich cookies, a bag of unsalted blue corn chips, and an organically grown watermelon that gushed pink juice down their chins while they laughed.

Stuffed, satisfied, and sticky-sweet they returned to bed and fell asleep in a warm tangle.

Perhaps it wasn't love that they had in common; perhaps it was only a need for escape and forgetting. But they found it.

Three hours later the alarm clock sounded and Jenny left to go wait tables at H.P.'s Cafe. Travis slept dreamless, groaning and smiling when she kissed him good-bye on the forehead.

When the explosions started, Travis woke up screaming.

Part 4

MONDAY

The many men, so beautiful!
And they all dead did lie:
And a thousand slimy things
Lived on; and so did I.
—Samuel Taylor Coleridge,
Rime of the Ancient Marnier

23

RIVERA

Rivera came through the trailer door followed by two uniformed officers. Robert sat up on the couch and was immediately rolled over and handcuffed. Rivera read him his *Miranda* rights before he was completely awake. When Robert's vision cleared, Rivera was sitting in a chair in front of him, holding a piece of paper in his face.

"Robert, I am Detective Sergeant Alphonse Rivera." A badge wallet flipped open in Rivera's other hand. "This is a warrant for your and The Breeze's arrest. There's one here to search this trailer as well, which is what I and deputies Deforest and Perez will be doing in just a moment."

A uniformed officer appeared from the far end of the trailer. "He's not here, Sergeant."

"Thanks," Rivera said to the uniform. To Robert he said: "Things will go easier for you if you tell me right now where I can find The Breeze."

Robert was starting to get a foggy idea of what was going on.

"So you're not a dealer?" he asked sleepily.

"You're quick, Masterson. Where's The Breeze?"

"The Breeze didn't have anything to do with it. He's been gone for two days. I took the suitcase because I wanted to know who the guy was that was with my wife."

"What suitcase?"

Robert nodded toward the living-room floor. The Haliburton case lay there unopened. Rivera picked it up and tried the latches.

"It's got a combination lock," Robert said. "I couldn't get it open."

Sheriff's deputies were riffling through the trailer. From the back bedroom one shouted. "Rivera, we've got it."

"Stay here, Robert. I'll be right back."

Rivera rose and started toward the bedroom just as Perez appeared in the kitchen holding another aluminum suitcase.

"That it?" Rivera asked.

Perez, a dark Hispanic who seemed too small to be a deputy, threw the suitcase on the kitchen table and opened the lid. "Jackpot," he said.

Neat square blocks of plastic-covered green weed lay in even rows across the suitcase. Robert could smell a faint odor like skunk coming from the marijuana.

"I'll get the testing kit," Perez said.

Rivera took a deep sniff and looked at Perez quizzically. "Right, it could be just lawn clippings that they weighed out in pounds."

Perez looked hurt by Rivera's sarcasm. "But for the record?"

Rivera waved him away, then returned to the couch and sat down next to Robert.

"You are in deep trouble, my friend."

"You know," Robert said, "I felt really bad about being so rude to you yesterday when you came by." He smiled weakly. "I've been going through some really hard times."

"Make it up to me, Robert. Tell me where The Breeze is."

"I don't know."

"Then you are going to eat shit for all that pot over there on the table."

"I didn't even know it was there. I thought you guys were here about the suitcase I took. The other one."

"Robert, you and I are going to go back to the station and have a really long talk. You can tell me all about the suitcase and all the folks that The Breeze has been keeping company with."

"Sergeant Rivera, I don't mean to be rude or anything, but I wasn't quite awake when you were telling me the charges . . . sir."

Rivera helped Robert to his feet and led him out of the trailer. "Possession of marijuana for sale and conspiracy to sell marijuana. Actually the conspiracy charge is the nastier of the two."

"So you didn't even know about the suitcase I took?"

"I couldn't care less about the suitcase." Rivera pushed Robert into the cruiser. "Watch your head."

"You should bring it along just to see who the guy was that it belonged to. Your guys in the lab can open it and . . ."

Rivera slammed the car door on Robert's comment. He turned to Deforest, who was coming out of the trailer. "Grab that suitcase out of the living room and tag it."

"More pot, Sarge?"

"I don't think so, but the whacko seems to think it's important."

24

AUGUSTUS BRINE

Augustus Brine was sitting in his pickup, parked a block away from Jenny's house. In the morning twilight he could just make out the outline of Jenny's Toyota and an old Chevy parked in front. The king of the Djinn sat in the passenger seat next to Brine, his rheumy blue eyes just clearing the dashboard.

Brine was sipping from a cup of his special secret roast coffee. The thermos was empty and he was savoring the last full cup. The last cup, perhaps, that he would ever drink. He tried to call up a Zen calm, but it was not forthcoming and he berated himself; trying to think about it pushed it farther from his grasp. *"Like trying to bite the teeth,"* the Zen proverb went. *"There is not only nothing to grasp, but nothing with which to grasp it."* The closest he was going to get to no-mind was to go home and destroy a few million brain cells with a few bottles of wine—not an option.

"You are troubled, Augustus Brine." The Djinn had been silent for over an hour. At the sound of his voice Brine was startled and almost spilled his coffee.

"It's the car," Brine said. "What if the demon is in the car? There's no way to know."

"I will go look."

"Look? You said he was invisible."

"I will get in the car and feel around. I will sense him if he is that close."

"And if he's there?"

"I will come back and tell you. He cannot harm me."

"No." Brine stroked his beard. "I don't want them to know we're here until the last minute. I'll risk it."

"I hope you can move fast, Augustus Brine. If Catch sees you, he will be on you in an instant."

"I can move," Brine said with a confidence that he did not feel. He felt like a fat, old man—tired and a little wired from too much coffee and not enough sleep.

"The woman!" The Djinn poked Brine with a bony finger.

Jenny was coming out of the house in her waitress uniform. She made her way down the front steps and across the shallow front yard to her Toyota.

"At least she's still alive." Brine was preparing to move. With Jenny out of the house one of their problems was solved, but there would be little time to act. The demonkeeper could come out at any moment. If their trap was not set, all would be lost.

The Toyota turned over twice and died. A cloud of blue smoke coughed out of the exhaust pipe. The engine cranked, caught again, sputtered, and died; blue smoke.

"If she goes back to the house, we have to stop her," Brine said.

"You will give yourself away. The trap will not work."

"I can't let her go back in that house."

"She is only one woman, Augustus Brine. The demon Catch will kill thousands if he is not stopped."

"She's a friend of mine."

The Toyota cranked again weakly, whining like an injured animal, then fired up. Jenny revved the engine and pulled away leaving a trail of oily smoke.

"That's it," Brine said. "Let's go." Brine started the truck, pulled forward, and stopped.

"Turn off the engine," the Djinn said.

"You're out of your mind. We leave it running."

"How will you hear the demon if he comes before you are ready?"

Begrudgingly, Brine turned off the key. "Go!" he said.

Brine and the Djinn jumped out of the truck and ran around to the bed. Brine dropped the tailgate. There were twenty ten-pound bags of flour, each with a wire sticking out of the top. Brine grabbed a bag in each hand, ran to the middle of the yard, paying out wire behind him as he went. The Djinn wrestled one bag out of the truck and carried it like a babe in his arms to the far corner of the yard.

With each trip to the truck Brine could feel panic growing inside him. The demon could be anywhere. Behind him the Djinn stepped on a twig and Brine swung around clutching his chest.

"It is only me," the Djinn said. "If the demon is here, he will come after me first. You may have time to escape."

"Just get these unloaded," Brine said.

Ninety seconds after they had started, the front yard was dotted with flour bags, and a spider web of wires led back to the truck. Brine hoisted the Djinn into the bed of the truck and handed him two lead wires. The Djinn took the wires and crouched over a car battery that Brine had secured to the bed of the truck with duct tape.

"Count ten, then touch the wires to the battery," Brine said. "After they go off, start the truck."

Brine turned and ran across the yard to the front steps. The small porch was too close to the ground for Brine to crawl under, so he crouched beside it, covering his face with his arms, counting to himself, "seven, eight, nine, ten." Brine braced himself for the explosion. The seal bombs were not powerful enough to cause injury when detonated one at a time, but twenty at once might produce a considerable shock wave. "Eleven, twelve, thirteen, fourteen, shit!" Brine stood up and tried to see into the bed of the truck.

"The wires, Gian Hen Gian!"

"It is done!" Came the answer.

Before Brine could say anything else the explosions began—not a single blast, but a series of blasts like a huge string of firecrackers. For a moment the world turned white with flour. Then storms of flame swirled around the front of the house and mushroomed into the sky as the airborne flour was ignited by successive explosions. The lower branches of the pines were seared and pine needles crackled as they burned.

At the sight of the fire storms, Brine dove to the ground and covered his head. When the explosion subsided, he stood and tried to see through the fog of flour, smoke, and soot that hung in the air. Behind him he heard the front door open. He turned and reached up into the doorway, felt his hand close around the front of a man's shirt, and yanked back, hoping he was not pulling a demon down off the steps.

"Catch!" the man screamed. "Catch!"

Unable to see though the gritty air, Brine punched blindly at the squirming man. His meaty fist connected with something hard and the man went limp in his arms. Brine heard the truck start. He dragged the unconscious man across the yard toward the sound of the running engine. In the distance a siren began to wail.

He bumped into the truck before he saw it. He opened the door and threw the man onto the front seat, knocking Gian Hen Gian against the opposite door. Brine jumped into the truck, put it into gear, and sped out of the doughy conflagration into the light of morning.

"You did not tell me there would be fire," the Djinn said.

"I didn't know." Brine coughed and wiped flour out of his eyes. "I thought all the charges would go off at once. I forgot that the fuses would burn at different rates. I didn't know that flour would catch fire—it was just supposed to cover everything so we could see the demon coming."

"The demon Catch was not there."

Brine was on the verge of losing control. Covered in flour and soot, he looked like an enraged abominable snowman. "How do you know that? If we didn't have the cover of the flour, I might be dead now. You didn't know where he was before. How can you know he wasn't there? Huh? How do you know?"

"The demonkeeper has lost control of Catch. Otherwise you would not have been able to harm him."

"Why didn't you tell me that before? Why don't you tell me these things in advance?"

"I forgot."

"I might have been killed."

"To die in the service of the great Gian Hen Gian—what an honor. I envy you, Augustus Brine." The Djinn removed his stocking cap, shook off the flour, and held it to his chest in salute. His bald head was the only part of him that was not covered in flour.

Augustus Brine began to laugh.

"What is funny?" The Djinn asked.

"You look like a worn brown crayon." Brine was snorting with laughter. "King of the Djinn. Give me a break."

"What's so funny?" Travis said, groggily.

Keeping his left hand on the wheel, Augustus Brine snapped out his right fist and coldcocked the demonkeeper.

25

AMANDA

Amanda Elliot told her daughter that she wanted to leave early to beat the Monterey traffic, but the truth was that she didn't sleep well away from home. The idea of spending another morning in Estelle's guest room trying to be quiet while waiting for the house to awaken was more than she could stand. She was up at five, dressed and on the road before five-thirty. Estelle stood in the driveway in her nightgown waving as her mother drove away.

Over the last few years Amanda's visits had been tearful and miserable. Estelle could not resist pointing out that each moment she spent with her mother might be the last. Amanda responded, at first, by comforting her daughter and assuring her that she would be around for many more years to come. But as time passed, Estelle refused to let the subject lie, and Amanda answered her concern with pointed comparisons between her own energy level and that of Estelle's layabout husband, Herb. "If it weren't for his finger moving on the remote control you'd never know he was alive at all."

As much as Amanda was irritated by Effrom marauding around the house like an old tomcat, she needed only to think of Herb, permanently affixed to Estelle's couch, to put her own husband in a favorable light. Compared to Herb, Effrom was Errol Flynn and Douglas Fairbanks rolled into one: a connubial hero. Amanda missed him.

She drove five miles per hour over the speed limit, changing lanes aggressively, and checking her mirrors for highway patrol cars. She was an old woman, but she refused to drive like one.

She made the hundred miles to Pine Cove in just over an hour and a half. Effrom would be in his workshop now, working on his wood carvings and smoking cigarettes. She wasn't supposed to know about the cigarettes any more than she was supposed to know that Effrom spent every morning watching the women's exercise show. Men have to have their secret lives and forbidden pleasures, real or perceived. Cookies snitched from the jar are always sweeter than those served on a plate, and nothing evokes the prurient like puritanism. Amanda played her role for Effrom, staying on his tail, keeping him alert to the possibility of discovery, but never quite catching him in the act.

Today she would pull in the driveway and rev the engine, take a long time getting into the house to make sure that Effrom heard her coming so he could take a shot of breath spray to cover the smell of tobacco on his breath. Didn't it occur to the old fart that she was the one who bought the breath spray and brought it home with the groceries each week? Silly old man.

When Amanda entered the house, she noticed an acrid, burnt smell in the air. She had never smelled cordite, so she assumed that Effrom had been cooking. She went to the kitchen expecting to see the ruined remains of one of her frying pans, but the kitchen, except for a few cracker crumbs on the counter, was clean. Maybe the smell was coming from the workshop.

Amanda usually avoided going near Effrom's workshop when he was working, mainly to avoid the sound of the high-speed drills he used for carving, which reminded her of the unpleasantness of the dentist's office. Today there was no sound coming from the workshop.

She knocked on the door, gently, so as not to startle him. "Effrom, I'm home." He had to be able to hear her. A chill ran through her. She had imagined finding Effrom cold and stiff a thousand times, but always she was able to push the thought out of her mind.

"Effrom, open this door!" She had never entered the workshop. Except for a few toys that Effrom dragged out at Christmastime to donate to local charities, Amanda never even saw any of the carvings he produced. The workshop was Effrom's sacred domain.

Amanda paused, her hand on the doorknob. Maybe she should call someone. Maybe she should call her granddaughter, Jennifer, and have her come over. If Effrom were dead she didn't want to face it alone. But what if he was just hurt, lying there on the floor waiting for help. She opened the door. Effrom was not there. She breathed a sigh of relief, then her anxiety returned. Where was he?

The workshop's shelves were filled with carved wooden figures, some only a few inches high, some several feet long. Every one of them was a figure of a nude woman. Hundreds of nude women. She studied each figure, fascinated with this new aspect of her husband's secret life. The figures were running, reclining, crouching, and dancing. Except for a few figures on the workbench that were still in the rough stage, each of the carvings was polished and oiled and incredibly detailed. And they all had something in common: they were studies of Amanda.

Most were of her when she was younger, but they were unmistakably her. Amanda standing, Amanda reclining, Amanda dancing, as if Effrom were trying to preserve her. She felt a scream rising in her chest and tears filling her eyes. She turned away from the carvings and left the workshop. "Effrom! Where are you, you old fart?"

She went from room to room, looking in every corner and closet; no Effrom. Effrom didn't go for walks. And even if he'd had a car, he didn't drive anymore. If he had gone somewhere with a friend, he would have left a note. Besides, all his friends were dead: the Pine Cove Poker Club had lost its members, one by one, until solitaire was the only game in town.

She went to the kitchen and stood by the phone. Call who? The police? The hospital? What would they say when she told them she had been home almost five minutes and couldn't find her husband? They would tell her to wait. They wouldn't understand that Effrom *had* to be here. He couldn't be anywhere else.

She would call her granddaughter. Jenny would know what to do. She would understand.

Amanda took a deep breath and dialed the number. A machine answered the phone. She stood there waiting for the beep. When it came, she tried to keep her voice controlled, "Jenny, honey, this is Grandma, call me. I can't find your grandfather." Then she hung up and began sobbing.

The phone rang and Amanda jumped back. She picked it up before the second ring.

"Hello?"

"Oh, good, you're home." It was a woman's voice. "Mrs. Elliot, you've probably seen the bullet hole in your bedroom door. Don't be frightened. If you listen carefully and follow my instructions, everything will be fine."

26

TRAVIS'S STORY

Augustus Brine sat in one of the big leather chairs in front of his fireplace, drinking red wine from a balloon goblet and puffing away on his meerschaum. He had promised himself that he would have only one glass of wine, just to take the edge off the adrenaline and caffeine jangle he had worked himself into during the kidnapping. Now he was on his third glass and the wine had infused him with a warm, oozy feeling; he let his mind drift in a dreamy vertigo before attacking the task at hand: interrogating the demonkeeper.

The fellow looked harmless enough, propped up and tied to the other wing chair. But if Gian Hen Gian was to be believed, this dark young man was the most dangerous human on Earth.

Brine considered washing up before waking the demonkeeper. He had caught a glimpse of himself in the bathroom mirror—his beard and clothing covered with flour and soot, his skin caked with sweat-streaked goo—and decided that he would make a more intimidating impression in his current condition. He had found the smelling salts in the medicine cabinet and sent Gian Hen Gian to the bathroom to bathe while he rested. Actually he wanted the Djinn out of the room while he questioned the demonkeeper. The Djinn's curses and ravings would only complicate an already difficult task.

Brine set his wineglass and his pipe on the end table and picked up a cotton-wrapped smelling-salt capsule. He leaned over to the demonkeeper and snapped the capsule under his nose. For a moment nothing happened, and Brine feared that he had hit him too hard, then the demonkeeper started coughing, looked at Brine, and screamed.

"Calm down—you're all right," Brine said.

"Catch, help me!" The demonkeeper struggled against his bonds. Brine picked up his pipe and lit it, affecting a bored nonchalance. After a moment the demonkeeper settled down.

Brine blew a thin stream of smoke into the air between them. "Catch isn't here. You're on your own."

Travis seemed to forget that he had been beaten, kidnapped, and tied up. His concentration was focused on Brine's last statement. "What do you mean, Catch isn't here? You know about Catch?"

Brine considered giving him the I'm-asking-the-questions-here line that he had heard so many times in detective movies, but upon reflection, it seemed silly. He wasn't a hardass; why play the role? "Yes, I know about the demon. I know that he eats people, and I know you are his master."

"How do you know all that?"

"It doesn't matter," Brine said. "I also know that you've lost control of Catch."

"I have?" Travis seemed genuinely shaken by this. "Look, I don't know who you are, but you can't keep me here. If Catch is out of control again, I'm the only one that can stop him. I'm really close to ending all this; you can't stop me now."

"Why should you care?"

"What do you mean, why should I care? You might know about Catch, but you can't imagine what he's like when he's out of control."

"What I mean," Brine said, "is why should you care about the damage he causes? You called him up, didn't you? You send him out to kill, don't you?"

Travis shook his head violently. "You don't understand. I'm not what you think. I never wanted this, and now I have a chance to stop it. Let me go. I can end it."

"Why should I trust you? You're a murderer."

"No. Catch is."

"What's the difference? If I do let you go, it will be because you will have told me what I want to know, and how I can use that information. Now I'll listen and you'll talk."

"I can't tell you anything. And you don't want to know anyway, I promise you."

"I want to know where the Seal of Solomon is. And I want to know the incantation that sends Catch back. Until I know, you're not going anywhere."

"Seal of Solomon? I don't know what you're talking about."

"Look—what is your name, anyway?"

"Travis."

"Look, Travis," Brine said, "my associate wants to use torture. I don't like the idea, but if you jerk me around, torture might be the only way to go."

"Don't you have to have two guys to play good cop, bad cop?"

"My associate is taking a bath. I wanted to see if I could reason with you before I let him near you. I really don't know what he's capable of . . . I'm not even sure what he is. So if we could get on with this, it would be better for the both of us."

"Where's Jenny?" Travis asked.

"She's fine. She's at work."

"You won't hurt her?"

"I'm not some kind of terrorist, Travis. I didn't ask to be involved in this, but I am. I don't want to hurt you, and I would never hurt Jenny. She's a friend of mine."

"So if I tell you what I know, you'll let me go?"

"That's the deal. But I'll have to make sure that what you tell me is true." Brine relaxed. This young man didn't seem to have any of the qualities of a mass murderer. If anything, he seemed a little naive.

"Okay, I'll tell you everything I know about Catch and the incantations, but I swear to you, I don't know anything about any Seal of Solomon. It's a pretty strange story."

"I guessed that," Brine said. "Shoot." He poured himself a glass of wine, relit his pipe, and sat back, propping his feet up on the hearth.

"Like I said, it's a pretty strange story."

"Strange is my middle name," Brine said.

"That must have been difficult for you as a child," Travis said.

"Would you get on with it."

"You asked for it." Travis took a deep breath. "I was born in Clarion, Pennsylvania, in the year nineteen hundred."

"Bullshit," Brine interrupted. "You're not a day over twenty-five."

"This is going to take a lot more time if I have to keep stopping. Just listen—it'll all fall into place."

Brine grumbled and nodded for Travis to continue.

"I was born on a farm. My parents were Irish immigrants, black Irish. I was the oldest of six children, two boys and four girls. My parents were staunch Catholics. My mother wanted me to be a priest. She pushed me to study so I could get into seminary. She was working on the local diocese to recommend me while I was still in the womb. When World War I broke out, she begged the bishop to get me into seminary early. Everybody knew it was just a matter of time before America entered the war. My mother wanted me in seminary before the Army could draft me. Boys from secular colleges were already in Europe, driving ambulances, and some of them had been killed. My mother wasn't going to lose her chance to have a son become a priest to something as insignificant as a world war. You see, my little brother was a bit slow—mentally, I mean. I was my mother's only chance."

"So you went to seminary," Brine interjected. He was becoming impatient with the progress of the story.

"I went in at sixteen, which made me at least four years younger than the other boys. My mother packed me some sandwiches, and I packed myself into a threadbare black suit that was three sizes too small for me and I was on the train to Illinois.

"You have to understand, I didn't want any part of this stuff with the demon; I really wanted to be a priest. Of all the people I had known as a child, the priest seemed like the only one who had any control over things. The crops could fail, banks could close, people could get sick and die, but the priest and the church were always there, calm and steadfast. And all that mysticism was pretty nifty, too."

"What about women?" Brine asked. He had resolved himself to hearing an epic, and it seemed as if Travis needed to tell it. Brine found he liked the strange young man, in spite of himself.

"You don't miss what you've never known. I mean I had these urges, but they were sinful, right? I just had to say, 'Get thee behind me Satan', and get on with it."

"That's the most incredible thing you've told me so far," Brine said. "When I was sixteen, sex seemed like the only reason to go on living."

"That's what they thought at seminary, too. Because I was younger than the others, the prefect of discipline, Father Jasper, took me on as his special project. To keep me from impure thoughts, he made me work constantly. In the evenings, when the others were given time for prayer and meditation, I was sent to the chapel to polish the silver. While the others ate, I worked in the kitchen, serving and washing dishes. For two years the only rest I had from dawn until midnight was during classes and mass. When I fell behind in my studies, Father Jasper rode me even harder.

"The Vatican had given the seminary a set of silver candlesticks for the altar. Supposedly they had been commissioned by one of the early popes and were over six hundred years old. The candlesticks were the most prized possession of the seminary and it was my job to polish them. Father Jasper stood over me, evening after evening, chiding me and berating me for being impure in thought. I polished the silver until my hands were black from the compound, and still Father Jasper found fault with me. If I had impure thoughts it was because he kept reminding me to have them.

"I had no friends in seminary. Father Jasper had put his mark on me, and the other students shunned me for fear of invoking the prefect of discipline's wrath. I wrote home when I had a chance, but for some reason my letters were never answered. I began to suspect that Father Jasper was keeping my letters from getting to me.

"One evening, while I was polishing the silver on the altar, Father Jasper came to the chapel and started to lecture me on my evil nature.

"'You are impure in thought and deed, yet you do not confess,' he said. 'You are evil, Travis, and it is my duty to drive that evil out!'

"I couldn't take it any longer. 'Where are my letters?' I blurted out. 'You are keeping me from my family.'

"Father Jasper was furious. 'Yes, I keep your letters. You are spawned from a womb of evil. How else could you have come here so young. I waited for eight years to come to Saint Anthony's—waited in the cold of the world while others were taken into the warm bosom of Christ.'

"At last I knew why I had been singled out for punishment. It had nothing to do with my spiritual impurity. It was jealousy. I said, 'And you, Father Jasper, have you confessed your jealousy and your pride? Have you confessed your cruelty?'

"'Cruel, am I?' he said. He laughed at me, and for the first time I was really afraid of him. 'There is no cruelty in the bosom of Christ, only tests of faith. Your faith is wanting, Travis. I will show you.'

"He told me to lie with arms outstretched on the steps before the altar and pray for strength. He left the chapel for a moment, and when he returned I could hear something whistling through the air. I looked up and saw that he was carrying a thin whip cut from a willow branch.

"'Have you no humility, Travis? Bow your head before our Lord.'

"I could hear him moving behind me, but I could not see him. Why I didn't leave right then I don't know. Perhaps I believed that Father Jasper was actually testing my faith, that he was the cross I had to bear.

"He tore my robe up the back, exposing my bare back and legs. 'You will not cry out, Travis. After each blow a Hail Mary. Now,' he said. Then I felt the whip across my back and I thought I would scream, but instead I said a Hail Mary. He threw a rosary in front of me and told me to take it. I held it behind my head, feeling the pain come with every bead.

"'You are a coward, Travis. You don't deserve to serve our Lord. You are here to avoid the war, aren't you, Travis?'

"I didn't answer him and the whip fell again.

"After a while I heard him laughing with each stroke of the whip. I did not look back for fear he might strike me across the eyes. Before I had finished the rosary, I heard him gasp and drop to the floor behind me. I thought—no, I hoped—he had had a heart attack. But when I looked back he was kneeling behind me, gasping for air, exhausted, but smiling.

"'Face down, sinner!' he screamed. He drew back the whip as if he were going to strike me in the face and I covered my head.

"'You will tell no one of this,' he said. His voice was low and calm. For some reason that scared me more than his anger. 'You are to stay the night here, polish the silver, and pray for forgiveness. I will return in the morning with a new robe for you. If you speak of this to anyone, I will see that you are expelled from Saint Anthony's and, if I can manage it, excommunicated.'

"I hadn't ever heard excommunication used as a threat. It was something we studied in class. The popes had used it as an instrument of political control, but the reality of being excluded from salvation by someone else had never really occurred to me. I didn't believe that Father Jasper could really excommunicate me, but I wasn't going to test it.

"While Father Jasper watched, I began to polish the candle-sticks, rubbing furiously to take my mind off the pain in my back and legs, and to try to forget that he was watching. Finally, he left the chapel. When I heard the door close, I threw the candlestick I was holding at the door.

"Father Jasper had tested my faith, and I had failed. I cursed the Trinity, the Virgin, and all the saints I could remember. Eventually my anger subsided and I feared Father Jasper would return and see what I had done.

"I retrieved the candlestick and inspected it to see if I had done any damage. Father Jasper would check them in the morning as he always did, and I would be lost.

"There was a deep scratch across the axis of the candlestick. I rubbed at it, harder and harder, but it only seemed to get worse. Soon I realized that it wasn't a scratch at all but a seam that had been concealed by the silversmith. The priceless artifact from the Vatican was a sham. It was supposed to be solid silver, but here was evidence that it was hollow. I grabbed both ends of the candlestick and twisted. As I suspected, it unscrewed. There was a sort of triumph in it. I wanted to be holding the two pieces when Father Jasper returned. I wanted to wave them in his face. 'Here', I would say, 'these are as hollow and false as you are. I would expose him, ruin him, and if I was expelled and damned, I didn't care. But I never got the chance to confront him.

"When I pulled the two pieces apart, a tightly rolled piece of parchment fell out."

"The invocation," Brine interrupted.

"Yes, but I didn't know what it was. I unrolled it and started to read. There was a passage at the top in Latin, which I didn't have much trouble translating. It said something about calling down help from God to deal with enemies of the Church. It was signed by His Holiness, Pope Leo the Third.

"The second part was written in Greek. As I said, I had fallen behind in my studies, so the Greek was difficult. I started reading it aloud, working on each word as I went. By the time I was through the first passage, it had started to get cold in the chapel. I wasn't sure what I was reading. Some of the words were mysteries to me. I just read over them, trying to glean what I could from the context. Then something seemed to take over my mind.

"I started reading the Greek as if it were my native language, pronouncing the words perfectly, without having the slightest idea of what they meant.

"A wind whipped up inside the chapel, blowing out all the

candles. Except for a little moonlight coming through the windows, it was completely dark, but the words on the parchment began to glow and I kept reading. I was locked into the parchment as if I had grabbed an electric wire and couldn't let go.

"When I read the last line, I found I was screaming the words. Lightning flashed down from the roof and struck the candlestick, which was lying on the floor in front of me. The wind stopped and smoke filled the chapel.

"Nothing prepares you for something like that. You can spend your life preparing to be the instrument of God. You can read accounts of possession and exorcism and try to imagine yourself in the situation, but when it actually happens, you just shut down. I did, anyway. I sat there trying to figure out what I had done, but my mind wouldn't work.

"The smoke floated up into the rafters of the chapel and I could make out a huge figure standing at the altar. It was Catch, in his eating form."

"What's his eating form?" Brine asked.

"I assume from the deal with the flour that you know Catch is visible to others only when he is in his eating form. Most of the time I see him as a three-foot imp covered with scales. When he feeds or goes out of control, he's a giant. I've seen him cut a man in half with one swipe of his claws. I don't know why it works that way. I just know that when I saw him for the first time, I had never been so frightened.

"He looked around the chapel, then at me, then at the chapel. I was praying under my breath, begging God for protection.

"'Stop it!' he said. 'I'll take care of everything.' Then he went down the aisle and through the chapel doors, knocking them off their hinges. He turned and looked back at me. He said: 'You have to open these things, right? I forgot—it's been a while.'

"As soon as he was gone I picked up the candlesticks and ran. I got as far as the front gates before I realized that I was still wearing the torn robe.

"I wanted to get away, hide, forget what I had seen, but I had to go back and get my clothes. I ran back to my quarters. Since I was in my third year at seminary, I been given a small private room, so, thankfully, I didn't have to go through the dormitory ward rooms where the newer students slept. The only clothes I had were the suit I had worn when I came and a pair of overalls I wore when I worked in the seminary fields. I tried to put on the suit, but the pants were just too tight, so I put the overalls on and wore the suit jacket over them to cover my shoulders. I wrapped the candlesticks in a blanket and headed for the gate.

"When I was just outside the gate, I heard a horrible scream from the rectory. There was no mistaking; it was Father Jasper.

"I ran the six miles into town without stopping. The sun was coming up as I reached the train station and a train was pulling away from the platform. I didn't know where it was going, but I ran after it and managed to swing myself on board before I collapsed.

"I'd like to tell you I had some kind of plan, but I didn't. My only thought was to get as far away from St. Anthony's as I could. I don't know why I took the candlesticks. I wasn't interested in their value. I guess I didn't want to leave any evidence of what I'd done. Or maybe it was the influence of the supernatural.

"Anyway, I caught my breath and went into the passenger car to find a seat. The train was nearly full, soldiers and a few civilians here and there. I staggered down the aisle and fell into the first empty seat I could find. It was next to a young woman who was reading a book.

"'This seat is taken,' she said.

"'Please, just let me rest here for a minute,' I begged. 'I'll get up when your companion returns.'

"She looked up from her book and I found myself staring into the biggest, bluest eyes I'd ever seen. I will never forget them. She was young, about my age, and wore her dark hair pinned up under a hat, which was the style in those days. She looked genuinely frightened of me. I guess I was wearing my own fright on my face.

"'Are you all right? Shall I call the conductor?' she asked.

"I thanked her but told her that I just needed to rest a moment. She was looking at the strange way I was dressed, trying to be polite, but obviously perplexed. I looked up and noticed that everyone in the car was staring at me. Could they know about what I'd done? I wondered. Then I realized why they were staring.

There was a war on and I was obviously the right age for the Army, yet I was dressed in civilian clothes. 'I'm a seminary student,' I blurted out to them, causing a breeze of incredulous whispers. The girl blushed.

"'I'm sorry,' I said to her. 'I'll move on.' I started to rise, but she put her hand on my shoulder to push me back into my seat and I winced when she touched my injured shoulder.

"'No,' she said, 'I'm traveling alone. I've just been saving this seat to ward off the soldiers. You know how they can be sometimes, Father.'

"'I'm not a priest yet,' I said.

"'I don't know what to call you, then,' she said.

"'Call me Travis,' I said.

"'I'm Amanda,' she said. She smiled, and for a moment I completely forgot why I was running. She was an attractive girl, but when she smiled, she was absolutely stunning. It was my turn to blush.

"'I'm going to New York to stay with my fiancé's family. He's in Europe,' she said.

"'So this train is going east?' I asked.

"She was surprised. 'You don't even know where the train is going?' she asked.

"'I've had a bad night,' I said. Then I started to laugh—I don't know why. It seemed so unreal. The idea of trying to explain it to her seemed silly.

"She looked away and started digging in her purse. 'I'm sorry,' I said, 'I didn't mean to offend you.'

'You didn't offend me. I need to have my ticket ready for the conductor.'

"I'd completely forgotten about not having a ticket. I looked up and saw the conductor coming down the aisle. I jumped up and a wave of fatigue hit me. I almost fell into her lap.

"'Is something wrong?' she asked.

"'Amanda,' I said, 'you have been very kind, but I should find another seat and let you travel in peace.'

"'You don't have a ticket, do you?' she said.

"I shook my head. 'I've been in seminary. I'd forgotten. We don't have any need for money there and . . .'

"'I have some traveling money,' she said.

"'I couldn't ask you to do that,' I said. Then I remembered the candlesticks. 'Look, you can have these. They're worth a lot of money. Hold them and I'll send you the money for the ticket when I get home,' I said.

"I unrolled the blanket and dropped the candlesticks in her lap.

"'That's not necessary,' she said. "I'll loan you the money.'

"'No, I insist you take them,' I said, trying to be gallant. I must have looked ridiculous standing there in my overalls and tattered suit jacket.

"'If you insist,' she said. 'I understand. My fiancé is a proud man, too.'

"She gave me the money I needed and I bought a ticket all the way to Clarion, which was only about ten miles from my parent's farm.

"The train broke down somewhere in Indiana and we were forced to wait in the station while they changed engines. It was midsummer and terribly hot. Without thinking, I took off my jacket and Amanda gasped when she saw my back. She insisted that I see a doctor, but I refused, knowing that I would only have to borrow more money from her to pay for it. We sat on a bench in the station while she cleaned my back with damp napkins from the dining car.

"In those days the sight of a woman bathing a half-naked man in a train station would have been scandalous, but most of the passengers were soldiers and were much more concerned with being AWOL or with their ultimate destination, Europe, so we were ignored for the most part.

"Amanda disappeared for a while and returned just before our train was ready to leave. 'I've reserved a berth in the sleeping car for us,' she said.

"I was shocked. I started to protest, but she stopped me. She said, 'You are going to sleep and I am going to watch over you. You are a priest and I'm engaged, so there is nothing wrong with it. Besides, you are in no shape to spend the night sitting up in a train.'

"I think it was then that I realized that I was in love with her. Not that it mattered. It was just that after living so long with Father Jasper's abuse I wasn't prepared for the kindness she was showing me. It never occurred to me that I might be putting her in danger.

"As we pulled away from the station, I looked out on the platform, and for the first time I saw Catch in his smaller form. Why it happened then and not before I don't know. Maybe I didn't have any strength left, but when I saw him there on the platform, flashing a big razor-toothed grin, I fainted.

"When I came to, I felt like my back was on fire. I was lying in the sleeping berth and Amanda was bathing my back with alcohol.

"'I told them you'd been wounded in France,' she said. "The porter helped me get you in here. I think it's about time you told me who did this to you.'

"I told her what Father Jasper had done, leaving out the parts about the demon. I was in tears when I finished, and she was holding me, rocking me back and forth.

"I'm not sure how it happened—the passion of the moment and all that, I guess—but the next thing I knew, we were kissing, and I was undressing her. Just as we were about to make love she stopped me.

"'I have to take this off,' she said. She was wearing a wooden bracelet with the initials E + A burnt into it. 'We don't have to do this,' I said.

"Have you, Mr. Brine, ever said something that you know you will always regret? I have. It was: 'We don't have to do this.'

"She said: 'Oh, then let's not.'

"She fell asleep holding me while I lay awake, thinking about sex and damnation, which really wasn't any different from what I'd thought about each night in the seminary—a little more immediate, I guess.

"I was just dozing off when I heard a commotion coming from the opposite end of our sleeping car. I peeked through the curtains of the berth to see what was happening. Catch was coming down the aisle, looking into berths as he went. I didn't know at the time that Catch was invisible to other people, and I couldn't understand why they weren't screaming at the sight of him. People were shouting and looking out of their berths, but all they were seeing was empty air.

"I grabbed my overalls and jumped into the aisle, leaving my jacket and the candlesticks in the berth with Amanda. I didn't even thank her. I ran down the aisle toward the back of the car, away from Catch. As I ran, I could hear him yelling, 'Why are you running? Don't you know the rules?'

"I went through the door between the cars and slid it shut behind me. By now people were screaming, not out of fear of Catch, but because a naked man was running through the sleeping car.

"I looked into the next car and saw the conductor coming down the aisle toward me. Catch was almost to the door behind me. Without thinking, or even looking, I opened the door to the outside and leapt off the train, naked, my overalls still in hand.

"The train was on a trestle at the time and it was a long drop to the ground, fifty or sixty feet. By all rights I should have been killed. When I hit, the wind was knocked out of me and I remember thinking that my back was broken, but in seconds I was up and running through a wooden valley. I didn't realize until later that I had been protected by my pact with the demon, even through he was not under my control at the time. I don't really know the extent of his protection, but I've been in a hundred accidents since then that should have killed me and come out without a scratch.

"I ran through the woods until I came to a dirt road. I had no idea where I was. I just walked until I couldn't walk anymore and then sat down at the side of the road. Just after sunup a rickety wagon pulled up beside me and the farmer asked me if I was all right. In those days it wasn't uncommon to see a barefoot kid in overalls by the side of the road.

"The farmer informed me that I was only about twenty miles from home. I told him that I was a student on holiday, trying to hitchhike home, and he offered to drive me. I fell asleep in the wagon. When the farmer woke me, we were stopped at the gate of my parents' farm. I thanked him and walked up the road toward the house.

"I guess I should have known right away that something was wrong. At that time of the morning everyone should have been out working, but the barnyard was deserted except for a few chickens. I could hear the two dairy cows mooing in the barn when they should have already been milked and put out to pasture.

"I had no idea what I would tell my parents. I hadn't thought about what I would do when I got home, only that I wanted to get there.

"I ran in the back door expecting to find my mother in the kitchen, but she wasn't there. My family rarely left the farm, and they certainly wouldn't have gone anywhere without taking care of the animals first. My first thought was that there had been an accident. Perhaps my father had fallen from the tractor and they had taken him to the hospital in Clarion. I ran to the front of the house. My father's wagon was tied up out front.

"I bolted through the house, shouting into every room, but there was no one home. I found myself standing on the front porch, wondering what to do next, when I heard his voice from behind me.

"'You can't run from me,' Catch said.

"I turned. He was sitting on the porch swing, dangling his feet in the air. I was afraid, but I was also angry.

"'Where is my family?!' I screamed.

"He patted his stomach. 'Gone,' he said.

"'What have you done with them?' I said.

"'They're gone forever,' he said. 'I ate them.'

"I was enraged. I grabbed the porch swing and pushed it with everything I had. The swing banged against the porch rail and Catch went over the edge into the dirt.

"My father kept a chopping block and an ax in front of the house for splitting kindling. I jumped off the porch and snatched up the ax. Catch was just picking himself up when I him in the forehead with it. Sparks flew and the ax blade bounced off his head as if it had hit cast iron. Before I knew it I was on my back and Catch was sitting on my chest grinning like the demon in that Fuselli painting, *The Nightmare*. He didn't seem at all angry. I flailed under him but could not get up.

"'Look,' he said, 'this is silly. You called me up to do a job and I did it, so what's all the commotion about? By the way, you would have loved it. I clipped the priest's hamstrings and watched him crawl around begging for a while. I really like eating priests, they're always convinced that the Creator is testing them.'

"'You killed my family!' I said. I was still trying to free myself.

"'Well, that sort of thing happens when you run away. It's all your fault; if you didn't want the responsibility, you shouldn't have called me up. You knew what you were getting into when you renounced the Creator.'

"'But I didn't,' I protested. Then I remembered my curses in the chapel. I *had* renounced God. 'I didn't know,' I said.

"'Well, if you're going to be a weenie about it, I'll fill you in on the rules,' he said. 'First, you can't run away from me. You called me up and I am more or less your servant forever. When I say forever, I mean forever. You are not going to age, and you are not going to be sick. The second thing you need to know is that I am immortal. You whack me with axes all you want and all you'll get is a dull ax and a sore back, so just save your energy. Third, I am Catch. They call me the destroyer, and that's what I do. With my help you can rule the world and other really swell stuff. In the past my masters haven't used me to the best advantage, but you might be the exception, although I doubt it. Fourth, when I'm in this form, you are the only one who can see me. When I take on my destroyer form, I am visible to everyone. It's stupid, and why it's that way is a long story, but that's the way it is. In the past they decided to keep me a secret, but there's no rule about it.'

"He paused and climbed off my chest. I got to my feet and dusted myself off. My head was spinning with what Catch had told me. I had no way of knowing whether he was telling the truth, but I had nothing else to go on. When you encounter the supernatural, your mind searches for an explanation. I'd had the explanation laid in my lap, but I didn't want to believe it.

"I said, 'So you're from hell?' I know it was a stupid question, but even a seminary education doesn't prepare you for a conversation with a demon.

"'No,' he said, 'I'm from Paradise.'

"'You're lying,' I said. It was the beginning of a string of lies and misdirections that have gone on for seventy years.

"He said, 'No, really, I'm from Paradise. It's a little town about thirty miles outside of Newark.' Then he started laughing and rolling around in the dirt holding his sides.

"'How can I get rid of you?' I asked.

"'Sorry,' he said, 'I've told you everything that I have to.'

"At the time I didn't know how dangerous Catch was. Somehow I realized that I was in no immediate danger, so I tried to come up with some sort of plan to get rid of him. I didn't want to stay there at the farm, and I didn't have anywhere I could go.

"My first instinct was to turn to the Church. If I could get to a priest, perhaps I could have the demon exorcised.

"I led Catch into town, where I asked the local priest to perform an exorcism. Before I could convince him of Catch's existence, the demon became visible and ate the priest, piece by piece, before my eyes. I realized then that Catch's power was beyond the comprehension of any normal priest, perhaps the entire Church.

"Christians are supposed to believe in evil as an active force. If you deny evil, you deny good and therefore God. But belief in evil is as much an act of faith as belief in God, and here I was faced with evil as a reality, not an abstraction. My faith was gone. It was no longer required. There was indeed evil in the world and that evil was me. It was my responsibility, I reasoned, to not let that evil become manifest to other people and thereby steal their faith. I had to keep Catch's existence a secret. I might not be able to stop him from taking lives, but I could keep him from taking souls.

"I decided to remove him to a safe place where there were no people for him to feed on. We hopped a freight and rode it to Colorado, where I led Catch high into the mountains. There I found a remote cabin where I thought he would be without victims. Weeks passed and I found that I had some control over the demon. I could make him fetch water and wood sometimes, but other times he defied me. I've never understood the inconsistency of his obedience.

"Once I had accepted the fact that I couldn't run away from Catch, I questioned him constantly, looking for some clue that might send him back to hell. He was vague, to say the least, giving me little to go on except that he had been on Earth before and that someone had sent him back.

"After we had been in the mountains for two months, a search party came to the cabin. It seemed that hunters in the area of the cabin, as well as people in villages as far as twenty miles away, had been disappearing. When I was asleep at night, Catch had been ranging for victims. It was obvious that isolation wasn't going to keep the demon from killing. I sent the search party away and set myself on coming up with some kind of plan. I knew we would have to move or people would discover that Catch existed.

"I knew there had to be some sort of logic to his presence on Earth. Then, while we were hiking out of the mountains, it occurred to me that the key to sending Catch back must have been concealed in another candlestick. And I had left them on the train with the girl. Jumping off the train to escape Catch may have cost me the only chance I had to get rid of him. I searched my memory for anything that could lead me to the girl. I had never asked where she was going or what her last name was. In trying to recall details of my time with her I kept coming up with the image of those striking blue eyes. They seemed etched into my memory while everything else faded. Could I go around the eastern United States asking anyone if they had seen a young girl with beautiful blue eyes?

"Something nagged at me. There was something that could lead me to the girl; I just had to remember it. Then it hit me—the wooden bracelet she wore. The initials carved inside the heart were E + A. How hard could it be to search service records for a soldier with the first initial E? His service records would have his next of kin, and she was staying with his family. I had a plan.

"I took Catch back East and began checking local draft boards. I told them I had been in Europe and a man whose first name began with E had saved my life and I wanted to find him. They always asked about divisions and stations and where the battle had taken place. I told them I had taken a shell fragment in the head and could remember nothing but the man's first initial. No one believed me, of course, but they gave me what I asked for—out of pity, I think.

"Meanwhile, Catch kept taking his victims. I tried to point him toward thieves and grifters when I could, reasoning that if he must kill, at least I could protect the innocent.

"I haunted libraries, looking for the oldest books on magic and demonology I could find. Perhaps somewhere I could find an incantation to send the demon back. I performed hundreds of rituals—drawing pentagrams, collecting bizarre talismans, and putting myself through all sorts of physical rigors and diets that were supposed to purify the sorcerer so the magic would work. After repeated failures, I realized that the volumes of magic were nothing more than the work of medieval snake-oil salesmen. They always added the purity of the sorcerer as a condition so they would have an excuse for their customers when the magic did not work.

"During this same time I was still looking for a priest who would perform an exorcism. In Baltimore I finally found one who believed my story. He agreed to perform an exorcism. For his protection, we arranged to have him stand on a balcony while Catch and I remained in the street below. Catch laughed himself silly through the entire ritual, and when it was over, he broke into the building and ate the priest. I knew then that finding the girl was my only hope.

"Catch and I kept moving, never staying in one place longer than two or three days. Fortunately there were no computers in those days that might have tracked the disappearances of Catch's victims. In each town I collected a list of veterans, then ran leads to the ground by knocking on doors and questioning the families. I've been doing that for over seventy years. Yesterday I think I found the man I was looking for. As it turned out, E was his middle initial. His name is J. Effrom Elliot. I thought my luck had finally turned. I mean the fact that the man is still alive is pretty lucky in itself. I thought that I might have to trace the candlesticks through surviving relatives, hoping that someone remembered them, perhaps had kept them as an heirloom.

"I thought it was all over, but now Catch is out of control and you are keeping me from stopping him forever."

27

AUGUSTUS

Augustus Brine lit his pipe and played back the details of Travis's story in his mind. He had finished the bottle of wine, but if anything, it had brought clarity to his thoughts by washing away the adrenaline from the morning's adventure.

"There was a time, Travis, that if someone had told me a story like that, I would have called the mental-health people to come and pick him up, but in the last twenty-four hours reality has been riding the dragon's back, and I'm just trying to hang on myself."

"Meaning what?" Travis asked.

"Meaning I believe you." Brine rose from the chair and began untying the ropes that bound Travis.

There was a scuffling behind them and Brine turned to see Gian Hen Gian coming through the living room wearing a flowered towel around his waist and another around his head. Brine thought he looked like a prune in a Carmen Miranda costume.

"I am refreshed and ready for the torture, Augustus Brine." The Djinn stopped when he saw Brine untying the demonkeeper. "So, will we hang the beast from a tall building by his heels until he talks?"

"Lighten up, King," Brine said.

Travis flexed his arms to get the blood flowing. "Who is that?" he asked.

"That," Brine said, "is Gian Hen Gian, king of the Djinn."

"As in genie?"

"Correct," Brine said.

"I don't believe it."

"You are not in a position to be incredulous toward the existence of supernatural beings, Travis. Besides, the Djinn was the one who told me how to find you. He knew Catch twenty-five centuries before you were born."

Gian Hen Gian stepped forward and shook a knotted brown finger in Travis's face. "Tell us where the Seal of Solomon is hidden or we will have your genitals in a nine-speed reverse action blender with a five-year guarantee before you can say shazam!"

Brine raised an eyebrow toward the Djinn. "You found the Sears catalog in the bathroom."

The Djinn nodded. "It is filled with many fine instruments of torture."

"There won't be any need for that. Travis is trying to find the seal so he can send the demon back."

"I told you," Travis said, "I've never seen the Seal of Solomon. It's a myth. I read about it a hundred times in books of magic, but it was always described differently. I think they made it up in the Middle Ages to sell books of magic."

The Djinn hissed at Travis and there was a wisp of blue damask in the air. "You lie! You could not call up Catch without the seal."

Brine raised a hand to the Djinn to quiet him. "Travis found the invocation for calling up the demon in a candlestick. He never saw the seal, but I believe it was concealed in the candlestick where he could not see it. Gian Hen Gian, have you ever seen the Seal of Solomon? Would it be possible to conceal it in a candlestick?"

"It was a silver scepter in Solomon's time," the Djinn said. "I suppose it could have been made into a candlestick."

"Well, Travis thinks that the invocation for sending the demon back is concealed in the candlestick he didn't open. I'd guess that anyone who had that knowledge and the Seal of Solomon would also have an invocation for giving you your power. In fact, I 'd bet my life on it."

"It is possible, but it is also possible that the dark one is misdirecting you."

"I don't think so," Brine said. "I don't think he wanted to be involved in this any more than I did. In seventy years he's never figured out that it's his will that controls Catch."

"The dark one is retarded, then!"

"Hey!" Travis said.

"Enough!" Brine said. "We have things to do. Gian Hen Gian, go get dressed."

The Djinn left the room without protest and Brine turned again to Travis. "I think you found the woman you've been looking for," he said. "Amanda and Effrom Elliot were married right after he returned from World War One. They get their picture in the local paper every year on their anniversary—you know, under a caption that reads, 'And they said it wouldn't last.' As soon as the king is ready we'll go over there and see if we can get the candlesticks—if she still has them. I need your word that I can trust you not to try to escape."

"You have it," Travis said. "But I think we should go back to Jenny's house—be ready when Catch returns."

Brine said, "I want you to try to put Jenny out of your mind, Travis. That's the only way you'll regain control of the demon. But first, there's something you ought to know about her."

"I know—she's married."

"No. She's Amanda's granddaughter."

28

EFFROM

Never having died before, Effrom was confused about how he should go about it. It didn't seem fair that a man his age should have to adapt to new and difficult situations. But life was seldom fair, and it was probably safe to assume that death wasn't fair either. This wasn't the first time he had been tempted to firmly demand to speak to the person in charge. It had never worked at the post office, the DMV, or return counters at department stores. Perhaps it would work here.

But where was here?

He heard voices; that was a good sign. It didn't seem uncomfortably warm—a good sign. He sniffed the air—no sulfur fumes (brimstone, the Bible called it); that was a good sign. Perhaps he had done all right. He did a quick inventory of his life: good father, good husband, responsible if not dedicated worker. Okay, so he cheated at cards at the VFW, but eternity seemed like an awfully long sentence for shuffling aces to the bottom of the deck.

He opened his eyes.

He had always imagined heaven to be bigger and brighter. This looked like the inside of a cabin. Then he spotted the woman. She was dressed in an iridescent purple body stocking. Her raven-black hair hung to her waist. *Heaven?* Effrom thought.

She was talking on the phone. They have phones in heaven? Why not?

He tried to sit up and found that he was tied to the bed. Why was that? *Hell?*

"Well, which is it?" he demanded.

The woman covered the receiver with her hand and turned to him. "Say something so your wife will know you're okay," she said.

"I'm not okay. I'm dead and I don't know where I am."

The woman spoke into the phone, "You see, Mrs. Elliot, your husband is safe and will remain so as long as you do exactly as I have instructed."

The woman covered the mouthpiece again. "She says she doesn't know about any invocation."

Effrom heard a gravely male voice answer her, but he couldn't see anyone else in the cabin. "She's lying," the voice said.

"I don't think so—she's crying."

"Ask her about Travis," the voice said.

Into the phone the woman said: "Mrs. Elliot, do you know someone named Travis?" She listened for a second and held the receiver to her breast. "She says no."

"It might have been a long time ago," the voice said. Effrom kept looking for who was talking but could see no one.

"Think," the woman said into the phone, "it might have been a long time ago."

The woman listened and nodded with a smile. Effrom looked in the direction of her nod. Who the hell was she nodding to?

"Did he give you anything?" The woman listened. "Candlesticks?"

"Bingo!" the voice said.

"Yes," said the woman. "Bring the candlesticks here and your husband will be released unharmed. Tell no one, Mrs. Elliot. Fifteen minutes."

"Or he dies," the voice said.

"Thank you, Mrs. Elliot," the woman said. She hung up.

To Effrom she said, "Your wife is on the way to pick you up."

"Who else is in this room?" Effrom asked. "Who have you been talking to?"

"You met him earlier today," the woman said.

"The alien? I thought he killed me."

"Not yet," the voice said.

"Is she coming?" Catch asked.

Rachel was looking out the cabin window at a cloud of dust rising from the dirt road. "I can't tell," she said. "Mr. Elliot, what kind of car does your wife drive?"

"A white Ford," Effrom said.

"It's her." Rachel felt a shiver of excitement run through her. Her sense of wonder had been stretched and tested many times in the last twenty-four hours, leaving her open and raw to every emotion. She was afraid of the power she was about to gain, but at the same time, the myriad possibilities that power created diluted her fear with a breathless giddiness. She felt guilty about abusing the old couple in order to gain the invocation, but perhaps with her newfound power she could repay them. In any case, it would be over soon and they would be going home.

The actual nature of the Earth spirit bothered her as well. Why did it seem . . . well . . . so impious? And why did it seem so male?

The Ford pulled up in front of the cabin and stopped. Rachel watched a frail old woman get out of the car holding two ornate candlesticks. The woman clutched the candlesticks to her and stood by the car looking around, waiting. She was obviously terrified and Rachel, feeling a stab of guilt, looked away. "She's here," Rachel said.

Catch said, "Tell her to come in."

Effrom looked up from the bed, but he could not rise enough to see out the window. "What are you going to do to the wife?" he demanded.

"Nothing at all," Rachel said. "She has something I need. When I get it, you can both go home."

Rachel went to the door and threw it open as if she were welcoming home a long-lost relative. Amanda stood by the car, thirty feet away. "Mrs. Elliot, you'll need to bring the candlesticks in so we can inspect them."

"No." Amanda stood firm. "Not until I know that Effrom is safe."

Rachel turned to Effrom. "Say something to your wife, Mr. Elliot."

"Nope," Effrom said. "I'm not speaking to her. This is all her fault."

"Please cooperate, Mr. Elliot, so we can let you go home." To Amanda, Rachel said, "He doesn't want to talk, Mrs. Elliot. Why don't you bring the candlesticks in? I assure you that neither one of you will be harmed." Rachel couldn't believe that she was saying these things. She felt as if she were reading the script from a bad gangster movie.

Amanda stood clutching the candlesticks, uncertain of what she should do. Rachel watched the old woman take a tentative step toward the cabin, then, suddenly, the candlesticks were ripped from her grasp and Amanda was thrown to the ground as if she'd been hit by a shotgun blast.

"No!" Rachel screamed.

The candlesticks seemed to float in the air as Catch carried them to her. She ignored them and ran to where Amanda lay on the ground. She cradled the old woman's head in her arms. Amanda opened her eyes and Rachel breathed a sigh of relief.

"Are you all right, Mrs. Elliot? I'm so sorry."

"Leave her," Catch said. "I'll take care of both of them in a second."

Rachel turned toward Catch's voice. The candlesticks were shaking in the air. She still found it unsettling to talk to a disembodied voice.

"I don't want these people hurt, do you understand?"

"But now that we have the invocation, they are insignificant." The candlesticks turned in the air as Catch examined them. "Come now, I think there's a seam on one of these, but I can't grip it. Come open it."

"In a minute," Rachel said. She helped Amanda get to her feet.

"Let's go in the house, Mrs. Elliot. It's all over. You can go home as soon as you feel up to it."

Rachel led Amanda through the front door, holding her by the shoulders. The old woman seemed dazed and listless. Rachel was afraid she would drop any second, but when Amanda saw Effrom tied to the bed, she shrugged off Rachel's support and went to him.

"Effrom." She sat on the bed and stroked his bald head.

"Well, wife," Effrom said, "I hope you're happy. You go gallivanting all over the state and you see what happens? I get kidnapped by invisible moon-men. I hope you had a good trip—I can't even feel my hands anymore. Probably gangrene. They'll probably have to cut them off."

"I'm sorry, Effrom." Amanda turned to Rachel. "Can I untie him, please?"

The pleading in her eyes almost broke Rachel's heart. She had never felt so cruel. She nodded. "You can go now. I'm sorry it had to be this way."

"Open this," Catch said. He was tapping a candlestick on Rachel's shoulder.

While Amanda untied Effrom's wrists and ankles and rubbed them to restore the circulation, Rachel examined one of the candlesticks. She gave it a quick twist and it unscrewed at the seam. From the weight of it, Rachel would have never guessed that it was hollow. As she unscrewed it, she noticed that the threads were gold. That accounted for the extra weight. Whoever had made the candlesticks had gone to great lengths to conceal the hollow interior.

The two pieces separated. A piece of parchment was tightly rolled inside. Rachel placed the base of the candlestick on the table, slid out the yellow tube of parchment, and slowly began to unroll it. The parchment crackled, and the edges flaked away as it unrolled. Rachel felt her pulse increase as the first few letters appeared. When half the page was revealed, her excitement was replaced with anxiety.

"We may be in trouble," she said.

"Why?" Catch's voice emanated from a spot only inches away from her face.

"I can't read this; it's in some foreign language—Greek, I think. Can you read Greek?"

"I can't read at all," Catch said. "Open the other candlestick. Maybe what we need is in there.

Rachel picked up the other candlestick and turned it in her hands. "There's no seam on this one."

"Look for one; it might be hidden," the demon said.

Rachel went to the kitchen area of the cabin and got a knife from the silverware drawer to scrape away the silver. Amanda was helping Effrom get to his feet, urging him across the room.

Rachel found the seam and worked the knife into it. "I've got it." She unscrewed the candlestick and pulled out a second parchment.

"Can you read this one?" Catch said.

"No. This one's in Greek, too. We'll have to get it translated. I don't even know anyone who reads Greek."

"Travis," Catch said.

Amanda had Effrom almost to the door when she heard Travis's name. "Is he still alive?" she asked.

"For a while," Catch said.

"Who is this Travis?" Rachel asked. She was supposed to be the one in charge here, yet the old woman and the demon seemed to know more about what was going on than she did.

"They can't go," Catch said.

"Why? We have the invocation; we just need to get it translated. Let them go."

"No," Catch said. "If they warn Travis, he will find a way to protect the girl."

"What girl?" Rachel felt as if she had walked into the middle of a plot-heavy mystery movie and no one was going to tell her what was happening.

"We have to get the girl and hold her hostage until Travis translates the invocation."

"What girl?" Rachel repeated.

"A waitress at the cafe in town. Her name is Jenny."

"Jenny Masterson? She's a member of the coven. What does she have to do with this?"

"Travis loves her."

"Who is Travis?"

There was a pause. Rachel, Amanda, and Effrom all stared at empty air waiting for the answer.

"He is my master," Catch said.

"This is really weird," Rachel said.

"You're a little slow on the uptake, aren't you, honey?" Effrom said.

29

RIVERA

Right in the middle of the interrogation Detective Sergeant Alphonse Rivera had a vision. He saw himself behind the counter at Seven-Eleven, bagging microwave burritos and pumping Slush-Puppies. It was obvious that the suspect, Robert Masterson, was telling the truth. What was worse was that he not only didn't have any connection with the marijuana Rivera's men had found in the trailer, but he didn't have the slightest idea where The Breeze had gone.

The deputy district attorney, an officious little weasel who was only putting time in at the D.A.'s office until his fangs were sharp enough for private practice, had made the state's position on the case clear and simple: "You're fucked, Rivera. Cut him loose."

Rivera was clinging to a single, micro-thin strand of hope: the second suitcase, the one that Masterson had made such a big deal about back at the trailer. It lay open on Rivera's desk. A jumble of notebook paper, cocktail napkins, matchbook covers, old business cards, and candy wrappers stared out of the suitcase at him. On each one was written a name, an address, and a date. The dates were obviously bogus, as they went back to the 1920s. Rivera had riffled through the mess a dozen times without making any sort of connection.

Deputy Perez approached Rivera's desk. He was doing his best to affect an attitude of sympathy, without much success. Everything he had said that morning had carried with it a sideways smirk. Twain had put it succinctly: "Never underestimate the number of people who would love to see you fail."

"Find anything yet?" Perez asked. The smirk was there.

Rivera looked up from the papers, took out a cigarette, and lit it. A long stream of smoke came out with his sigh.

"I can't see how any of this connects with The Breeze. The addresses are spread all over the country. The dates run too far back to be real."

"Maybe it's a list of connections The Breeze was planning to dump the pot on," Perez suggested. "You know the Feds estimate that more than ten percent of the drugs in this country move through the postal system."

"What about the dates?"

"Some kind of code, maybe. Did the handwriting check out?"

Rivera had sent Perez back to the trailer to find a sample of The Breeze's handwriting. He had returned with a list of engine parts for a Ford truck.

"No match," Rivera said.

"Maybe the list was written by his connection."

Rivera blew a blast of smoke in Perez's face. "Think about it, dipshit. I was his connection."

"Well, someone blew your cover, and The Breeze ran."

"Why didn't he take the pot?"

"I don't know, Sergeant. I'm just a uniformed deputy. This sounds like detective work to me." Perez had stopped trying to hide his smirk. "I'd take it to the Spider if I were you."

That made a consensus. Everyone who had seen or heard about the suitcase had suggested that Rivera take it to the Spider. He sat back in his chair and finished his cigarette, enjoying his last few moments of peace before the inevitable confrontation with the

Spider. After a few long drags he stubbed the cigarette in the ashtray on his desk, gathered the papers into the suitcase, closed it, and started down the steps into the bowels of the station and the Spider's lair.

Throughout his life Rivera had known half a dozen men nicknamed Spider. Most were tall men with angular features and the wiry agility that one associates with a wolf spider. Chief Technical Sergeant Irving Nailsworth was the exception.

Nailsworth stood five feet nine inches tall and weighed over three hundred pounds. When he sat before his consoles in the main computer room of the San Junipero Sheriff Department, he was locked into a matrix that extended not only throughout the county but to every state capital in the nation, as well as to the main computer banks at the FBI and the Justice Department in Washington. The matrix was the Spider's web and he lorded over it like a fat black widow.

As Rivera opened the steel door that led into the computer room, he was hit with a blast of cold, dry air. Nailsworth insisted the computers functioned better in this environment, so the department had installed a special climate control and filtration system to accommodate him.

Rivera entered and, suppressing a shudder, closed the door behind him. The computer room was dark except for the soft green glow of a dozen computer screens. The Spider sat in the middle of a horseshoe of keyboards and screens, his huge buttocks spilling over the sides of a tiny typist's chair. Beside him a steel typing table was covered with junk food in various stages of distress, mostly cupcakes covered with marshmallow and pink coconut. While Rivera watched, the Spider peeled the marshmallow cap off a cupcake and popped it in his mouth. He threw the chocolate-cake insides into a wastebasket atop a pile of crumpled tractor-feed paper.

Because of the sedentary nature of the Spider's job, the department had excused him from the minimum physical fitness standards set for field officers. The department had also created the position of chief technical sergeant in order to feed the Spider's ego and keep him happily clicking away at the keyboards. The

Spider had never gone on patrol, never arrested a suspect, never even qualified on the shooting range, yet after only four years with the department, Nailsworth effectively held the same rank that Rivera had attained in fifteen years on the street. It was criminal.

The Spider looked up. His eyes were sunk so far into his fat face that Rivera could see only a beady green glow.

"You smell of smoke," the Spider said. "You can't smoke in here."

"I'm not here to smoke, I need some help."

The Spider checked the data spooling across his screens, then turned his full attention to Rivera. Bits of pink coconut phosphoresced on the front of his uniform.

"You've been working up in Pine Cove, haven't you?"

"A narcotics sting." Rivera held up the suitcase. "We found this. It's full of names and addresses, but I can't make any connections. I thought you might . . ."

"No problem," the Spider said. "The Nailgun will find an opening where there was none." The Spider had given himself the nickname "Nailgun." No one called him the Spider to his face, and no one called him Nailgun unless they needed something.

"Yeah," Rivera said, "I thought it needed some of the Nailgun's wizardry."

The Spider swept the junk food from the top of the typing table into the wastebasket and patted the top of the table. "Let's see what you have."

Rivera placed the suitcase on the table and opened it. The Spider immediately began to shuffle through the papers, picking up a piece here or there, reading it, and throwing it back into the pile.

"This is a mess."

"That's why I'm here."

"I'll need to put this into the system to make any sense of it. I can't use a scanner on handwritten material. You'll have to read it to me while I input."

The Spider turned to one of his keyboards and began typing. "Give me a second to set up a data base format."

As far as Rivera was concerned, the Spider could be speaking

Swahili. Despite himself, Rivera admired the man's efficiency and expertise. His fat fingers were a blur on the keyboard.

After thirty seconds of furious typing the Spider paused. "Okay, read me the names, addresses, and dates, in that order."

"So you need me to sort them out?"

"No. The machine will do that."

Rivera began to read the names and addresses from each slip of paper, deliberately pausing so as not to get ahead of the Spider's typing.

"Faster, Rivera. You won't get ahead of me."

Rivera read faster, throwing each paper on the floor as he finished with it.

"Faster," the Spider demanded.

"I can't go any faster. At this speed if I mispronounce a name, I could lose control and get a serious tongue injury."

For the first time since Rivera had known him the Spider laughed.

"Take a break, Rivera. I get so used to working with machines that I forget people have limitations."

"What's going on here?" Rivera said. "Is the Nailgun losing his sarcastic edge?"

The Spider looked embarrassed. "No. I wanted to ask you about something."

Rivera was shocked. The Spider was almost omniscient, or so he pretended. This was a day for firsts. "What do you need?" he said.

The Spider blushed. Rivera had never seen that much flaccid flesh change color. He imagined that it put an incredible strain on the Spider's heart.

"You've been working in Pine Cove, right?"

"Yes."

"Have you ever run into a girl up there named Roxanne?"

Rivera thought for a moment, then said no.

"Are you sure?" The Spider's voice had taken on a tone of desperation. "It's probably a nickname. She works at the Rooms-R-Us Motel. I've run the name against Social Security records, credit reports, everything. I can't seem to find her. There are over ten thousand women in California with the name Roxanne, but none of them check out."

"Why don't you just drive up to Pine Cove and meet her?"

The Spider's color deepened. "I couldn't do that."

"Why not? What's the deal with this woman, anyway? Does it have to do with a case?"

"No, it's . . . it's a personal thing. We're in love."

"But you've never met her?"

"Well, yes, sort of—we talk by modem every night. Last night she didn't log on. I'm worried about her."

"Nailsworth, are you telling me that you are having a love affair with a woman by computer?"

"It's more than an affair."

"What do you want me to do?"

"Well, if you could just check on her. See if she's all right. But she can't know I sent you. You mustn't tell her I sent you."

"Nailsworth, I'm an undercover cop. Being sneaky is what I do for a living."

"Then you'll do it?"

"If you can find something in these names that will bail me out, I'll do it."

"Thanks, Rivera."

"Let's finish this." Rivera picked up a matchbook and read the name and address. The Spider typed the information, but as Rivera began to read the next name, he heard the Spider pause on the keyboard.

"Is something wrong?" Rivera asked.

"Just one more thing," Nailsworth said.

"What?"

"Could you find out if she's modeming someone else?"

"Santa Maria, Nailsworth! You are a real person."

Three hours later Rivera was sitting at his desk waiting for a call from the Spider. While he was in the computer room, someone had left a dog-eared paperback on his desk. Its title was *You Can Have a Career in Private Investigation*. Rivera suspected Perez. He had thrown the book in the wastebasket.

Now, with his only suspect back out on the street and nothing forthcoming from the Spider, Rivera considered fishing the book out of the trash.

The phone rang, and Rivera ripped it from its cradle.

"Rivera," he said.

"Rivera, it's the Nailgun."

"Did you find something?" Rivera fumbled for a cigarette from the pack on his desk. He found it impossible to talk on the phone without smoking.

"I think I have a connection, but it doesn't work out."

"Don't be cryptic, Nailsworth. I need something."

"Well, first I ran the names through the Social Security computer. Most of them are deceased. Then I noticed that they were all vets."

"Vietnam?"

"World War One."

"You're kidding."

"No. They were all World War One vets, and all of them had a first or middle initial E. I should have caught that before I even input it. I tried to run a correlation program on that and came up with nothing. Then I ran the addresses to see if there was a geographical connection."

"Anything there?"

"No. For a minute I thought you'd found someone's research project on World War One, but just to be sure, I ran the file through the new data bank set up by the Justice Department in Washington. They use it to find criminal patterns where there aren't any. In effect it makes the random logical. They use it to track serial killers and psychopaths."

"And you found nothing?"

"Not exactly. The files at the Justice Department only go back thirty years, so that eliminated about half of the names on your list. But the other ones rang the bell."

"Nailsworth, please try to get to the point."

"In each of the cities listed in your file there was at least one unexplained disappearance around the date listed—not the vets;

other people. You can eliminate the large cities as coincidence, but hundreds of these disappearances were in small towns."

"People disappear in small towns too. They run away to the city. They drown. You can't call that a connection."

"I thought you'd say that, so I ran a probability program to get the odds on all of this being coincidence."

"So?" Rivera was getting tired of Nailsworth's dramatics.

"So the odds of someone having a file of the dates and locations of unexplained disappearances over the last thirty years and it being a coincidence is ten to the power of fifty against."

"Which means what?"

"Which means, about the same odds as you'd have of dragging the wreck of the *Titanic* out of a trout stream with a fly rod. Which means, Rivera, you have a serious problem."

"Are you telling me that this suitcase belongs to a serial killer?"

"A very old serial killer. Most serial killers don't even start until their thirties. If we assume that this one was cooperative enough to start when the Justice Department's files start, thirty years ago, he'd be over sixty now."

"Do you think it goes farther back?"

"I picked some dates and locations randomly, going back as far as 1925. I called the libraries in the towns and had them check the newspapers for stories of disappearances. It checked out. Your man could be in his nineties. Or it could be a son carrying on his father's work."

"That's impossible. There must be another explanation. Come on, Nailsworth, I need a bailout here. I can't pursue an investigation of a geriatric serial killer."

"Well, it could be an elaborate research project that someone is doing on missing persons, but that doesn't explain the World War One vets, and it doesn't explain why the researcher would write the information on matchbook covers and business cards from places that have been out of business for years."

"I don't understand." Rivera felt as if he were stuck in the Spider's web and was waiting to be eaten.

"It appears that the notes themselves were written as far back as fifty years ago. I could send them to the lab to confirm it if you want."

"No. Don't do that." Rivera didn't want it confirmed. He wanted it to go away. "Nailsworth, isn't it possible that the computer is making some impossible connections? I mean, it's programmed to find patterns—maybe it went overboard and made this one up?"

"You know the odds, Sergeant. The computer can't make anything up; it can only interpret what's put into it. If I were you, I'd pull my suspect out of holding and find out where he got the suitcase."

"I cut him loose. The D.A. said I didn't have enough to charge him."

"Find him," Nailsworth said.

Rivera resented the authoritarian tone in Nailsworth's voice, but he let it go. "I'm going now."

"One more thing."

"Yes?"

"One of your addresses was in Pine Cove. You want it?"

"Of course."

Nailsworth read the name and address to Rivera, who wrote it down on a memo pad.

"There was no date on this one, Sergeant. Your killer might still be in the area. If you get him, it would be the bailout you're looking for."

"It's too fantastic."

"And don't forget to check on Roxanne for me, okay?" The Spider hung up.

30

JENNY

Jenny had arrived at work a half hour late expecting to find Howard waiting behind the counter to reprimand her in his own erudite way. Strangely enough, she didn't care. Even more strange was the fact that Howard had not shown up at the cafe all morning.

Considering that she had drunk two bottles of wine, eaten a heavy Italian meal and everything in the refrigerator, and stayed up all night making love, she should have been tired, but she wasn't. She felt wonderful, full of humor and energy, and not a little excited. When she thought of her night with Travis, she grinned and shivered. There should be guilt, she thought. She was, technically, a married woman. Technically, she was having an illicit affair. But she had never been very technically minded. Instead of guilt she felt happy and eager to do it all again.

From the moment she got to work she began counting the hours until she got off after the lunch shift. She was at one hour and counting when the cook announced that there was a call for her in the office.

She quickly refilled her customer's coffee cups and headed to the back. If it was Robert, she would just act like nothing had happened. She wasn't exactly in love with someone else as he suspected. It was . . . it didn't matter what it was. She didn't have to explain anything. If it was Travis—she hoped it was Travis.

She picked up the phone. "Hello."

"Jenny?" It was a woman's voice. "It's Rachel. Look, I'm having a special ritual this afternoon at the caves. I need you to be there."

Jennifer did not want to go to a ritual.

"I don't know, Rachel, I have plans after work."

"Jennifer, this is the most important thing we've ever done, and I need you to be there. What time do you get off?"

"I'm off at two, but I need to go home and change first."

"No, don't do that. Come as you are—it's really important."

"But I really . . ."

"Please, Jenny. It will only take a few minutes."

Jennifer had never heard Rachel sound so adamant. Maybe it really was important.

"Okay. I guess I can make it. Do you need me to call any of the others?"

"No. I'll do it. You just be at the caves as soon as you can after two."

"Okay, fine, I'll be there."

"And Jenny"—Rachel's voice had lowered an octave—"don't tell anyone where you are going." Rachel hung up.

Jennifer immediately dialed her home phone and got the answering machine. "Travis, if you're there, pick up." She waited. He was probably still sleeping. "I'm going to be a little late. I'll be home later this afternoon." She almost said, "I love you," but decided not to. She pushed the thought out of her mind. "Bye," she said, and hung up.

Now, if she could only avoid Robert until she could think of a way to destroy his hope for their reconciliation. Returning to the floor of the cafe, she realized that somewhere along the way her feeling of well-being had vanished and she felt very tired.

31

GOOD GUYS

Augustus Brine, Travis, and Gian Hen Gian were squeezed into the seat of Brine's pickup. As they approached Effrom and Amanda's house, they spotted a beige Dodge parked in the driveway.

"Do you know what kind of car they drive?" Travis asked.

Brine was slowing down. "An old Ford, I think."

"Don't slow down. Keep going," Travis said.

"But why?"

"I'd bet anything that Dodge is a police car. There's a whip antenna pinned down on the back."

"So what? You haven't done anything illegal." Brine wanted to get it over with and get some sleep.

"Keep going. I don't want to answer a lot of questions. We don't know what Catch has been doing. We can come back later, after the police leave."

The Djinn said, "He has a point, Augustus Brine."

"All right." Brine gunned the pickup and sped by.

In a few minutes they were sitting in Jenny's kitchen listening to the answering machine. They had gone in the back way to avoid the burnt, doughy mess in the front yard.

"Well," Travis said, resetting the machine, "that buys us a little time before we have to explain it to Jenny."

"Do you think Catch will come back here?" Brine asked.

"I hope so," Travis said.

"Can't you concentrate your will on bringing him back until we can find out if Amanda still has the candlesticks?"

"I've been trying. I don't understand this much more than you do."

"Well, I need a drink," Brine said. "Is there anything in the house?"

"I doubt it. Jenny said she couldn't keep anything in the house or her husband would drink it. She drank all the wine last night."

"Even some cooking sherry would be fine," Brine said, feeling a little sleazy as he spoke.

Travis began going through the cupboards.

"Should you find a small quantity of salt, I would be most grateful," the Djinn said.

Travis found a box of salt among the spices and was handing it to the Djinn when the phone rang.

They all froze and listened as the machine played Jenny's outgoing message. After the beep there was a pause, then a woman's voice. "Travis, pick up." It was not Jenny.

Travis looked to Brine. "No one knows I'm here."

"They do now. Pick it up."

Travis picked up the phone, and the answering machine clicked off.

"This is Travis."

Brine watched the color drain out of the demonkeeper's face as he listened. "Is she all right?" Travis said into the phone. "Let me talk to her. Who are you? Do you know what you're getting yourself into?"

Brine couldn't imagine what was going on in the conversation.

Suddenly Travis screamed into the phone, "He's not an Earth spirit—he's a demon. How can you be so stupid?"

Travis listened for a moment more, then looked at Augustus Brine and covered the receiver with his hand. "Do you know where there are some caves to the north of town?"

"Yes," Brine said, "the old mushroom farm."

Travis spoke into the phone, "Yes, I can find it. I'll be there at four." He sat down hard on one of the kitchen chairs and let the phone fall into its cradle.

"What's going on?" Brine demanded.

Travis was shaking his head. "Some woman is holding Jennifer and Amanda and her husband hostage. Catch is with her and she has the candlesticks. And you were right, there are three invocations."

"I don't understand," Brine said. "What does she want?"

"She thinks that Catch is some kind of benevolent Earth spirit. She wants his power."

"Humans are so ignorant," the Djinn said.

"But what does she want with you?" Brine asked. "She has the candlesticks and the invocations."

"They're in Greek. They want me to translate the invocations or they'll kill Jenny."

"Let them," the Djinn said. "Perhaps you can bring Catch under control with the woman dead."

Travis exploded. "They thought of that, you little troll! If I don't show up at four, they'll kill Jenny and destroy the invocation. Then we'll never be able to send Catch back."

Augustus Brine checked his watch. "We've got exactly an hour and a half to come up with a plan."

"Let us retire to the saloon and consider our options," the Djinn said.

32

THE HEAD OF THE SLUG

Augustus Brine led the way into the Head of the Slug. Travis followed, and Gian Hen Gian shuffled in last. The saloon was nearly empty: Robert was sitting at the bar, another man sat in the dark at a table in the back, and Mavis was behind the bar. Robert turned as they entered. When he saw Travis, he jumped off the stool.

"You fucking asshole!" Robert screamed. He stormed toward Travis with his fist cocked for a knockout blow. He got four steps before Augustus Brine threw out a massive forearm that caught him in the forehead. There was a flash of tennis shoes flailing in the air as Robert experienced the full dynamic range of the clothesline effect. A second later he lay on the floor unconscious.

"Who is that?" Travis asked.

"Jenny's husband," Brine answered, bending over and inspecting Robert's neck for any jutting vertebrae. "He'll be okay."

"Maybe we should go somewhere else."

"There isn't time," Brine said. "Besides, he might be able to help."

Mavis Sand was standing on a plastic milk box peering over the bar at Robert's supine form. "Nice move, Asbestos," she said. "I like a man that can handle himself."

Brine ignored the compliment. "Do you have any smelling salts?"

Mavis climbed down from her milk box, rummaged under the bar for a moment, and came up with a gallon bottle of ammonia. "This should do it." To Travis and the Djinn she said: "You boys want anything?"

Gian Hen Gian stepped up to the bar. "Could I trouble you for a small quantity . . ."

"A salty dog and a draft, please," Travis interrupted.

Brine wrapped one arm under Robert's armpits and dragged him to a table. He propped him up in a chair, retrieved the ammonia bottle from the bar, and waved it under Robert's nose.

Robert came to, gagging.

"Bring this boy a beer, Mavis," Brine said.

"He ain't drinking today. I've been pouring him Cokes since noon."

"A Coke, then."

Travis and the Djinn took their drinks and joined Brine and Robert at the table, where Robert sat looking around as if he were experiencing reality for the first time. A nasty bump was rising on his forehead. He rubbed it and winced.

"What hit me?"

"I did," Brine said. "Robert, I know you're angry at Travis, but you have to put it aside. Jenny's in trouble."

Robert started to protest, but Brine raised a hand and he fell silent.

"For once in your life, Robert, do the right thing and listen."

It took fifteen minutes for Brine to relate the condensed version of the demon's story, during which time the only interruption was the screeching feedback of Mavis Sand's hearing aid, which she had cranked up to maximum so she could eavesdrop. When Brine finished, he drained his beer and ordered a pitcher. "Well?" he said.

Robert said, "Gus, you're the sanest man I know, and I believe that you believe Jenny is in trouble, but I don't believe this little man is a genie and I don't believe in demons."

"I have seen the demon," came a voice from the dark end of the bar. The figure who had been sitting quietly when they came in stood and walked toward them.

They all turned to see a rumpled and wrinkled Howard Phillips staggering out of the dark, obviously drunk.

"I saw it outside of my house last night. I thought it was one of the slave creatures kept by the Old Ones."

"What in the hell are you talking about, Howard?" Robert asked.

"It doesn't matter any longer. What matters is that these men are telling you the truth."

"So now what?" Robert said. "What do we do now?"

Howard pulled a pocket watch from his vest and checked the time. "You have one hour to plan a course of action. If I can be of any assistance . . ."

"Sit down, Howard, before you fall down," Brine said. "Let's lay it out. I think it's obvious from what we know that there is no way to hurt the demon."

"True," Travis said.

"Therefore," Brine continued, "the only way to stop him and his new master is to get the invocation from the second candlestick, which will either send Catch back to hell or empower Gian Hen Gian."

"When Travis meets them, why don't we just rush them and take it?" Robert said.

Travis shook his head. "Catch would kill Jenny and the Elliotts before we ever got close. Even if we got hold of the invocation, it has to be translated. That takes time. It's been years since I've read any Greek. You would all be killed, and Catch would find another translator."

"Yes, Robert," Brine added. "Did we mention that unless Catch is in his eating form, which must have been what Howard saw, no one can see him but Travis?"

"I am fluent in Greek," Howard said. They all looked at him.

"No," Brine said. "They expect Travis to be alone. The mouth of the cave is at least fifty yards from any cover. As soon as Howard stepped out, it would be over."

"Maybe we should let it be over," Travis said.

"No. Wait a minute," Robert said. He took a pen from Howard's pocket and began scribbling figures on a cocktail napkin. "You say there's cover fifty yards from the caves?" Brine nodded. Robert did some scribbling. "Okay, Travis, exactly how big is the print on the invocation? Can you remember?"

"What does it matter?"

"It matters," Robert insisted. "How big is the print?"

"I don't know—it's been a long time. It was handwritten, and the parchment was pretty long. I'd guess the characters were maybe a half-inch tall."

Robert scribbled furiously on the napkin, then put the pen down. "If you can get them out of the cave and hold up the invocation— tell them you need more light or something—I can set up a telephoto lens on a tripod in the woods and Howard can translate the invocation."

"I don't think they'll let me hold the parchment up long enough for Howard to translate. They'll suspect something."

"No, you don't understand." Robert pushed the napkin he had been writing on in front of Travis. It was covered with fractions and ratios.

Looking at it, Travis was baffled. "What does this mean?"

"It means that I can put a Polaroid back on one of my Nikons and when you hold up the parchments, I can photograph them, hand the Polaroid to Howard, and thirty seconds later he can start translating. The ratios show that the print will be readable on the Polaroid. I just need enough time to focus and set exposure, maybe three seconds." Robert looked around the table.

Howard Phillips was the first to speak. "It sounds feasible, although fraught with contingencies."

Augustus Brine was smiling.

"What do you think, Gus?" Robert asked.

"You know, I always thought you were a lost cause, but I think I've changed my mind. Howard's right, though—there's a lot of *ifs* involved. But it might work."

"He is still a lost cause," the Djinn chimed in. "The invocation is useless without the silver Seal of Solomon, which is part of one of the candlesticks."

"It's hopeless," Travis said.

Brine said, "No, it's not. It's just very difficult. We have to get the candlesticks before they know about the seal. We'll use a diversion."

"Are you going to explode more flour?" asked Gian Hen Gian.

"No. We're going to use you as bait. If Catch hates you as much as you say, he'll come after you and Travis can grab the candlesticks and run."

"I don't like it," Travis said. "Not unless we can get Jenny and the Elliotts clear."

"I agree," said Robert.

"Do you have a better idea?" Brine asked.

"Rachel is a bitch," Robert said, "but I don't think she's a killer. Maybe Travis can send Jenny down the hill from the caves with the candlesticks as a condition to translating the invocation."

"That still leaves the Elliotts," Brine said. "And besides, we don't know if the demon knows the seal is in the candlesticks. I think we go for the diversion plan. As soon as Howard has the invocation translated, Gian Hen Gian should step out of the woods and we all go for it."

Howard Phillips said, "But even if you have the seal and the invocation, you still have to read the words before the demon kills us all."

"That's right," said Travis. "And the process should begin as soon as Rachel starts reading the words I translate, or Catch will know something is up. I can't bluff on the translation at my end."

"You don't have to," Brine said. "You simply have to be slower than Howard, which doesn't sound like a problem."

"Wait a second," Robert said. He was out of his seat and across the bar to where Mavis was standing. "Mavis, give me your recorder."

"What recorder?" she said coyly.

"Don't bullshit me, Mavis. You've got a microcassette recorder under the bar so you can listen to people's conversations."

Mavis pulled the recorder out from under the bar and reluctantly handed it over to Robert. "This is the solution to the time problem," Robert said. "We read the invocation into this before the genie comes out of the woods. When and if we get the candlesticks, we play it back. This thing has a high speed for secretaries to use when typing dictation."

Brine looked at Travis. "Will it work?"

"It's not any more risky than anything else we're doing."

"Who's voice do we use?" Robert asked. "Who gets the responsibility?"

The Djinn answered, "It must be Augustus Brine. He has been chosen."

Robert checked his watch. "We've got a half hour and I still have to pick up my cameras at The Breeze's trailer. Let's meet at the U-PICK-EM sign in fifteen minutes."

"Wait—we need to go over this again," Travis said.

"Later," Brine said. He threw a twenty-dollar bill on the table and headed toward the door. "Robert, use Howard's car. I don't want this whole thing depending on your old truck starting. Travis, Gian Hen Gian, you ride with me."

33

RIVERA

During the drive to Pine Cove, Rivera was nagged by the idea that he had forgotten something. It wasn't that he hadn't reported where he was going; he had planned that. Until he had physical evidence that there was a serial killer in the area, he wasn't saying a word. But when he knocked on the Elliotts' front door and it swung open, he suddenly remembered that his bullet-proof vest was hanging in his locker back at the station.

He called into the house and waited for an answer. None came.

Only cops and vampires have to have an invitation to enter, he thought. But there is probable cause. The part of his mind that functioned like a district attorney kicked in.

"So, Sergeant Rivera," the lawyer said, "you entered a private residence based on a computer data base that could have been no more than a mailing list?"

"I believed that Effrom Elliott's name on the list represented a clear and present danger to a private citizen, so I entered the residence."

Rivera drew his revolver and held it in his right hand while he held his badge out in his left.

"Mr. and Mrs. Elliott, this is Sergeant Rivera from the Sheriff's Department. I'm coming in the house."

He moved from room to room announcing his presence before he entered. The bedroom door was closed. He saw the splintered bullet hole in the door and felt his adrenaline surge.

Should he call for backup?

The D.A. said: "And so you entered the house on what basis?"

Rivera came through the door low and rolled. He lay for a moment on the floor of the empty room, feeling stupid.

What now? He couldn't call in and report a bullet hole in a residence that he had probably entered illegally, especially when he hadn't reported that he was in Pine Cove in the first place.

One step at a time, he told himself.

Rivera returned to his unmarked car and reported that he was in Pine Cove.

"Sergeant Rivera," the dispatcher said, "there is a message for you from Technical Sergeant Nailsworth. He said to tell you that Robert Masterson is married to the granddaughter of Effrom Elliott. He said he doesn't know what it means, but he thought you should know."

It meant that he had to find Robert Masterson. He acknowledged the message and signed off.

Fifteen minutes later he was at The Breeze's trailer. The old pickup was gone and no one answered the door. He radioed the station and requested a direct patch to the Spider.

"Nailgun, can you get me Masterson's wife's home address? He gave the trailer as residence when we brought him in. And give me the place where she works."

"Hold on, it'll be just a second for her address." Rivera lit a cigarette while he waited. Before he took the second drag, Nailsworth came back with the address and the shortest route from Rivera's location.

"It will take a little longer for the employer. I have to access the Social Security files."

"How long?"

"Five, maybe ten minutes."

"I'm on my way to the house. Maybe I won't need it."

"Rivera, there was a fire call at that address this morning. That mean anything to you?"

"Nothing means anything to me anymore, Nailsworth."

Five minutes later Rivera pulled up in front of Jenny's house. Everything was covered with a gummy gray goo, a mix of ashes, flour, and water from the fire hoses. As Rivera climbed out of the car, Nailsworth called back.

"Jennifer Masterson is currently employed at H.P.'s Cafe, off Cypress in Pine Cove. You want the phone number?"

"No," Rivera said. "If she's not here, I'll go over there. It's just a few doors down from my next stop."

"You need anything else?" Nailsworth sounded as if he was holding something back.

"No," Rivera said. "I'll call if I do."

"Rivera, don't forget about that other matter."

"What matter?"

"Roxanne. Check on her for me."

"As soon as I can, Nailsworth."

Rivera threw the radio mike onto the passenger seat. As he walked up to the house, he heard someone come on the radio singing a chorus to the song "Roxanne" in a horrible falsetto. Nailsworth had shown his weakness over an open frequency, and now, Rivera knew, the whole department would ride the fat man's humiliation into the ground.

When this was over, Rivera promised himself, he would concoct a story to vindicate the Spider's pride. He owed him that. Of course, that depended on Rivera vindicating himself.

The walk to the door covered his shoes with gray goo. He waited for an answer and returned to the car, cursing in Spanish, his shoes converted to dough balls.

He didn't get out of the car at H.P.'s Cafe. It was obvious from the darkened windows that no one was inside. His last chance was the Head of the Slug Saloon. If Masterson wasn't there, he was out of leads, and he would have to report what he knew, or, what was more embarrassing, what he didn't know, to the captain.

Rivera found a parking place in front of the Slug behind Robert's truck, and after taking a few minutes to get his right shoe unstuck from the gas pedal, he went in.

34

U - P I C K - E M

The Pagan Vegetarians for Peace called them the Sacred Caves because they believed that the caves had once been used by Ohlone Indians for religious ceremonies. This, in fact, was not true, for the Ohlone had avoided the caves as much as possible due to the huge population of bats that lived there, bats that were inextricably locked into the destiny of the caves.

The first human occupation of the caves came in the 1960s, when a down-and-out farmer named Homer Styles decided to use the damp interior of the caves to cultivate mushrooms. Homer started his business with five hundred wooden crates of the sort used for carting soda bottles, and a half-gallon carton of mail-order mushroom spores; total investment: sixteen dollars. Homer had stolen the crates from behind the Thrifty-Mart, a few at a time, over the period of weeks that it took him to read the pamphlet *Fungus for Fun and Profit,* put out by the U.S. Department of Agriculture.

After filling the crates with moist peat and laying them out on the cave floor, Homer spread his spores and waited for the money to roll in. What Homer didn't figure on was the rapid growth rate of the mushrooms (he'd skipped that part of the pamphlet), and within days he found himself sitting in a cave full of mushrooms with no market and no money to pay for help in harvesting.

The solution to Homer's problem came from another government pamphlet entitled *The Consumer-Harvested Farm,* which had come, by mistake, in the same envelope with *Fungus for Fun.* Homer took his last ten dollars and placed an ad in the local paper: *Mushrooms, $.50 lb. U-PICK-EM, your container. Old Creek Road. 9-5 daily.*

Mushroom-hungry Pine Covers came in droves. As fast as the mushrooms were harvested, they grew back, and the money rolled in.

Homer spent his first profits on a generator and a string of lights for the caves, figuring that by extending his business hours into the evening, his profits would grow in proportion. It would have been a sound business move had the bats not decided to rear their furry heads in protest.

During the day the bats had been content to hang out on the roof of the cave while Homer ran his business below. But on the first night of Homer's extended hours when the bats woke to find their home invaded by harshly lit mushroom pickers, their tolerance ended.

There were twenty customers in the caves when the lights went on. In an instant the air above them was a maelstrom of screeching, furry, flying rodents. In the rush to exit, one woman fell and broke a hip and another was bitten on the hand while extracting a bat from her hair. The cloud of bats soon disappeared into the night, only to be replaced the next day by an equally dense cloud of landbound vermin: personal-injury lawyers.

The varmints prevailed in court. Homer's business was destroyed, and once again the bats slept in peace.

A depressed Homer Styles went on a binge in the Head of the Slug. He spent four days in an Irish whiskey haze before his money ran out and Mavis Sand sent him to an Alcoholics Anonymous meeting. (Mavis could tell when a man had hit bottom, and she felt no need to pump a dry well.)

Homer found himself in the meeting room of the First National Bank, telling his story. It happened that at that same meeting a young surfer who called himself The Breeze was working off a court-ordered sentence he had earned by drunkenly crashing a '62 Volkswagen into a police cruiser and promptly puking on the arresting officer's shoes.

The farmer's story touched off an entrepreneurial spark in the surfer, and after the meeting The Breeze cornered Homer with a proposition.

"Homer, how would you like to make some heavy bread growing magic mushrooms?"

The next day the farmer and the surfer were hauling bags of manure into the caves, spreading it over the peat, and scattering a completely different type of spore.

According to The Breeze their crop would sell for ten to twenty dollars an ounce instead of the fifty cents a pound that Homer received for his last crop. Homer was enraptured with the possibility of becoming rich. And he would have, if not for the bats.

As the day of their first harvest neared, The Breeze had to take his leave of their plantation to serve the weekend in the county jail (the first of fifty—the judge had not been amused at having barf-covered police shoes presented as evidence in his courtroom). Before he left, The Breeze assured Homer that he would return Monday to help with the drying and marketing of the mushrooms.

In the meantime, the woman who had been bitten during the debacle of the bats, came down with rabies. County animal-control agents were ordered to the caves to destroy the bat colony. When the agents arrived, they found Homer Styles crouched over a tray of psychedelic mushrooms.

The agents offered Homer the option of walking away and leaving the mushrooms, but Homer refused, so they radioed the sheriff. Homer was led away in handcuffs, the animal-control agents left with their pockets filled with mushrooms, and the bats were left alone.

When The Breeze was released on Monday, he found himself in search of a new scam.

A few months later, while incarcerated at the state prison in Lompoc, Homer Styles received a letter from The Breeze. The letter was covered with a fine yellow powder and read: "Sorry about your bust. Hope we can bury the hatchet."

Homer buried the letter in a shoe box he kept under his bunk and spent the next ten years living in relative luxury on the profits he made from selling psychedelic mushrooms to the other inmates. Homer sampled his crop only once, then swore off mushrooms for life when he hallucinated that he was drowning in a sea of bats.

35

BAD GUYS, GOOD GUYS

Rachel was drawing figures in the dirt of the cave floor with a dagger when she heard something flutter by her ear.

"What was that?"

"A bat," Catch said. He was invisible.

"We are out of here," Rachel said. "Take them outside."

Effrom, Amanda, and Jenny were sitting with their backs against the cave wall, tied hand and foot, and gagged.

"I don't know why we couldn't have waited at your cabin," Catch said.

"I have my reasons. Help me get them outside, now."

"You're afraid of bats?" Catch asked.

"No, I just feel that this ritual should take place in the open," Rachel insisted.

"If you have a problem with bats, you're going to love it when you see me."

* * *

A quarter mile down the road from the cave, Augustus Brine, Travis, and Gian Hen Gian were waiting for Howard and Robert to arrive.

"Do you think we can pull this off?" Travis asked Brine.

"Why ask me? I know less about this than the two of you. Whether we pull it off depends mostly on your powers of persuasion."

"Can we go over it again?"

Brine checked his watch. "Let's wait for Robert and Howard. We still have a few minutes. And I don't think that it will hurt to be a little late. As far as Catch and Rachel are concerned, you are the only game in town."

Just then they heard a car down-shifting and turned to see Howard's old black Jag turning onto the dirt road. Howard parked behind Brine's truck. He and Robert got out and Robert reached into the backseat and began handing things to Brine and Travis: a camera bag, a heavy-duty tripod, a long aluminum lens case, and finally, a hunting rifle with a scope. Brine did not take the rifle from Robert.

"What's that for?"

Robert stood up, rifle in hand. "If it looks like it isn't going to work, we use it to take out Rachel before she gets power over Catch."

"What will that accomplish?" Brine asked.

"It will keep Travis in control of the demon."

"No," Travis said. "One way or another it ends here, but we don't shoot anyone. We're here to end the killing, not add to it. Who's to say that Rachel won't have more control over Catch than I do?"

"But she doesn't know what she is getting into. You said that yourself."

"If she gets power over Catch, he has to tell her, just like he told me. At least I will be free of him."

"And Jenny will be dead," Robert spat.

Augustus Brine said, "The rifle stays in the car. We are going to do this on the assumption that it will work, period. Normally I'd say that if anyone wants out, they can go now, but the fact is, we all have to be here for it to work."

Brine looked around the group. They were waiting. "Well, are we going to do this?"

Robert threw the rifle into the backseat of the car. "Let's do it, then."

"Good," Brine said. "Travis, you have to get them out of the cave and into the open. You have to hold the invocation up long enough for Robert to get a picture, and you have to get the candlesticks back to us, preferably by sending them down the hill with Jenny and the Elliotts."

"They'll never go for that. Without the hostages, why should I translate the invocation?"

"Then hold it as a condition. Play it the best you can. Maybe you can get one of them down."

"If I make the candlesticks a condition, they'll be suspicious."

"Shit," Robert said. "This isn't going to work. I don't know why I thought it would."

Through the whole discussion the Djinn had remained in the background. Now he stepped into the circle. "Give them what they want. Once the woman has control of Catch, they will have no need to be suspicious."

"But Catch will kill the hostages, and probably all of us," Travis said.

"Wait a minute," Robert said. "Where is Rachel's van?"

"What does that have to do with anything?" Brine said.

"Well, they didn't walk here with hostages in tow. And the van isn't parked here. That means that her van must be up by the cave."

"So?" Travis said.

"So, it means that if we have to storm them, we can go in Gus's truck. The road must come out of the woods and loop around the hill to the caves. We already have the recorder, so the invocation can be played back fast. Gus can drive up the hill, Travis can throw the candlesticks into the truck, and all Gus has to do is hit the play button."

They considered it for a moment, then Brine said, "Everyone in the bed of the truck. We park it in the woods as close to the caves as we can without it being seen. It's the closest thing to a plan that we have."

On the grassy hill outside the cave Rachel said, "He's late."

"Let's kill one of them," the demon said.

Jenny and her grandparents sat on the ground, back to back.

"Once this ritual is over, I won't have you talking like that," Rachel said.

"Yes, mistress, I yearn for your guidance."

Rachel paced the hill, making an effort not to look at her hostages. "What if Travis doesn't come?"

"He'll come," Catch said.

"I think I hear a car." Rachel watched the point where the road emerged from the woods. When nothing came, she said, "What if you're wrong? What if he doesn't come?"

"There he is," Catch said.

Rachel turned to see Travis walking out of the woods and up the gentle slope toward them.

Robert screwed the tripod into the socket of the telephoto lens, tested its steadiness, then fitted the camera body on the back of the lens and turned it until it clicked into place. From the camera bag at his feet he took a pack of Polaroid film and snapped it into the bottom of the Nikon's back.

"I've never seen a camera like that," said Augustus Brine.

Robert was focusing the long lens. "The camera's a regular thirty-five millimeter. I bought the Polaroid back for it to preview results in the studio. I never got around to using it."

Howard Phillips stood poised with notebook in hand and a fountain pen at ready.

"Check the batteries in that recorder," Robert said to Brine. "There are some fresh ones in my camera bag if you need them."

Gian Hen Gian was craning his neck to see over the undergrowth into the clearing where Travis stood. "What is happening? I cannot see what is happening."

"Nothing yet," Brine said. "Are you set, Robert?"

"I'm ready," Robert said without looking up from the camera. "I'm filling the frame with Rachel's face. The parchment should be easily readable. Are you ready, Howard?"

"Short of the unlikely possibility that I may be stricken with writer's cramp at the crucial moment, I am prepared."

Brine snapped four penlight batteries into the recorder and tested the mechanism. "It's up to Travis now," he said.

Travis topped halfway up the hill. "Okay, I'm here. Let them go and I'll translate the invocation for you."

"I don't think so," Rachel said. "Once the ritual has been performed and I'm sure it has worked, then you can all go free."

"You don't have any idea what you're talking about. Catch will kill us all."

"I don't believe you. The Earth spirit will be in my control, and I won't allow it."

Travis laughed sarcastically. "You haven't even seen him, have you? What do you think you have there, the Easter Bunny? He kills people. That's the reason he's here."

"I still don't believe you." Rachel was beginning to lose her resolve.

Travis watched Catch move to where the hostages were tied. "Come, do it now, Travis, or the old woman dies." He raised a clawed hand over Amanda's head.

Travis trudged up the hill and stood in front of Rachel. Very quietly her said to her, "You know, you deserve what you are going to get. I never thought I could wish Catch on anyone, but you deserve it." He looked at Jenny, and her eyes pleaded for an explanation. He looked away. "Give me the invocation," he said to Rachel. "I hope you brought a pencil and paper. I can't do this from memory."

Rachel reached into an airline bag that she had brought and pulled out the candlesticks. One at a time she unscrewed them and removed the invocations, then replaced the pieces in the airline bag. She handed Travis the parchments.

"Put the candlesticks over by Jenny," he said.

"Why?" Rachel asked.

"Because the ritual won't work if they are too close to the parchments. In fact, you'd be better off if you untied them and sent them away with the candlesticks. Get them out of the area altogether." The lie seemed so obvious that Travis feared he had ruined everything by putting too much importance on the candlesticks.

Rachel stared at him, trying to make sense of it. "I don't understand," she said.

"Neither do I," Travis said. "But this is mystical stuff. You can't tell me that taking hostages so you can call up a demon is consistent with the logical world."

"Earth spirit! Not demon. And I will use this power for good."

Travis considered trying to convince her of her folly, then decided against it. The lives of Jenny and the Elliotts depended on Catch maintaining his charade as a benevolent Earth spirit until it was too late. He glared at the demon, who grinned back.

"Well?" Travis said.

Rachel picked up the airline bag and took it to a spot a few feet down the hill from the hostages.

"No. Farther away," Travis said.

She slung the bag over her shoulder and took it another twenty yards down the hill, then turned to Travis for approval.

"What is this about?" Catch asked.

Travis, afraid to push his luck, nodded to Rachel and she set the bag down. Now the candlesticks were twenty yards closer to the road that ran around the back of the hill—the road that Augustus Brine would drive when the shit hit the fan.

Rachel returned to the hilltop.

"I'll need that pencil and paper now," he said.

"It's in the bag." Rachel went back toward the bag.

While she was retrieving the pencil and paper from the airline bag, Travis held the parchments out before him, one at a time, counting to six before he put the first one down and picked up the next. He hoped he had the angle to Robert's camera right and that his body was not in the way of the lens.

"Here." Rachel handed him a pencil and a steno pad.

Travis sat down cross-legged with the parchments out in front
of him. "Sit down and relax, this is going to take some time."

He started on the parchment from the second candlestick,
hoping to buy some time. He translated the Greek letter by letter,
searching his memory first for each letter, then for the meaning of
the words. By the time he finished the first line, he had fallen into
a rhythm and had to make an effort to slow down.

"Read what he has written," Catch said.

"But he's just done one line—" Rachel said.

"Read it."

Rachel took the steno pad from Travis and read, "Being in
possession of the Power of Solomon I call upon the race that
walked before man . . ." She stopped. "That's all there is."

"It's the wrong paper," Catch said. "Travis, translate the other
one. If it's not right this time, the girl dies."

"That's the last time I buy you a Cookie Monster comic book,
you scaly fucker."

Reluctantly Travis shuffled the parchments and began to translate the invocation he had spoken in Saint Anthony's chapel
seventy years before.

Howard Phillips had two Polaroid prints out on the ground
before him. He was writing a translation out on a notepad while
Augustus Brine and Gian Hen Gian looked over his shoulder.
Robert was looking through the camera.

"They've made him change parchments. He must have been
translating the wrong one."

Brine said, "Howard, are you translating the one we need?"

"I am not sure yet. I've only translated a few lines of the Greek.
This Latin passage at the top appears to be a message rather than
an invocation."

"Can't you just scan it? We don't have time for mistakes."

Howard read what he had written. "No, this is wrong." He tore
the sheet from the notepad and began again, concentrating on the
other Polaroid. "This one seems to have two shorter invocations.
The first one seems to be the one that empowers the Djinn. It
talks about a race that walked before man."

"That is right. Translate the one with two invocations," the Djinn said.

"Hurry," Robert said, "Travis has half a page. Gus, I'm going to ride up the hill in the bed of the truck when you go. I'll jump out and grab the bag with the candlesticks. They're still a good thirty yards from the road and I can move faster than you can."

"I'm finished," Howard said. He handed his notebook to Brine.

"Record it at normal speed," Robert said. "Then play it back at high speed."

Brine held the recorder up to his face, his finger on the record button. "Gian Hen Gian, is this going to work? I mean is a voice on a tape going to have the same effect as speaking the words?"

"It would be best to assume that it will."

"You mean you don't know?"

"How would I know?"

"Swell," Brine said. He pushed the record button and read Howard's translation into the recorder. When he finished, he rewound the tape and said, "Okay, let's go."

"Police! Don't anyone move!"

They turned to see Rivera standing in the road behind them, his .38 in hand, panning back and forth to cover them. "Everybody down on the ground, facedown."

They stood frozen in position.

"On the ground, now!" Rivera cocked his revolver.

"Officer, there must be a mistake," Brine said, feeling stupid as he said it.

"Down!"

Reluctantly, Brine, Robert, and Howard lay facedown on the ground. Gian Hen Gian remained standing, cursing in Arabic. Rivera's eyes widened as blue swirls appeared in the air over the Djinn's head.

"Stop that," Rivera said.

The Djinn ignored him and continued cursing.

"On your belly, you little fucker."

Robert pushed himself up on his arms and looked around. "What's this about, Rivera? We were just out here taking some pictures."

"Yeah, and that's why you have a high-powered rifle in your car."

"That's nothing," Robert said.

"I don't know what it is, but it's more than nothing. And none of you are going anywhere until I get some answers."

"You're making a mistake, Officer," Brine said. "If we don't continue with what we were doing, people are going to die."

"First, it's Sergeant. Second, I'm getting to be a master at making mistakes, so one more is no big deal. And third, the only person who is going to die is this little Arab if he doesn't get his ass on the ground."

What was taking them so long? Travis had dragged the translation out as long as he could, stalling on a word here and there, but he could tell that Catch was getting impatient and to delay any long would endanger Jenny.

He tore two sheets from the steno pad and handed them to Rachel. "It's finished, now you can untie them." He gestured to Jenny and the Elliotts.

"No," Catch said. "First we see if it works."

"Please, Rachel, you have what you want. There's no reason to keep these people here."

Rachel took the pages. "I'll make it up to them once I have the power. It won't hurt to keep them here a few more minutes."

Travis fought the urge to look back toward the woods. Instead he cradled his head in his hands and sighed deeply as Rachel began to read the invocation aloud.

Augustus Brine finally convinced Gian Hen Gian to lie down on the ground. It was obvious that Rivera would not listen to anyone until the Djinn relented.

"Now, Masterson, where in the hell did you get that metal suitcase?"

"I told you, I stole it out of the Chevy."

"Who owns the Chevy?"

"I can't tell you that."

"You can tell me or you can go up on murder charges."

"Murder? Who was murdered?"

"About a thousand people, it looks like. Where is the owner of that suitcase? Is it one of these guys?"

"Rivera, I will tell you everything I know about everything in about fifteen minutes, but now you've got to let us finish what we started."

"And what was that?"

Brine spoke up, "Sergeant, my name is Augustus Brine. I'm a businessman here in town. I have done nothing wrong, so I have no reason to lie to you."

"So?" Rivera said.

"So, you are right. There is a killer. We are here to stop him. If we don't act right now, he will get away, so please, please, let us go."

"I'm not buying it, Mr. Brine. Where is this killer and why didn't you call the police about him? Take it nice and slow, and don't leave anything out."

"We don't have time," Brine insisted.

Just then they heard a loud thump and the sound of a body slumping to the ground. Brine turned around to see Mavis Sand standing over the collapsed detective, her baseball bat in hand.

"Hi, cutie," she said to Brine.

They all jumped to their feet.

"Mavis, what are you doing here?"

"He threatened to close me down if I didn't tell him where you went. After he left, I got to feeling like a shit about telling him, so here I am."

"Thanks, Mavis," Brine said. "Let's go. Howard, you stay here. Robert, in the bed of the truck. Whenever you're ready, King," he said to the Djinn.

Brine jumped into the truck, fired it up, and engaged the four-wheel drive.

Rachel read the last line of the invocation with a grandiose flourish of her arm. "In the name of Solomon the King, I command thee to appear!"

Rachel said, "Nothing happened."

Catch said, "Nothing happened, Travis."

Travis said, "Give it a minute." He had almost given up hope. Something had gone horribly wrong. Now he was faced with either telling them about the candlesticks or keeping his bond with the demon. Either way, the hostages were doomed.

"Fine, Travis," Catch said. "The old man is the first to go."

Catch wrapped one hand around Effrom's neck. As Travis and Rachel watched, the demon grew into his eating form and lifted Effrom off the ground.

"Oh my God!" Rachel put her fist to her mouth and started backing away from the demon. "Oh no!"

Travis tried to focus his will on the demon. "Put him down, Catch," he commanded.

From somewhere down the hill came the sound of a truck starting.

Gian Hen Gian stepped out of the woods. "Catch," he shouted, "will you never give up your toys?" The Djinn started up the hill.

Catch threw Effrom to the side. He landed like a rag doll, ten yards away. Rachel was shaking her head violently, as if trying to shake away the demon's image. Tears streamed down her cheeks.

"So someone let the little fart out of his jar," Catch said. He stalked down the hill toward the Djinn.

An engine roared and Augustus Brine's pickup broke out of the tree line and bounced up the dirt road, throwing up a cloud of dust in its wake. Robert stood in the bed, holding onto the roll bar for support.

Travis darted past Catch to Amanda and Jenny.

"Still a coward, King of the Djinn?" Catch said, pausing a second to look at the speeding truck.

"I am still your superior," the Djinn said.

"Is that why you surrendered your people to the netherworld without a fight?"

"This time you lose, Catch."

Catch spun to watch the truck slide around the last turn and off the road to bound across the open grass toward the candlesticks.

"Later, Djinn," Catch said. He began to run toward the truck. Taking five yards at a stride the demon was over the hill and past Travis and the women in seconds.

Augustus Brine saw the demon coming at them. "Hold on, Robert." He wrenched the wheel to the side to throw the truck into a slide.

Catch lowered his shoulder and rammed into the right front fender of the truck. Robert saw the impact coming and tried to decide whether to brace himself or jump. In an instant the decision was made for him as the fender crumpled under the demon and the truck went up on two wheels, then over onto its roof.

Robert lay on the ground trying to get his wind back. He tried to move, and a searing pain shot through his arm. Broken. A thick cloud of dust hung in the air, obscuring his vision. He could hear the demon roaring behind him and the screeching sound of tearing metal.

As the dust settled, he could just make out the shape of the upside-down truck. The demon was pinned under the hood, ripping at the metal with his claws. Augustus Brine hung by his seat belt. Robert could see him moving.

Robert climbed to his feet, using his good arm to push himself up.

"Gus!" he shouted.

"The candlesticks!" came back.

Robert looked around on the ground. There was the bag. He had almost landed on it. He started to reach for it with both hands and nearly passed out when the pain from his broken arm hit him. From his knees he was able to scoop up the bag, heavy with the candlesticks, in his good arm.

"Hurry," Brine shouted.

Catch had stopped clawing at the metal. With a great roar he shoved the truck up and off of him. Standing before the truck, he threw his head back and roared with such intensity that Robert nearly dropped the candlesticks.

Every bone in Robert's body said flee, get the hell out of here. He stood frozen.

"Robert, I'm stuck. Bring them to me." Brine was struggling with the seat belt. At the sound of his voice the demon leapt to the driver's side of the truck and clawed at the door. Brine heard the skin of the door go with the first slash. He stared at the door in terror, expecting a claw to come through the window at any second. The demon's claws raked the support beam inside the door.

"Gus, here. Ouch. Shit." Robert was lying outside the passenger side window, pushing the bag with the candlesticks across the roof of the truck. "The play button, Gus. Push it."

Brine felt the pocket of his flannel shirt. Mavis's recorder was still clipped there. He fumbled for the play button, found it, and pushed, just as a daggerlike claw ripped into his shoulder.

A hundred miles south, at Vandenberg Air Force Base, a radar technician reported a UFO. entering restricted air space from over the Pacific. When the aircraft refused to respond to radio warning, four jet fighters were scrambled to intercept. Three of the fighter pilots would report no visual contact. The fourth, upon landing, would be given a urinalysis and confined to quarters until he could be debriefed by an officer from the Air Force Department of Stress Management.

The bogey would be officially explained as radar interference caused by unusually high swell conditions offshore.

Of the thirty-six reports, filed in triplicate with various departments of the military complex, not one would mention an enormous white owl with an eighty-foot wingspan.

However, after some consideration, the Pentagon would award seventeen million dollars to the Massachusetts Institute of Technology for a secret study on the feasibility of an owl-shaped aircraft. After two years of computer simulations and wind-tunnel prototype tests, the research team would conclude that an owl-shaped aircraft would, indeed, be an effective weapon, but only if the enemy should ever mobilize a corps of field-mouse-shaped tanks.

Augustus Brine realized that he was going to die. In that same moment he realized that he was not afraid and that it did not matter. The monster clawing to get at him didn't matter. The chipmunk chatter of his voice playing back double-speed on the recorder didn't matter. The shouting of Robert, and now Travis, outside the truck didn't matter. He was acutely aware of it all, he was part of it all, but it did not matter. Even the gunfire didn't matter. He accepted it and let it go.

Rivera came to when Brine had started the truck. Mavis Sand was standing over the policeman with his revolver, but she and Howard were watching what was going on up the hill. Rivera glanced up the hill to see Catch materializing in his eating form, holding Effrom by the throat.

"Santa Maria! What the hell is that?"

Mavis trained the gun on him. "Stay right there."

Ignoring her, Rivera stood and ran down the road toward his patrol car. At his car he popped the trunk lid and pulled the riot gun out of its bracket. As he ran back past Howard's Jag, he paused, then opened the back door and grabbed Robert's hunting rifle.

By the time he was again in view of the hill, the truck was upside down and the monster was clawing at the door. He threw the riot gun to the ground and shouldered the rifle. He braced the barrel against a tree, threw the bolt to jack a shell into the chamber, sighted through the scope, and brought the cross-hairs down on the monster's face. Resisting the urge to scream, he squeezed the trigger.

The round hit the demon in his open mouth and knocked him back a foot. Rivera quickly jacked another shell into the chamber and fired. Then another. When the firing pin clicked on an empty chamber, the monster had been knocked back from the truck a few feet but was still coming.

"Santa fucking Maria," Rivera said.

Gian Hen Gian had reached the top of the hill where Travis knelt by Amanda and Jenny.

"It is done," the Djinn said.

"Then do something!" Travis said. "Help Gus."

"Without his orders I may carry out only the command of my last master." Gian Hen Gian pointed to the sky. Travis looked up to see something white coming out of the clouds, but it was too far away to make out what it was.

Catch recovered from the rifle slugs and went forward. He hooked his huge hand behind the reinforcement beam of the truck's door, ripped it off, and threw it behind him. Inside the truck, still hanging from the seat belt, Augustus Brine turned calmly and looked at the demon. Catch drew back his hand to deliver a blow that would rip Brine's head from his shoulders.

Brine smiled at him. The demon paused.

"What are you, some kind of wacko?" Catch said.

Brine didn't have time to answer. The reverberation of the owl's screech shattered the windshield of the truck. Catch looked up as the talons locked around his body, and he was swept into the air flailing at the owl's legs.

The owl climbed into the sky so rapidly that in seconds it was nothing more than a tiny silhouette against the sun, which was making its way toward the horizon.

Augustus Brine continued to smile as Travis released the seat belt. He hit the roof of the truck with his injured shoulder and passed out.

When Brine regained consciousness, they were all standing over him. Jenny was holding Amanda's head to her shoulder. The old woman was sobbing.

Brine looked from face to face. Someone was missing.

Robert spoke first. "Tell Gian Hen Gian to heal your shoulder, Gus. He can't do it until you tell him. While you're at it, tell him to fix my arm."

"Do it," Brine said. As he said it, the pain was gone from his shoulder. He sat up.

"Where's Effrom?"

"He didn't make it, Gus," Robert said. "His heart gave out when the demon threw him."

Brine looked to the Djinn. "Bring him back."

The Djinn shook his head balefully. "This I cannot do."

Brine said, "I'm sorry, Amanda." Then to Gian Hen Gian, "What happened to Catch?"

"He is on his way to Jerusalem."

"I don't understand."

"I have lied to you, Augustus Brine. I am sorry. I was bound to the last command of my last master. Solomon bade me take the demon back to Jerusalem and chain him to a rock outside the great temple."

"Why didn't you tell me that?"

"I thought you would never give me my power if you knew. I am a coward."

"Don't be ridiculous."

"It is as Catch said. When the angels came to drive my people into the netherworld, I would not let them fight. There was no battle as I told you. We went like sheep to the slaughter."

"Gian Hen Gian, you are not a coward. You are a creator—you told me that yourself. It's not in your nature to destroy, to make war."

"But I did. So I have tried to vindicate myself by stopping Catch. I wanted to do for the humans what I did not do for my own people."

"It doesn't matter," Brine said. "It's finished."

"No, it's not," Travis said. "You can't chain Catch to a rock in the middle of Jerusalem. You have to send him back. You have to read the last invocation. Howard translated it while we were waiting for you to wake up."

"But Travis, you don't know what will happen to you. You may die on the spot."

"I'm still bound to him, Gus. That isn't living anyway. I want to be free." Travis handed him the invocation and the candlestick with the Seal of Solomon concealed in it. "If you don't, I will. It has to be done."

"All right, I'll do it," Brine said.

Travis looked up at Jenny. She looked away. "I'm sorry," Travis said. Robert went to Jenny's side and held her. Travis walked down the hill, and when he was out of sight, Augustus Brine began reading the words that would send Catch back to hell.

They found Travis slumped in the backseat of Howard's Jaguar. Augustus Brine was the first to reach the car.

"I did it, Travis. Are you all right?"

As Travis looked up, Brine had to fight the urge to recoil. The demonkeeper's face was deeply furrowed and shot with broken veins. His dark hair and brows had turned white. But for his eyes, which were still young with intensity, Brine would not have recognized him. Travis smiled. There were still a couple of teeth left in front.

His voice was still young. "It didn't hurt. I expected one of those wrenching Lon Chaney transformations, but it didn't happen. Suddenly I was old. That was it."

"I'm glad it didn't hurt," Brine said.

"What am I going to do?"

"I don't know, Travis. I need to think."

36

JENNY, ROBERT, RIVERA, AMANDA, TRAVIS, HOWARD, AND THE SPIDER

Rivera drove Robert and Jennifer to their house. They sat in the, back, holding each other the whole way, not saying a word until they thanked him when he dropped them off. On the drive back to the station Rivera tried to formulate a story that would save his career. Any version of the true story seemed like a sure ticket to a psychological disability retirement. In the end he decided to tell the story as far as the point where The Breeze disappeared.

A month later Rivera was pumping Slush-Puppies at the Seven-Eleven, working undercover for the robbery division. However, with the arrest of a team of robbers that had terrorized convenience stores in the county for six months, he was promoted to lieutenant.

Amanda and Travis rode with Howard. At Amanda's request, Gian Hen Gian saw that Effrom's body was turned to stone and placed inside the cave. When Howard stopped in front of Amanda's house, she invited Travis to come inside. He refused at first, wanting to leave her alone with her grief.

"Have you completely missed the significance of all this, Travis?" she asked.

"I guess so," he said.

"Did it occur to you that the presence of Catch and Gian Hen Gian proves that Effrom is not gone completely? I will miss him, but he goes on. And I don't want to be alone right now. I helped you when you needed it," she said, and she waited.

Travis went in.

Howard went home to work on a new menu for his restaurant.

Chief Technical Sergeant Nailsworth never found out what happened to Roxanne or who she really was, and he was heartbroken. Because of his grief he was unable to eat, lost a hundred and fifty pounds, met a girl at a computer user's meeting, and married her. He never had computer sex again outside the privacy of his home.

37

GOOD GUYS

Augustus Brine declined offers for a ride home. He wanted to walk. He needed to think. Gian Hen Gian walked at his side.

"I can repair your truck, make it fly if you wish," the Djinn said.

"I don't want it," Brine said. "I'm not even sure I want to go home."

"You may do as you wish, Augustus Brine."

"I don't want to go back to the store either. I think I'll give the business to Robert and Jenny."

"Is it wise to put the drunkard in the wine barrel?"

"He won't drink anymore. I want them to have the house, too. I'll start the paperwork in the morning."

"It is done."

"Just like that?"

"You doubt the word of the King of the Djinn?"

They walked in silence for a while before Brine spoke again.

"It seems wrong that Travis has lived so long without having a life, without love."

"Like yourself, you mean?"

"No, not like myself. I've had a good life."

"Would you have me make him young again?"

Brine thought for a moment before he answered. "Could you make him age in reverse? For each year that passes he is a year younger?"

"It can be done."

"And her, too?"

"Her?"

"Amanda. Could you make them grow young together?"

"It can be done, if you command it."

"I do."

"It is done. Will you tell them?"

"No, not right away. It will be a nice surprise."

"And what of yourself, Augustus Brine? What is it you wish?"

"I don't know. I always thought I'd make a good madam."

Before the Djinn could say anything else, Rachel's van sputtered up beside them and stopped. She rolled down the window and said, "Do you need a ride, Gus?"

"He is trying to think," the Djinn snapped.

"Don't be rude," Brine said to the Djinn. "Which way are you going?"

"I don't know for sure. I don't feel like going home—maybe ever."

Brine walked around the front of the van and slid open the cargo door. "Get in, Gian Hen Gian."

The Djinn got into the van. Brine slammed the cargo door and climbed into the passenger seat next to Rachel.

"Well?" she said.

"East," Brine said. "Nevada."

It was called King's Lake. When it appeared in the desert, it simultaneously appeared on every map of Nevada that had ever been printed. People who had passed through that part of the state swore that they had never seen it before, yet there it was on the map.

Above the tree-lined banks of King's Lake stood a palace with a hundred rooms. Atop the palace a massive electric sign read, BRINE'S BAIT, TACKLE, AND FINE WOMEN.

Anyone who visited the palace was greeted by a beautiful, dark-haired woman, who took their money and led them to a room. On their way out a tiny brown man in a rumpled suit returned their money and wished them well.

Upon returning home the visitors told of a white-haired man who sat all day in the lotus position at the end of a pier in front of the palace, fishing and smoking a pipe. They said that when evening approached, the dark-haired woman would join the man and together they would watch the sun go down.

The visitors were never quite clear as to what had happened to them while they were at the palace. It didn't seem to matter. But after a visit they found that they appreciated the simple pleasures that life presented to them and they were happy. And although they recommended Brine's to their friends, they never returned themselves.

What went on in the rooms is another story altogether.

Perennial

STRAP YOURSELVES IN, LADIES AND GENTLEMEN, IT'S CHRISTOPHER MOORE TIME!

THE STUPIDEST ANGEL: *A Heartwarming Tale of Christmas Terror*

ISBN 0-06-059025-4 (Coming in hardcover Fall 2004 from William Morrow)

Ah, Christmas—the hap-happiest season of all! Except for Pine Cove Constable Theo Crowe, who's looking for the local evil developer who disappeared after playing Santa at the Caribou Lodge Christmas party. Meanwhile the town braces for the annual onslaught of holiday tourists and the storm of the century. Oh, and did we mention the tall dark stranger with supernatural strength who arrives looking for "a child," and the clueless angel sent to Earth on a mysterious mission? Yikes! Pass the eggnog.

FLUKE: *Or, I Know Why the Winged Whale Sings*

ISBN 0-06-056668-X (paperback)

Every winter, whale researchers Nate Quinn and Clay Demolocus, partners in the Maui Whale Research Foundation, ply the warm Pacific waters, trying to solve an age-old mystery: Just why *do* humpback whales sing? Then one day a whale moons Nate, lifting its tail to display a cryptic scrawled message: Bite Me. But no one else saw a thing—not Clay, not fetching research assistant Amy, not even spliff-puffing white-boy Rastaman Kona (né Preston Applebaum). The weirdness only gets weirder when Nate gets a call telling him a whale has made contact—by phone.

LAMB: *The Gospel According to Biff, Christ's Childhood Pal*

ISBN 0-380-81381-5 (paperback)

The birth of Jesus has been well chronicled, as have his glorious teachings, acts, and divine sacrifice after his thirtieth birthday. But no one knows about the early life of the Son of God—"the missing years"—except Biff. Ever since the day he came upon six-year-old Joshua of Nazareth resurrecting lizards in the village square, Levi bar Alphaeus, a.k.a. "Biff," had the distinction of being the Messiah's best bud. That's why the angel Raziel has resurrected Biff from the dust of Jerusalem and brought him to America to write a new gospel, one that tells the real, untold story.

THE LUST LIZARD OF MELANCHOLY COVE

ISBN 0-06-073545-7 (paperback)

The town psychiatrist has decided to switch everybody in Pine Cove, California, from their normal antidepressants to placebos, so naturally—well, to be accurate, artificially—business is booming at the local blues bar. Trouble is, those lonely slide-guitar notes have also attracted a colossal sea-beast with a thing for explosive oil tanker trucks. Suddenly, morose Pine Cove turns libidinous and is hit by a mysterious crime wave, and a beleaguered constable has to fight off his own gonzo appetites to find out what's wrong and what, if anything, to do about it.

ISLAND OF THE SEQUINED LOVE NUN
ISBN 0-06-073544-9 (paperback)

A wonderfully crazed excursion into the demented heart of a tropical paradise—a world of cargo cults, cannibals, mad scientists, ninjas, and talking fruit bats. Our bumbling hero is Tucker Case, a hopeless geek trapped in a cool guy's body, who makes a living as a pilot for the Mary Jean Cosmetics Corporation. But when he demolishes his boss's pink plane, Tuck must make a run for his life. Now there's only one employment opportunity left for him: piloting shady secret missions for an unscrupulous medical missionary and a sexy blond High Priestess on the remotest of Micronesian hells.

BLOODSUCKING FIENDS: *A Love Story*
ISBN 0-06-073541-4 (paperback)

Jody never asked to become a vampire. But when she wakes up under an alley Dumpster with a badly burned arm, an aching neck, superhuman strength, and a thirst for blood, she realizes the decision has been made for her. An eternity of nocturnal prowlings is going to take some getting used to, and that's where Tommy fits in. Biding his time night-clerking and frozen turkey bowling in a San Francisco Safeway, Tommy's world is turned upside-down when a beautiful, undead redhead walks through the door and proceeds to rock Tommy's life—and afterlife—in ways he never imagined possible.

COYOTE BLUE
ISBN 0-06-073543-0 (paperback)

As a boy, he was Samson Hunts Alone—until a deadly misunderstanding with the law forced him to flee the Crow reservation at age fifteen. Now a successful Santa Barbara insurance salesman celebrating his thirty-fifth birthday and his hollow, invented life, Samuel Hunter is offered the dangerous gift of love in the exquisite form of Calliope Kincaid, *and* a curse in the unheralded appearance of an ancient Indian god. For Coyote, the trickster, has arrived to transform tranquility into chaos, to reawaken the mystical storyteller within Sam . . . and to seriously screw up his existence in the process.

PRACTICAL DEMONKEEPING
ISBN 0-06-073542-2 (paperback)

Moore's ingenious debut novel introduces the reader to one of the most memorably mismatched pairs in the annals of literature. The good-looking one is one-hundred-year-old ex-seminarian and "roads" scholar Travis O'Hearn. The green one is Catch, a demon with a nasty habit of eating most of the people he meets. Behind the fake Tudor façade of Pine Cove, California, Catch sees a four-star buffet. Travis, on the other hand, thinks he sees a way of ridding himself of his toothy traveling companion. The winos, neo-pagans, and deadbeat Lotharios of Pine Cove, meanwhile, have other ideas.